Death
of a Doxy

Chris Longmuir

To Isobel

Enjoy

Chris Longmuir

B&J

Published by Barker & Jansen

Copyright © Chris Longmuir, 2018

Cover design by Cathy Helms www.avalongraphics.org

ISBN: 978-0-9574153-7-9

DEDICATION

This book is dedicated to the memory of Dundee's first
policewoman, Jean Forsyth Thomson

.

1

Splotches of blood combined with other stains created a grim kaleidoscope of colour on the faded blue mattress.

He had meant to save her, not kill her. But her depravity overwhelmed him when she mocked him and laughed in his face.

Bile burned his throat and he leaned over the box sink in front of the window waiting for the pain to pass. Outside, footsteps on the landing caused him to draw back and he slid into a shadowy corner of the room, his hand tightening on the poker which he still clutched. When the sound disappeared he returned to the sink, turned the tap, bent over, and swilled water around his mouth. The burning sensation faded. He closed his eyes and leaned his head on the cool glass of the window, in the vain hope the scene behind him would disappear and everything would be the same as when he entered the room less than half an hour ago.

An image of her flashed through his mind. Innocent blue eyes; now so knowing. Hair, golden as daffodils on a spring morning, streaming behind her in the breeze; now dull and lank. Skin, translucent in the sunshine; now caked in thick face paint.

Where had that innocent young girl gone?

He opened his eyes and turned to survey the room. A dingy place containing nothing more than a rickety wardrobe, a bed, one chair, and a table holding a guttering oil lamp. The last embers of a fire glowed in the black grate of the fireplace which spilled ash over the floor. And on the mantelpiece, a candle dripped wax into a saucer.

But the thing that held his eyes more than anything else was the body which sprawled on the mattress before him, beaten and bloodied, and no longer the girl he remembered. His hand loosened on the poker which clattered onto the wooden floorboards to lie in a widening pool of blood.

Unaware he had been holding his breath, it now whispered out from between his lips, and the anger that consumed him was replaced by exhilaration rushing through his body, reviving him, exciting him.

He had saved her, although not in the way he intended. He could see now. This way was better. It was the only way to eradicate the depraved life she led. But he couldn't leave her like this, with her clothing in disarray. No, that wouldn't do. He would make her respectable, lay her out before her body stiffened, and arrange her dress to provide her with a modesty she hadn't experienced for a long time.

Her limbs moved easily under his tender hands. He rolled her onto her back and straightened her legs, smoothing the dress over them. Next, he crossed her hands over her chest and arranged her blood-soaked hair around her shoulders.

Pleased with his work he rinsed her blood from the poker. Then, taking one last look at the scene in front of him, he left the room, closing and locking the door behind him.

At the bottom of the stairs, he sidled around the final corner and hurried across the backlands behind the tenement. This was an area of grass, weeds and rubbish which serviced the tenements that bordered it. The place where the tenants kept their bins and hung their washing on ropes to dry. He slipped through a close at the other side of this waste ground, opposite the building he'd left, and emerged onto the street. After taking a circuitous route and keeping to side streets he eventually reached Magdalen Green. From there it was a short walk to where the River Tay flowed to meet the North Sea. With one last look around to make sure no one observed him, he raised his arm and threw the poker into the water.

He smiled to himself as he walked homeward. His job was done.

2

'I'll sort that little bitch out, see if I don't.' Aggie heaved herself out of the chair, staggering as the room swayed gently around her. 'What gives her the right to insult good customers like yourself?' She smiled at the portly, little man sitting opposite.

'Ach. I didn't mean it to be a complaint like. She said she wasn't in the mood. And Rita wasn't so bad although I'd have preferred Lily.'

'She's no right not to be in the mood. She's paid good money to be in the mood.' Aggie staggered through the door. 'Sorting out, that's what she needs, and I'll soon see to that.'

Fresh air swirled around Aggie's head as she lurched along the stone landing with only her grasp on the blisteringly cold iron rail preventing her from falling. She almost welcomed the sour warmth of the stairwell as she entered it to make her way to the next landing.

The thumping of her feet on the sticky steps leading down the spiral stair turret resounded upwards, giving her the impression she was not alone. Her head swam as she tried to focus her eyes in the darkness, and she stopped her downward progress to lean against the wall and catch her breath. She listened for a moment, but there was only the sound of her own breathing and the echo of her feet.

Several steps later she emerged from the choking closeness of the stairwell onto the second-floor landing, a stone platform similar to the one above and known locally as a plattie, which jutted out from the rear of the building to overhang the backlands below. She turned to the right.

Laughter and the low buzz of voices filtered out from the first door Aggie passed, while a curtain fluttered briefly at the window of the next flat. The last house on the landing appeared silent and empty, although she knew the girl was inside because of the faint glimmer of light showing.

She banged on the door. 'I know you're in there,' she shouted. After listening for a moment and hearing nothing, she thumped again. 'Let me in if ye know what's good for ye.' She listened once more. 'Little bitch,' she said as she fumbled in her skirt pocket for her master keys. 'I'll show you who is boss of this outfit.'

The door swung open and, pushing her way inside, Aggie prepared to give Lily a tongue lashing. She opened her mouth to speak but gagged on the words. Unable to move she stood for a moment struggling to understand what lay on the bed in front of her. But her mind rejected it. The girl was playing a twisted game with her. Well, she'd show her who was boss and Lily would think twice before playing funny games again.

Aggie moved closer. Her feet slipped on something wet and she sat down with a thud. She thrust out a hand but the substance beneath her oozed between her fingers and something dripped from the girl's hair onto the back of Aggie's hand.

She opened her mouth again and roared at the top of her voice, 'Murder! Bloody murder!'

3

Kirsty Campbell hovered between sleeping and waking, slipping from one nightmare to the next until something disturbed her. The sound tipped the balance and she was fully awake. She held her breath to listen but all she could hear were the rustles of the night. The wind rattling her window frame, the ticking of her clock, and the scrape of mice behind the skirting boards.

Allowing her breath to escape she snuggled under the scratchy warmth of the grey blanket. She was letting her imagination run away with itself.

The dreams started when they took Angel away to the lunatic asylum because even though she'd saved the girl from the hangman, she'd failed her. All Kirsty had wanted was to help the girl, but she hadn't known how to empty Angel's mind of the horror of that night in the Howff graveyard, nor had she been able to bring the girl's sister back. Now, Angel rocked and crooned in her locked room at the asylum while Kirsty's dreams were plagued with nightmares.

The door to the building closed with a slight click and footsteps tapped their way up the stairs. For a moment her dreams became confused with reality and she thought it was Edward even though she knew that was impossible.

The steps halted outside her door and a fist thumped on it.

She swung her legs out of the bed onto the skin-chilling linoleum, stood up, pulled the blanket around her and felt her way out of the bedroom, across her living room and over to the door.

'Who's there?' she whispered, her voice hoarse with nervousness.

'Open up, Kirsty. It's me, Brewster.'

'What on earth d'you want at this time of night?' Kirsty felt her way to the mantelpiece and fumbled for matches. After striking one, she held it to the hissing gas jet until it lit with a plop.

'Come on, Kirsty. Open the door, I need to speak to you.' The doorknob rattled.

Each step Kirsty took chilled her feet even more but pulling the blanket around her body and up to her chin, she hobbled across the room to open the door.

'Damn it, Brewster. You'll break the door off its hinges and where am I going to find the money to replace it? Certainly not from the pittance Dundee Police pay me. You should know better than to visit a lady in the middle of the night. You'll have my reputation in tatters. What would my family think? My father would probably shoot you and he would disown me again.'

Detective Inspector Brewster paid no attention to her complaints and strode into the room. 'In the name of the wee man, Kirsty, this place is a dump. Can't you find anything better?'

Kirsty's muscles tensed. 'This flat suits me fine,' she said. 'Anyway is that what you came to tell me, or is there something else you wanted?' Her voice was as brittle as the icicles that hung outside her window.

Amusement shone in his grey eyes. 'Relax, Kirsty, you're always getting riled up about something. Usually, it's me, when I come to think about it.' Looking around him, he said, 'Where do you sit in this place?' He bent over, scooped clothes from an armchair and threw them onto the rickety sofa.

The chair creaked when he sat on it and for a moment Kirsty thought it might collapse. 'Well, what's so important you have to wake me in the middle of the night?' She pushed the garments aside and perched on the edge of the sofa but not before making sure the blanket covered her completely.

Brewster rubbed his hands on the knees of his trousers and leaned forward.

'There's been a murder over in the Scouringburn district and we want you to interview a suspect.' He studied his hands. 'She won't talk to policemen, says they're ruffians and rogues.'

Kirsty laughed. 'She's maybe not far wrong. Who is she?'

'Oh, you've met this one before, and she remembers you. Says you're that nice policewoman who finds homes for children and she doesn't intend to talk to anyone else but you.'

Brewster looked up from his knees and Kirsty thought she detected an amused glint in his eyes. Her fingers tightened on the edge of the blanket. He was laughing at her again.

'This woman is evidently well informed,' she snapped. 'Who did you say she was?'

'There you go again, biting my head off when I mean no harm.' His voice was soothing but the gleam of amusement had intensified and a smile lurked around the corners of his mouth.

She darted a suspicious look towards him. 'You still haven't told me who?'

He sighed. 'I was saving that as a surprise but if you must know, it's Aggie West.'

'Big Aggie asked for me?' Kirsty almost choked, and she could have sworn Brewster was enjoying himself.

'That's right. She wants you and no one else.' Brewster seemed to be struggling to keep his expression solemn.

Kirsty wanted to tell him to get lost but decided to play him at his own game. 'Well, it's apparent I've misjudged Aggie. She's obviously a woman of considerable intelligence. Now get out of here, so I can put my clothes on, and then you can take me to see her.'

The chair creaked as he stood up. 'I could turn my back.'

'Out.' Kirsty pointed to the door.

He made an odd snuffling noise as he passed her but, ignoring it, she clicked the door shut behind him and turned the key in the lock.

Shrugging the blanket from her shoulders she crossed the room to the sink in front of the window. The water tap was stiff and she needed both hands to turn it. At last, the pipes shuddered and water spurted out into the enamel basin. She tried not to think how chilly it would be as she plunged her cupped hands into the water, scooping it up and over her face. The icy, coldness made her gasp, but once she rubbed her face dry with a towel, she was fully awake.

Her uniform hung on a hanger in the wardrobe in her bedroom because, despite leaving clothes littered on the back of chairs, she treated her police uniform more reverently. As one of Britain's first policewomen and the only one attached to Dundee City Police, she took an immense pride in the uniform although she would be the first to admit it wasn't the most attractive of attire.

It didn't take long for her to dress despite fingers, numb with cold, which struggled to fasten her shirt and jacket buttons. Her hairbrush was missing from the table beside her bed and it took her a moment before she remembered throwing it across the room last night when the scrabbling noises got too much for her to bear. Deciding she didn't have time to look for it, she combed her fingers through her short, auburn hair and pulled on her hat. She reckoned no one would know the difference.

When she opened the door to leave, she found Brewster sitting on the top step of the stairs with his arms resting on his legs and his hands dangling down between his knees.

'Took your time, didn't you?' He grinned, giving the impression he was laughing at her again.

Kirsty ignored the comment and, after a moment, he rose and led the way down the stairs into the darkness and silence of the sleeping building. She was accustomed to feeling her way up and down but Brewster muttered and stumbled all the way down until she feared he would wake her neighbours. After the entrance door slammed behind her, she breathed freely again.

Stars pricked glittering points of brilliance into the darkened sky and the frost haze around the moon seemed to increase its silvery radiance. The pavement sparkled with the sheen of gathering ice and Kirsty slithered on the glassy surface underneath her leather-soled boots.

Air sliced into Kirsty's lungs with a sharp pain and it was unusually silent without even a whisper of wind. Nothing moved on the street which was empty apart from an unfamiliar motor car parked in front of the door.

Brewster put his hand under her elbow and led her towards it. 'In you go,' he said as he opened the door, 'before you catch your death of cold.'

Kirsty's foot slipped on the running board forcing her to grab the framework. Her fingers throbbed with pain as they stuck to the freezing metal but she did not release her grasp until after she swung herself into the car. Snow had blown under the hooded cover sprinkling on the leather seats like a dusting of icing sugar and Kirsty wondered how long the dampness would take to seep through her thick serge skirt.

She turned her collar up and adjusted her skirt while she watched Brewster walk to the front of the car and lean over to crank the starter. After a few shudders and groans, the engine took hold with a vibrating beat. He paused a moment to listen to the throb before he let go of the starting handle and jumped into the driving seat.

Kirsty gripped the side of the car. 'D'you know how to drive this thing?' The coldness of the air made her voice rasp out in a hoarse croak.

'Of course, I do. I had a good half hour's practice yesterday.'

The car surged forward throwing Kirsty into the back of his seat.

'Where did you get the car anyway? I'm sure your salary doesn't run to this kind of expense.' She was having trouble moving her lips as the wind sliced into her face.

'A grateful client.' Brewster turned to grin at her.

'Watch the road,' she screamed.

'I am watching it,' he said as they turned the corner into the Marketgait. There was silence for a time until he turned off into the Scouringburn.

'What d'you mean – a grateful client? Anyway, isn't that bribery?'

'Not at all. The grateful client donated the car to Dundee Police Force as a way of saying thanks to us for finding his daughter. I thought it would be somewhat ungracious to refuse.' Brewster turned and grinned at her again while the car veered off course.

'Watch the road,' Kirsty yelled again. 'You'll overturn the car.'

'Well, I thought you'd have something to say about that instead of worrying about my driving.'

'I'm thinking,' she muttered. 'Anyway, you shouldn't have accepted it.'

'Why not? It was a gift.'

'Because it compromises me. Of all the people to accept a gift from you had to choose my father. I thought you'd know better.'

Her body shook with anger and when she heard him chuckling under his breath it made her even angrier.

'You're a fool, a damned fool, and if you weren't my superior officer I'd hit you.' The words were out before she could stop them and she waited for the anticipated reprimand. But Brewster gave no indication he'd heard.

She subsided into an angry silence.

4

Kirsty prised her fingers off the top of the car door when it shuddered to a halt in the narrow cobbled road.

She looked up at the dark face of the tenement. From memory, the four-storey stone building contained many flats although in Scotland no one ever referred to living in a flat or an apartment. The occupants thought of their homes as houses irrespective of their size or situation. Kirsty, having lived for many years in England found this strange and in her own mind, she always thought of these houses as flats.

These tenements were unlike anything Kirsty had seen before coming to Dundee. Doors to the ground floor houses faced the street. The upper ones were entered from the rear through a close which was a narrow entry passage carved through the middle of the building. A circular stair, encased in a tower which jutted from the back of the tenement, led to the upper houses on three different levels. Each level had an open-air stone landing, bordered by an iron railing. Local people referred to these landings as platties which Kirsty thought might be short for platforms because that was what they resembled.

Kirsty turned to face Brewster. 'I thought Big Aggie was in a cell?'

'Don't you want to look at the scene of the crime first?' He got out of the car. 'Come on. We don't have all night.'

It was obvious Brewster wasn't going to help her out of the car. Not that she would want that anyway, she told herself as she slithered on the running board before joining him on the pavement.

The opening of the close, which cut a black channel through the middle of the building, loomed in front of her and she entered its cave-like mouth. Darkness enveloped her, suffocating in its intensity, while menace hovered in the air around her, setting her nerves on edge. She just wanted to feel the wall in order to make sure she was still in an ordinary tenement close instead of some black, endless vacuum, but she'd done that once before and imagined the slime on her fingers for weeks after. Brewster walked in front of her and she was glad of his tuneless whistle, for it signified she was not alone.

A change of smell and a subtle variation in the intensity of the darkness told Kirsty she had emerged into the rodent-infested backlands that lay behind every tenement in Dundee. A jungle of lank grass, wash-houses, coal sheds and dustbin recesses where cats roamed nightly in search of their prey. Something more sinister could, even now, be moving from close to close and from tenement to tenement, searching for an escape into the night.

'He could be anywhere,' Brewster said as if he sensed her thoughts. 'A labyrinth of closes lead out onto at least four different streets. That's why Aggie chose this type of building to run her business. It makes sure her clients retain their anonymity. After all, most men don't want to be recognized visiting a doxy.'

'No doubt the doxy, as you call her, deserved all she got, while some poor misguided man is scuttling around, out there in the dark, terrified out of his wits.'

She glared at Brewster's back as he disappeared into the yawning mouth of the stairwell.

Kirsty had a lot of sympathy for the prostitutes but little time for the men who made their services necessary, and she certainly didn't agree with the common belief it was the girls' fault for leading the men into temptation.

The foul stench in the stairwell was worse than either the close or the back green and Kirsty tried to suspend her breathing for the length of time it took to climb the stairs. Something furry brushed against her legs and she hoped it was a cat but it carried on its silent way and she knew it was not. She clamped her mouth tightly closed and although her mind screamed no sound passed her lips.

At the top of the second flight, a shadow flitted over the grey oblong that indicated the way out from the stairwell and she collided with Brewster as he stopped. 'What is it?' she hissed.

He ignored her as he called up to the shape. 'Is that you, constable?'

'Aye, sir. The doctor went in a while ago. I told him you'd be coming but he wouldn't wait although he said I was to watch out for you. Charlie's guarding the door to keep the girls from going inside. We tried to get them to go back to their own rooms but they wouldn't budge.'

Brewster patted the constable on the shoulder as he passed him. 'That's all right, Jock. I'm sure the doctor is aware of the procedures by this time.' His breath, a white vapour floating in the night air, hung suspended before him like an eerie ectoplasm escaping from his body. 'Come on, Kirsty,' he said without turning around. 'Time to inspect the crime scene.'

The constable bent forward to peer at her as she emerged from the gloom of the stairwell. Kirsty was a curiosity to the majority of the police force who had not yet become accustomed to a woman in their ranks, but she had her own way of dealing with them. However, on this occasion there was no point in staring him down, so she kept her eyes fixed on the middle of Brewster's back as she pushed her way past the constable.

Faint light shone through the windows of the first two flats and the curtains twitched as invisible hands pulled them aside, signifying the watching eyes Kirsty could sense but not see. The sound of her feet, clattering on the icy surface of the stone landing, bounced upwards into the stillness of the night while the iron rails at their side glistened frostily in the moonlight as they walked and slithered to the furthest away door. A small crowd of girls clustered in front of it.

'Come on Charlie, let's have a look,' one of them said to the constable on duty.

'Now, ladies, stand back. Can't have you mucking up our crime scene.'

'Ladies, is it? That's not what you usually call us.'

Some of the girls sniggered and one of them stroked the policeman's arm. 'I could make it worth your while,' she said.

The policeman jerked his arm back. 'I'll run you in if you're not careful. A night in the cells will cool you down.'

'And all the big, bad bobbies will be queueing up for their share, will they?'

'Behave yourselves, girls,' Brewster said as he pushed past them. 'Stop intimidating my officer.'

'We want to know what's going on.'

Compared to the icy coldness outside, the one-roomed flat felt comfortably warm although the fire had died down to a few embers glowing dully through the metal bars of the grate. An oil lamp struggled to illuminate the room through a glass chimney stained with smoke from the flickering wick, while the faintly nauseating aroma of paraffin hung in the air.

'Ah, you've got here.' The grey-haired man kneeling beside the bed looked up and peered at them through thick-lensed spectacles. He struggled to a standing position and flexed first one leg, then the other. 'Damned knees. They're not as good as they used to be,' he muttered. 'High time I retired.'

Brewster snorted. 'You've been saying that for as long as I've known you, and you're still here. Admit it. You couldn't live without the excitement of your work.'

'Some excitements I could do without. Like this one here.' He gestured in the direction of the bed.

Kirsty bit hard on her lip. She never liked to see dead bodies but wouldn't acknowledge this to her male colleagues for fear they would think she was just a silly woman who had no right to be working with the police force. It would never have entered her mind that perhaps some of them felt much the same way she did.

She forced herself to approach the bed to inspect the slight figure lying there. Bile rose at the back of her throat when she saw the injuries to the girl's head and face. Blood seeped through her pale gold hair, turning the strands into a horrendous henna, and saturated the bed on which she lay.

Kirsty felt an overwhelming urge to speak in order to hide her feelings. 'She's very small, probably not much older than a child,' she said and then felt foolish because she should have said something more profound.

'Her name's Lily Petrie, and she's about nineteen or twenty.' Brewster touched Kirsty on the elbow. 'She's been a working girl for about three years.'

He turned to face the grey-haired man who was now busy packing instruments into a black doctor's bag. 'Well, Dr Savage, what can you tell me about her?'

'Not a lot so far. I'll be able to tell you more after the post-mortem. What I can tell you is rigor has started although liver mortis isn't complete yet. For what it's worth, she probably died about three to six hours ago which would make it between midnight and three o'clock. The light's not good in here but she seems to have been killed by several blows from a blunt instrument. You're looking for an iron bar or a poker or something similar.'

Dr Savage snapped his bag shut and straightened up. 'I'm off home, back to my bed. Try not to find any more bodies for me to examine tonight. There's a good lad, Brewster.' He paused in the doorway, 'Nice meeting you too, Miss Campbell. Maybe we'll do business again sometime.' He pulled his hat down over his eyes, turned his collar up and with a slight shiver he left the flat.

'What d'you make of it, Kirsty? Is it a crime of passion? An argument between working girls? Or has Big Aggie decided to cut down on her overheads?' Brewster raised an eyebrow.

'What I think is the last thing we should do is jump to conclusions. We need to find the murder weapon and speak to people before we can make a judgment.' Kirsty's tone was clipped and business-like because it was obvious to her Brewster was in danger of making his mind up before considering everything. 'Another thing. I think we have to investigate Lily and her life because who knows what might be hidden there.'

'I was hoping you'd say that and you might start by talking to the girls on the landing. Get their names and find out if any of them saw anything. Let them know we'll be speaking to them again.'

5

Brewster waited until Kirsty left the flat before standing in the doorway to survey the scene in front of him. He had expected the body to be sprawled on the mattress, but the girl lay on the bed at the rear of the room with her hands crossed over her chest in a macabre pose. Blood pooled around her head and soaked into her hair while her face bore witness to the ferocity of the blows.

The next thing to strike him was how small and childlike she appeared, cloaking her in a mantle of vulnerability. Sadness swept through Brewster and tears pricked the back of his eyelids.

Forcing his eyes away from her, he blinked and steadied his breathing. There was a job to be done which meant objectivity was important and he couldn't allow himself to be affected by his own reactions. Emotion had no place in an investigation.

The room was a typical single end, one room which served as kitchen, living room and bedroom combined. After surveying the entire room, he pulled out his notebook ready to follow the normal investigative procedure of starting at the left side of the door and noting every detail in a methodical manner. He remained in the doorway while he examined each item in the room by moving his gaze in a clockwise direction until he returned to the area to the right of the door.

He scribbled the details in his notebook. Jaw-box sink underneath the window to the left of the door. Water droplets at the bottom indicated recent use. A sideboard with one end tucked into the corner of the room stretched along part of the adjoining wall while its other end bordered the black metal fireplace. Above the fireplace was a shelf, bare apart from an unlit candle which sat in a puddle of wax in the saucer that held it while feeble flickering embers remained in the grate which contained mainly ash.

Most of the wall facing the door was taken up by the bed and a ramshackle wardrobe, while a wooden table and solitary chair occupied the right-hand wall. An oil lamp sat on the table casting its light over a tablecloth. Linoleum, the colour and pattern indistinguishable in the flickering glow of the oil lamp, covered the floor. He noted where the bloodstains were and swiftly drew a diagram, noting as he did so that there was no sign of a weapon. After that, he wrote his description of the body.

Slipping the notebook into his pocket he acknowledged to himself his examination of the scene had been cursory because the smoky oil lamp hadn't thrown enough light on its surroundings. He made a mental note to do another inspection during daylight hours.

'Do you mind if I have a word with you?' Kirsty approached the group of girls on the landing.

'I'd much rather have a word with this fine man here,' one of them said.

'Aggie told me there was a policewoman in Dundee, but I didn't believe her,' another said.

'You should have listened to her. She knew what she was talking about.'

Kirsty pulled a pencil and notebook from her pocket. 'I'll take your names first.'

The small fair-haired girl to Kirsty's left said, 'I'm Maud.'

'And your surname?'

'Gillespie.'

Kirsty peered at her notepad. 'Blast I can't see to write.'

'I'm Elsie Johnston and my room is two doors along the landing,' one of the girls said. 'We could go there.'

'If you wouldn't mind, that would be helpful.'

'I've never been asked if I minded before,' Elsie said. 'Follow me.'

The room looked exactly the same as Lily's room but a lot cosier. A fire burned in the grate. There were ornaments on the mantelpiece, and a patchwork quilt covered the bed.

The girl pulled a chair away from the table. 'You sit here, miss, the rest of you can sit on the floor or stand.'

'Thank you,' Kirsty said. 'I was admiring your quilt. It must be a lot of work to make.'

Colour tinged the girl's cheeks. 'I like to sew when I'm not working.'

Kirsty wrote down Maud's and Elsie's names. 'Right, I've got Maud and Elsie so if the rest of you can tell me who you are, we'll get that out of the way.'

'Now you've got our names in your book, what are you going to do with them?' Maud demanded.

'Yes, are you going to use them to have us arrested and put before the beak?'

Resentment seemed to hang over the girls who muttered among themselves but Kirsty had expected their hostility. These girls had no cause to like or trust the police. It would be part of her job to allay their fears and persuade them to trust her. Not an easy task.

'I have no intention of doing that,' Kirsty said. 'The reason I need to know who you are is so we can find Lily's killer.'

'How will that help?'

'You might have seen something suspicious around the time of her death.'

'None of us saw anything.'

'It might be something innocuous you think is unrelated.'

'What's innocuous mean?' Daisy asked.

'Something you think doesn't matter,' Kirsty replied. 'I also want to find out about Lily. What was she like? What about her family? Who are her friends? That kind of thing. I need to build a picture of her as a person in order to try to find out who would want her dead.'

'She didn't mix much. Thought herself better than us. Kept reminding any of us who would listen that she was a minister's daughter, not some slag from the streets.' Elsie's voice held a note of bitterness.

'That's right. Thought she was a cut above us, she did.'

'None of us liked her.'

'But we wouldn't kill her.'

'I didn't suggest you would,' Kirsty said although the possibility of one of the girls beating Lily to a pulp couldn't be ruled out.

'She wouldn't see just anyone,' Maud said. 'Aggie was never able to get her to take on some of the scruffs she sends to the rest of us.'

'Aggie didn't lose out. She used to charge more for Lily.'

'What about her regular clients?' Kirsty felt she wasn't getting any helpful information from the girls who were venting their dislike of the dead girl.

'One of her regulars is an ex-soldier. Calls himself the Captain. I don't think anyone knows his real name.'

'What about the chap who says he's a laird? Keeps boasting about his land. Says he's got a lot of farms and loads of money. Doesn't he come to you as well, Daisy?'

'He's nice, treats me well. Says he can't make up his mind whether he likes me or Lily best. But I'm not sure he has as much money as he claims.'

'Then there's him as owns all the tenements over in the next street. Mr Armstrong's his name. He's been seeing her recently.'

Kirsty jotted the names and details in her notebook. 'Anyone else you can think of?'

'I heard tell she had a boyfriend she kept secret from Aggie.'

'I saw her in the Overgate about a week ago and that pimp Freddie Simpson was hanging about her.'

'I don't think Lily would entertain him as a boyfriend, she was too high and mighty for that.' Elsie lifted a poker from the hearth and stirred the coals in the fireplace.

Brewster's voice sounded outside on the landing so Kirsty closed her notebook and stuffed it, along with the pencil, in her pocket.

'Thank you for your assistance, ladies,' she said. 'On my return, I would like to speak to you separately. If you can think of anything that might help that would be good.'

Elsie rose and opened the door for her. 'Lily brought an old school friend to Aggie about six months ago,' she whispered.

'She'll know more about her than any of us.'

'What's her name?'

'Nancy Allardyce. Her room is on the landing below this, number nine.'

Kirsty turned to thank Elsie but the door had closed.

6

Jamie Brewster opened the door and beckoned to the constable on duty.

'Keep an eye on this lot and don't let anyone near. I'll be back once daylight's arrived. That lamp's no damn use, can't see a thing the way it's flickering.'

The constable, slouching against the iron railing, tried to hide his cigarette.

Brewster watched the red tip arcing away from him into the darkness of the night. The landing was empty and neither Kirsty nor the girls, who had clustered there, were anywhere to be seen.

'If you're looking for the young lady, sir, she's in Elsie's house two doors along.'

Brewster nodded his thanks and strode to the door the constable indicated. He raised his hand to knock but before his fist made contact with the wood the door opened and Kirsty emerged.

'I heard you talking so I thought you'd be finished with your inspection of the crime scene,' she said.

'Did you get anything from the girls?'

'Not a lot, but it's a start and I've told them I'll be questioning them further.'

He nodded his approval. 'Big Aggie is waiting for you in the cells. Are you ready to go?'

'Yes, sir.' Kirsty walked past him.

With a nod to the policeman on duty, he followed her.

The icy roads and darkness made it an exciting drive back to the police station. The steering wheel seemed to have a life of its own and he wrestled with it as he tried to prevent the car from sliding while trying to ignore Kirsty's reaction to each bump and swerve.

At last, they drove under the arch into the courtyard and he drew up at the door.

'I'll be back later,' he said. 'Write me a full report after you've interviewed Big Aggie.'

'Yes, sir.' She got out of the car and marched into the police station without a backward look.

Brewster's hands tightened on the steering wheel. Kirsty could be aggravating and he couldn't quell his own annoyance at the sound of the resentment in her voice. She probably thought he should discuss his thoughts about the crime scene but he was busy wrestling with the car and that was the last thing on his mind.

Kirsty seemed to forget he was her senior officer and she should show him respect. But she made no pretence of hiding her resentment of male police officers and it riled him. She never stopped reminding him she was a trained policewoman and therefore entitled to be involved with investigations.

He glared at the door through which she'd vanished, he should do something about her but he didn't have time to ponder on that at the moment. There was too much to do.

After releasing the handbrake he guided the car to the rear of the courtyard, turned off the engine and got out. Then he walked through the arch to the street outside and turned in the direction of home. He had been away too long and Maggie would need him.

Once he turned the corner into the narrow lane leading to his house the pavement and cobbles were icier and he was glad he'd left the car at the Police Station. He slipped and slid as he walked homeward, swearing softly under his breath when he saved himself taking a tumble by grabbing the top of the fence that bordered the lane.

The cottage was in darkness and he knew Maggie would be awake and fretting. But she wouldn't say anything although sometimes he wished she would because her stoicism increased his guilt feelings.

The gate creaked when he opened it because he still hadn't found time to oil the hinges. He let it swing shut behind him, walked down the garden path and up the wooden ramp to the front door. Inside, the house was as cold as it was outside.

'Is that you, Jamie?' Maggie's voice floated through the open bedroom door.

'Yes, my love. I don't want you to freeze so I'll set the fire before I help you dress.'

It didn't take him long to rake the ash out of the grate and dump it in a tin bucket. He scrunched up yesterday's newspaper, pushed it into the fireplace, laid some kindling and nuggets of coal on top. Then, striking a match to light the paper, he waited until flames licked around the sticks and coal.

'The house isn't very warm yet,' he said when he walked into the bedroom.

Maggie grasped the bar hanging over the bed and pulled herself up to a sitting position. 'I'll survive.'

Brewster leaned over and hugged her. She was so brave it broke his heart to see her struggle. If it had been him, he would have given up long ago.

'I'm such a trial for you,' Maggie said as he helped to dress her.

'Don't be silly. We wed for better or worse, and I'm not the best husband in the world. You could have done a lot better.'

'You're the one being silly. You didn't bargain on getting an invalid for a wife.'

'Just because you're in a wheelchair doesn't mean you're an invalid. You're the best thing that ever happened to me.' Brewster tried to disguise the catch in his voice as he remembered her as the vibrant young woman he married. She didn't deserve this.

Once he settled her with a cushion at her back and a blanket over her knees, he pushed the wheelchair to the sitting room and positioned it in front of the fire.

'I'll peel potatoes before I put the porridge pot on,' he said. 'There's still beef stew left from yesterday which will do your dinner. Mrs McCormack will be in later in case you need any help.'

'I'm not helpless, Jamie. I could boil the potatoes and heat the stew myself.'

Brewster sighed. She could do a lot of things but couldn't

move around without her wheelchair. Apoplexy the doctor called it, something that usually didn't affect younger people. When he demanded why her legs were paralysed and would she recover, the doctor had explained her condition was due to a blood vessel bursting in her brain which made it unlikely she would ever walk again. That was eight years ago on their second marriage anniversary and he'd been right. Maggie hadn't recovered the use of her legs.

'You know I don't like you lifting pots,' he said. 'You might scald yourself.'

'You fuss too much.'

After he readied everything for Mrs McCormack and they had eaten the porridge, he said, 'I'll have to go back to work now and I'm not sure when I'll get finished.' He leaned over and kissed her.

He left the house, fighting the guilt that consumed him every time he had to leave her.

7

The cell door slammed behind Kirsty with a metallic thud that seemed to shake the building.

'Took your time getting here, didn't you?' The woman lying on the mattress-covered stone slab propped herself up on her elbows and glared at her. 'I was beginning to think those shits of policemen weren't going to send for you.'

Kirsty leaned against the door. 'I understand you wanted to talk to me.'

'I'm certainly not going to talk to those pillocks who can never get their brains separated from their dicks when they're speaking to me. All they see is girls and sex and booze. They don't see me. They don't see Big Aggie, the person.'

'I thought that was the way you liked it. After all, that's how you make your money.'

'Oh, it's how I make my money all right, but that doesn't make me any less of a person.' Aggie glared at Kirsty. 'Lippy, aren't you? But that's all right, I don't have much time for milk sops. I need someone who'll stand up for me when the men have it in for me.'

'You don't know that I'll stand up for you, though, do you? Maybe you're guilty and if that's the case I'll make sure you hang.' Kirsty stared back at the big woman, determined not to be intimidated by her.

Big Aggie laughed. It was surprisingly light and musical considering her size. 'How do I convince you I'm innocent?'

'To begin with, you can answer my questions.'

'Will I get out of here if I do?'

'Maybe yes, maybe no.'

'You'd better come and sit down.' Aggie patted the mattress beside her. 'It'll be more comfortable.'

Kirsty crossed the cell and balanced on the edge of the bed

despite wondering about the possibility of fleas.

'Tell me about last night.'

'Same as any other night, sitting in my own wee house getting a heat at the fire.'

'Anyone with you?'

'No, I don't need to work so I never have company.'

Aggie's gaze was bland and innocent but she didn't fool Kirsty.

'You went to Lily's flat. What time was that?'

'Two o'clock in the morning or thereabouts, I reckon. Yes, must have been two because I looked at the clock on the mantelpiece as I left my own house. Not sure if it had the right time but I wound it up earlier in the evening so I suppose it did.'

'Why did you go to the flat?'

'Why not? She's one of my girls and I like to check up on them now and then.'

Kirsty hardened her voice. 'That's not good enough. Lily could have had a customer at two o'clock.'

Aggie glared at her. 'You're not daft, are you? All right, I'd had a complaint and I wanted to sort her out. They need sorting out now and then those girls do.'

'Did you sort her out? Really sort her out?'

'Don't be silly. Can't sort anyone out when they're already dead. Can I now?'

Far off sounds of doors clanging and feet echoing in the corridors broke the silence that engulfed both women. Kirsty stared at Aggie who returned the look with a glare of her own. Despite that, Kirsty believed her.

'All right. Tell me what you found?'

'It was awful. She lay there all covered in blood. Then I thought maybe she wasn't dead and I went over to try and wake her up, but that didn't work. That's when it hit me. She was dead and I had her blood all over me, and that's when I started to scream.' Aggie paused for breath. 'Then when the bobbies came, they clapped me in here. That's the god's honest truth.'

'I see.' Kirsty scribbled in her notebook before looking up. 'What about a weapon, did you see anything lying in the flat?'

'Didn't see nothing like that although everything was a mess so I suppose there could have been something. Wouldn't have known what to look for in any case.' Aggie shuddered. 'I never seen nothing like that before and I don't want to see anything like it again. Horrible it was.'

'One other thing, Aggie. I'm not clear about how you got in. Was the door open or what?'

'Naw, it was locked, but I got my master keys. Property's mine after all.'

'What about Lily's key?'

'The girls keep their keys in the keyhole on the inside of the door. Hers wasn't there, otherwise, my key wouldn't have worked.'

Kirsty scribbled in her notebook.

'Well, am I getting out of here or not?'

'It doesn't look good, Aggie. You were the one who found her. So I want more from you. I'll need to know if she had any gentleman callers that night. I'm sure you must have a system for keeping track of them. And I need to interview the other girls who work for you before any decision can be made.'

'Who says they work for me? I just rent them rooms.'

'Whatever you say. But I am going to question them. I'm also going to need the names of all Lily's clients.'

'Can't do it,' Aggie said. 'That's confidential information, that is. It'd be my ruination if I told the bobbies the names of anyone who visited my girls.'

'That's up to you. It's either ruination or the hangman's rope. You decide.' Kirsty closed her notebook. 'I'll leave you to think about it but I'll expect you to deliver the next time I come to see you.'

She walked to the door and thumped it to let the turnkey know she'd finished.

8

'Did Aggie give you any trouble?' The large woman in the navy blue dress turned the key in the lock of the heavy iron door.

Kirsty shook her head. 'Nothing I couldn't handle and you were in the corridor if I needed help.'

The turnkey reached for the cover of the peephole and sliding it to the side she looked into the cell. 'She's sitting there like butter wouldn't melt in her mouth. But she's not to be trusted, you be careful when you come back to see her.'

'I'll keep that in mind.'

Kirsty liked the gruff turnkey who ran a tight ship and stood no nonsense. The men were wary but she'd struck up an unlikely friendship with her because she sensed a kind heart beating in that stern frame.

Annie certainly presented an imposing appearance. Older and more buxom than Kirsty, she towered over even the tallest men and had a build to match. Her grey hair scraped into a tight bun gave her a severe appearance and her navy blue attire looked more like a uniform than a dress. Attached to the leather belt which circled her waist hung several iron rings from which dangled iron keys reaching to her knees. These keys jangled as they strode along the corridor to the barred door which gave access to the cell area.

The turnkey unlocked the door and swung it open. She waited until Kirsty passed through to the other side and clanged it shut again.

Kirsty raised her hand in a farewell wave. 'Like as not I'll be back to talk to Aggie again,' she said.

Annie grinned. 'I'll try to keep her in a good mood.'

Traversing the warren of corridors beneath the police station was starting to get easier for Kirsty and she only took one wrong turn. Once she realized her mistake she retraced her steps and soon emerged in the upper corridor at the rear of the charge room. She turned to the left, walking past the canteen, the constables' room and the sergeants' room, all showing no signs of life apart from the smell of cigarette smoke hanging in the air.

The door to her own small office, converted from a cloakroom, stood open and she wondered if any of the men had been having a poke around. It wouldn't have done them any good because the room was so small it was impossible to leave anything inside.

She squeezed past the ancient desk and sat in the wooden chair. But when she reached for a pencil she realized all her pencils had gone. That was why her door was open, they were thieving things from her office.

Kirsty suppressed her anger. If that was the way it was, well two could play at that game.

She stalked down the corridor until she came to the constables' room. After entering she rummaged in their desk drawers until she found pencils. She appropriated two from each desk and marched back to her own office.

It didn't take long to write up her interview with Big Aggie. Then she wrote a report on her interviews with the girls which didn't amount to much more than their names and the snippets of information they'd provided. She ended with an assessment of what she would do next.

Nancy Allardyce was top of her list to interview. According to Elsie, Nancy was an old school friend of Lily and should be able to provide information about the murdered girl.

Then, Kirsty wanted to interview Elsie again as well as Daisy who apparently shared the client called the Laird, with Lily.

After replacing the pencil in her drawer she gathered the sheets of paper together and placed the reports on Brewster's desk. Instead of returning to her own office, she followed the corridor to the charge room.

Warm air met her when she pushed the door open. 'It's warmer in here than in my room.' She deliberately didn't say office because she knew this was a sore point with the men.

Even the sergeants didn't get an office of their own.

'I keep the stove topped up,' the desk sergeant said without looking up. 'It helps cut the draught when the door opens.'

He finished writing in the ledger in front of him, then laid the pen down with a sigh. 'Paperwork, it'll be the death of me. Give me a night on the beat anytime.' He lifted his foot and closed the door of the potbellied stove, hiding the glowing coals inside.

'I'm looking for Inspector Brewster. I take it he hasn't returned yet.'

The desk sergeant looked at the large wall clock. 'I saw him head off down the road when he dropped you off, miss. Seeing as that was about an hour ago I expect he'll be back soon.'

'Where is everyone else? The place is empty. I thought there might be some bobbies in the constables' room.'

'Ah! That's because of the murder. Sergeant Brodie's in charge of the search and the bobbies not out on the beat are off to the Scouringburn. But the first patrol is due to finish soon, so we won't be quiet for long.' He leaned on the polished wood counter. 'Did the inspector say what he wanted you to do?'

Kirsty nodded. 'I've done what he asked. Interviewed Big Aggie and written my reports.'

'Better you than me,' he said. 'Big Aggie's not someone we like messing with.'

'She wasn't so bad. But I suppose I'll have to go and twiddle my thumbs until Brewster returns.'

'There's a fire lit in the canteen, miss, and the kettle was hot not long ago. I'd lay odds you haven't had anything to eat this morning, you could make yourself a cuppa and toast some bread.'

Kirsty smiled her thanks and headed in the direction of the canteen.

9

'Any new developments, Geordie?' Brewster kicked the charge room door shut.

'Nothing so far,' the desk sergeant said, 'but Miss Campbell was looking for you. She's in the canteen.'

Brewster shrugged away the twinge of guilt that nagged him about leaving her here while he went to attend to Maggie. As Kirsty's superior officer he should be playing more of a guiding role. But his wife needed him and he couldn't neglect her.

The canteen was empty apart from Kirsty.

He sat on a bench opposite her and watched as she struggled to spread hard margarine on a piece of toast.

'There's tea made.' She nodded at the teapot simmering on the black hob over the open fire.

'I thought you didn't like stewed tea.' He grabbed the handle and poured some into a tin mug.

'I've got accustomed to it but I'll never get used to margarine. When are they going to take butter off the ration? It's not as if we're still at war.' She lifted the toasting fork. 'D'you want toast?'

He shook his head. 'I had breakfast with Maggie.' He expected her to say something, but she didn't.

She leaned back against the wall and took a bite of the toast.

He suppressed a laugh as her face indicated disgust at what she was eating. She had shed her armour and didn't seem to be so brittle this morning and he was reluctant to spoil the moment by laughing out of turn. Her hat lay on the end of the bench and her tousled hair made her look younger. But her uniform was as immaculate as usual despite him rousing her from her bed at an unearthly hour.

'How was your interview with Aggie? Did she tell you anything?'

'No more than we knew already. She told me Lily was dead when she found her and described what she did. You know what? I believe her.'

'Aggie's not daft. She knows the rest of us wouldn't believe a word she says, that's why she asked for you.'

'She probably knew you'd be biased.'

'It's not bias, it's common sense. When the bobbies arrived they found Aggie, covered in blood, beside the body. That means she's the most likely person to have killed Lily.'

'What's her motive?'

'That doesn't concern me for the moment, we'll find out eventually. What does matter is the evidence before us and that all points to Aggie.'

'I still think we need to look further afield.'

Brewster sighed. Kirsty was doing it again, trying to take over the investigation, but he was her senior officer and he couldn't allow her to forget that. So, although he recognized the sense in her argument, it increased his determination to prove her wrong.

'Have you written the reports I asked for?' His voice was sterner than he meant it to be.

'Of course,' she snapped. 'They're on your desk.'

He rose and moved to the door. 'Did you find out how Aggie operates her business? How the men access the girls and whether she keeps records?'

Kirsty shifted her position on the bench. 'I didn't think about that. I was busy finding out what happened.'

'You'd best find out then. Interview her again and report back to me. We'll be going back to the scene of the crime in about an hour when there is more daylight.'

'Yes, sir.'

Brewster marched down the corridor without looking back.

Kirsty seethed as she strode through the corridors to Aggie's cell. Brewster couldn't resist wielding his authority over her when she was only trying to be helpful. He'd seemed human when he joined her in the canteen and she thought he would be receptive to her ideas but he clammed up again when she doubted his conclusions. But he didn't have to gloat when he found something she'd missed.

'Back again, so soon?' The turnkey unlocked the cell door for her. 'I'll be outside if you need me.'

Kirsty nodded her thanks and entered, wrinkling her nose at the smell. A mixture of stale urine, sweat and indistinguishable odours seemed to be ingrained into the stains on the concrete floor.

Aggie rose from the narrow, mattress-covered bench. 'That was quick. Can I go now?'

'I'm afraid not, but I want to check one or two other things with you.'

'I told you all I know about Lily and how I found her.'

'We'll be going back to your building this morning and I need to understand how your business works.'

'I told you. I rent rooms to the girls, what they do in them is their own concern.'

'Now you and I know that's not strictly true.'

Aggie shrugged. 'Believe what you like but that's all I'll be telling you.'

'Have it your own way, but if you are renting the rooms there must be some system for paying rent and you must keep records.'

'You're not daft, are you?'

'No, so come on, Aggie, how is the rent paid?'

'The bottom house in the building, the one with the door on the street before you enter the close. That's the office. William Simpson is responsible for the keys. When the money is handed over a key is issued for the room they are paying for. And that's as much as I'm saying.'

'What about your accounts and records?'

'I told you. That's all I'm saying until my solicitor gets here. I've said too much already.'

'You've got a solicitor?'

'Oh, yes! And he's the best one in town.' Aggie flashed her a triumphant smile. 'Simon Harvie. He'll get me out of here.'

Kirsty didn't doubt it. Simon Harvie had helped her confront the influential Bogue family when they threatened to apply for custody of her own sister, Ailsa. Anyone who could get the better of old Mr Bogue was someone to be reckoned with.

Aggie leaned back against the wall, folded her arms across her chest and looked at Kirsty through narrowed eyes.

It was evident nothing more was to be gained during this interview so Kirsty banged on the cell door and waited for the turnkey to let her out. She would be glad to escape this confined space with its white tiled walls, barred window, and stained concrete floor.

She heard the thud of feet before she pushed open the door to the main part of the building. Several constables passed her, hurrying to the outer door.

'I want every inch of the backlands searched for the murder weapon.' Brewster's voice soared over the hubbub.

The door slammed and the corridor was empty apart from Brewster.

'Does that mean you didn't find the weapon when you searched Lily's room last night?' She was tempted to add this confirmed her belief in Aggie's innocence, but she refrained.

Brewster stared at her as if reading her mind. 'That doesn't let Big Aggie off the hook. She probably threw it over the railing before we arrived.'

'Let's hope the constables find something then because Aggie informed me she's engaged Simon Harvie as her solicitor.'

'Damn! It had to be him.'

'She reckons he'll get her out of police custody as soon as she sees him and she's maybe not far wrong.'

Brewster's shoulders slumped and he ran a hand over his face. Kirsty wondered how much sleep he'd had. Probably not much.

'What did Aggie tell you?'

Kirsty followed him into his office. 'Not much. She doesn't want to incriminate herself. But she did say William Simpson takes the money and hands out keys for the girls' rooms.'

'William Simpson.' Brewster's voice was thoughtful. 'He's a bit of a mystery man. I know his brother, Freddie, though.

He's an ex-boxer, a hard man who gets into fights, and he's pimped for girls on the street from time to time. As far as I'm aware, he works for Aggie now.'

'If William gives the keys out he's bound to know the identity of the last person to visit Lily in her room.'

Brewster nodded. 'Be ready in fifteen minutes. We're going back to the Scouringburn.'

10

Freddie Simpson inhaled, filling his lungs with air, before stepping out of the door of the ground floor flat. Sweat trickled down his back but no one would see the damp patches which were covered by his jacket.

'Where do you think you're going?' One of the two bobbies on duty stepped forward blocking his way to the close.

'Can't a man go to the cludgie when he needs? What am I supposed to do, piss in the sink?'

The constable frowned and looked at his partner.

'It'll be all right if you accompany him to make sure he doesn't go up to the crime scene.'

'Come on then, make it quick.'

'Don't think you're coming inside with me,' Freddie said as they walked through the close to the back of the building.

The constable laughed. 'What would I want to do that for? I'll wait outside.'

As they climbed the stairs Freddie could hear activity above but he ignored it. All he needed to do was get into the cludgie and retrieve Lily's journal before anyone else found it.

'I'll manage now,' he said when they reached the lavatory on the middle half-landing.

'That place stinks.' The constable wrinkled his nose. 'But, I don't suppose you'd notice.'

Freddie glowered at him. 'Needs must,' he said, going in and closing the door.

Once inside, he poked his fingers behind the cistern, moving them around until he found the journal.

Lily was good at ferreting out secrets and she kept meticulous notes. But she always made sure no one else knew apart from Freddie which was why she didn't keep any information in her room.

He slipped the notebook into the inside pocket of his jacket before pulling the chain to flush the toilet.

The constable escorted him downstairs and through the close, only leaving to return to his post when Freddie entered the flat and shut the door.

Freddie wiped his damp hands on his trouser legs and walked through to the room that overlooked the rear of the building. He peered out the window, watching the bobbies searching the backlands. They had been at it for hours and the longer they took the more frazzled his nerves became.

He wasn't the only one who was nervous. During the night, the girls clustered on the landings talking among themselves. Their voices had drifted down to him through the still night air. He'd listened but kept well clear. He didn't want the bobbies poking their noses into his affairs.

Freddie leaned forward and gripped the windowsill. He didn't know what to do. William, whose place it was to be here, had gone walkabout saying he didn't feel well and would Freddie mind looking after things until he got back. And Aggie wasn't here to tell him. She'd been carted off by the bobbies in the middle of the night, her cursing and swearing echoing down the stairs when they took her away.

One of the two bobbies guarding the end of the close leading to the stairs turned his head to look at him and he drew back into the room. He paced through to the kitchen, walked around the table in the middle, and peered out the front window to the street outside. If the road was clear he'd sneak out and be off. But two other bobbies guarded the entrance to the close, lounging against the wall, smoking their cigarettes. There was no way he could leave without them seeing him and they might think he was the one who did for Lily.

Despair surged through him. His body sagged. He slumped in a chair, leaned his elbows on the table and cradled his head in his hands.

After a moment he fumbled in his pocket for his packet of Woodbines and with shaking fingers slid a cigarette out of the pack. A fag would calm him. He reached for the matches but they fell from the box onto the table. The first three he selected broke when he struck them on the side of the box but the fourth flamed long enough for him to light his fag. The tip glowed red and he inhaled the smoke deep into his lungs in an effort to calm his nerves. It was in vain because shaking engulfed his body. He couldn't get the image of Lily out of his head. Lily, beautiful Lily, he was nothing without her.

Warning her Aggie wouldn't take kindly to her leaving and setting up her own house had made Lily laugh. 'What can she do? Besides, I have you to protect me so it will all work out fine.'

She'd laughed at him again when he suggested they seal their relationship in the usual way. 'Later,' she'd said, 'when it will mean more. If I give you what you want before I've left Aggie, it will make you another one of them.' Even though he understood she didn't want him to be another customer it didn't stop him wondering if she only used him to get what she wanted. In any case, it didn't matter now because all their plans collapsed when she died.

Loud knocking on the door pushed thoughts of Lily out of his mind. Alarmed, he jumped to his feet and the chair crashed to the floor. His heart pounded as he crossed the room. Had they come to take him away as well?

Inspector Brewster barged his way in, followed by the woman in the outlandish uniform. Aggie had told him about the policewoman although this was the first time he'd seen her. But he knew the inspector from way back and didn't like him. More than once he'd narrowly avoided prison and it was all down to this man. Now he was here, looking for someone to blame for Lily's death.

Freddie laid his fag on the table and wiped his hands on his trousers. Sweat dripped from his forehead. 'What d'you want with me? I haven't done anything.'

'I never said you had, but now you're making me think.' Brewster picked up the toppled chair and set it upright. 'Sit down, Freddie, we need to have a chat.'

Freddie, a big, muscle-bound man, knew he could easily get the better of the inspector in a fight, but he felt intimidated by this man and couldn't explain it to himself. He wiped the sweat from his forehead. 'What can I do for you, Inspector?'

'You can start by telling me all about Aggie's business. I'll also need a list of the men who visit the girls and I want access to the records.'

Brewster nodded to the policewoman. 'You take notes while Freddie here provides the information.'

She responded by pulling her notebook from her pocket.

'Why would I be knowing anything about that? I'm only standing in for William. He's the one you want.' A drop of sweat dripped from his face onto the table.

'Your boss, Aggie, told Miss Campbell,' Brewster pointed at Kirsty, 'you and your brother book the men in when they come to visit the girls. She said both of you are responsible for the business side of her enterprise.'

Freddie's mind whirled. Aggie never described her business to anyone and woe betide any employee who discussed it, particularly with the police. No one was more aware of the consequences of indiscretion than him because he was the one who beat up the last person who ratted on her.

'That's not true. William's the one responsible for that. It's nothing to do with me.'

'But William doesn't seem to be here. Where is he?'

'How would I know. He just asked me to mind things until he got back.'

'William wouldn't leave anyone in charge he couldn't trust and who didn't understand the business. Am I right?'

Freddie stared into Brewster's eyes but the inspector's gaze never wavered. Damn William for leaving him in this position.

'Come on, stop thinking about it and tell me what I want to know.' Brewster drummed his fingers on the table. 'I can't wait all day.'

Freddie hesitated, uncertain what to do. But one thing was clear, they wouldn't know he worked for Aggie unless she told them, so what was she up to? Was she trying to drop him in the shit, trying to shift the blame? He wouldn't put it past her.

'What do you want to know?'

'You can start off by telling me how the business works. What happens when a client arrives and wants to see one of the girls? Talk me through the process.'

'They come here first. They pay their money for the service they want and they get a token and the key to one of the houses upstairs. The girls keep their doors locked so no one who hasn't paid gets in. After they're admitted to the flat they give the token to the girl and she can cash it here the next day. That way, there's no danger of robbery and it keeps the girls safe.'

'Does that mean no one is able to gain access to any of the rooms without a key?'

'That's right although the girls also have their own key so I suppose they could let someone in. They're not likely to do that unless they know them.'

'You're a pimp, Freddie. You're selling the girls to men for sexual services.'

Freddie's tongue stuck to the roof of his mouth. The inspector was twisting his words. Thinking back to what he'd said he realized his mistake. He should have said time, not service.

'No, Mr Brewster, my job is to protect the girls and it's William who sells the tokens.'

'But you stand in for him and sell them when he's not here, and you said the tokens buy the girls' services.'

Freddie squirmed. 'What the tokens buy isn't up to me. It's up to Aggie. Each token buys an hour of time with a girl. What they do during that time isn't my concern.'

'You know perfectly well what they do in that time, though. Don't you?'

'You can't prove that.'

'We'll see.' The inspector stared at him. 'So that means you know who the customers are, which girls they visit, and have a record of when they visit.'

'I didn't say nothing about records.'

'Ah! But if there are no records how would Aggie know you and William aren't on the fiddle?'

Freddie wiped sweat from his brow while he tried to think of an answer. Nothing came to mind. The inspector was too clever for him.

'I'll need the records, as well as a list of customers.'

'They don't belong to me so I can't hand them over. Only Aggie can do that.'

The inspector's eyes narrowed. 'That's all right. I'll apply for a warrant, and those records had better be here when I come back or you'll be looking at the inside of a police cell.'

Freddie heaved a sigh of relief once he was alone again. He grabbed a towel and rubbed the sweat from his face and hair. His cigarette had burned down but he flicked the ash off the end and drew the smoke deep into his lungs, before throwing the butt into the fireplace. It was time to move, he didn't fancy being here when the inspector returned with his warrant and if William didn't return soon, brother or no brother, he would be off for good. But there were things he needed to do before he left.

He locked the door to the street before hurrying into the other room. Lucky the inspector hadn't asked to see through here. This was the hub of the business. The front room, set out like any other living area with an armchair, a table and four kitchen chairs, was for show. The back room, however, which in any other flat would be a bedroom, contained a massive desk along one wall and a large wooden filing cabinet opposite. Above the desk, on rows of hooks, hung twenty labelled keys, one for each of the flats. The twenty-first key was in Aggie's possession and gave access to the top floor shebeen. In this drinking den, any kind of alcohol could be purchased before or after a visit to one of the girls.

Freddie ran his finger over the drawers in the filing cabinet and pulled out the one labelled K to L. All the girls were filed under their first names, not their surnames and he blessed his brother for being fastidious. William might not be the muscle employed in the business but he was definitely the brain.

He riffled through the files to locate the one for Lily, opened it and removed everything inside before replacing the empty envelope. There were too many secrets in Lily's file and he had no intention of allowing it to be seen by the bobbies.

He walked through to the front room, placed the documents in the grate, struck a match and watched them burn. Satisfied nothing was left he returned to the desk and grabbed several sheets of paper. What had happened to Lily was a tragedy but there was money to be made out of it.

Freddie grasped a pencil and wrote, 'I know what you done. Bring £20 to the Howff graveyard at nine of the night on Thursday. Leave it underneath Jonathan Bogue's stone.'

That should do it. Satisfied with what he'd written he copied the words onto several other pieces of paper but put a different time on each one.

He knew more about Lily than any of the others They'd been close. He even knew about that flash geezer who pranced about at the picture house in his ridiculous red and gold suit. No one else here knew about him but, when he followed Lily on her days off, he saw what the two of them got up to. But she was just playing and had more sense than tie herself to anyone because if she did, her plan to open a grand house in competition with Aggie would never come about.

Freddie mourned Lily as well as the loss of his partnership with her and the loss of the wealth this would have brought. But, Lily had known everyone's secrets and, because she planned for him to be her enforcer, he knew them as well. Secrets they wouldn't want anyone else to know. These men would gladly pay him to keep quiet.

11

'Do a door-to-door and talk to all the girls. Find out if any of them saw or knew anything about what happened last night.'

'Yes, sir.'

He stopped at the bottom of the stairwell. 'What did you think of Freddie?'

'I think he's scared, sir. He knows more than he's telling.'

Brewster reflected on the interview. Freddie had a fearsome reputation for violence and he'd expected him to be more aggressive, so he was inclined to agree with Kirsty. She didn't miss much.

The smell in the stairwell had increased in intensity since last night. Halfway up the spiral stairs, they passed a cludgie with the door hanging off giving a clear view of the lavatory pan inside and allowing the stench to escape and envelop them.

'I'll start door-knocking here,' Kirsty said when they emerged into the open air on the first landing, 'and work my way upwards.

Brewster nodded and, holding his breath, he continued his upward climb in the turret stairwell.

The policeman on duty at Lily's house stood to attention at his approach.

'Relax, Archie. How have things been, any problems?' Brewster patted the man's shoulder.

'No, sir. Some of the girls wanted to go into the room but they didn't argue when I said they couldn't. I did let the photographer in, though. He showed me some authorization and said you sent him to take photographs of the crime scene. I hope that was all right, sir?'

'You did well, Archie.'

He frowned when Kirsty emerged from the stairwell accompanied by one of the girls. What was she up to? No doubt she'd tell him later.

He turned back to Archie. 'Find someone to fetch Davvy and tell him to bring the barrow. By the time he gets here I'll have finished checking the body and he can take it to the mortuary.'

Brewster entered Lily's room. Nothing had changed since last night although he hoped daylight would allow him to see anything he might have missed.

He examined the body first, noting the position, posed with hands crossed over her chest. Her clothing was intact with no signs of disarray and arranged so she was fully covered. He surmised that meant she was not sexually attacked.

The post-mortem might reveal something, although given Lily's profession, he wasn't sure how helpful such a finding would be.

Lastly, he looked at her injuries. Blood pooled under her head and her face was unrecognizable owing to the vicious beating it had received. Whatever delivered the blows to Lily's face and head had been something solid. An iron bar or poker, Dr Savage had said, although there was no sign of a weapon in the room.

For the briefest moment, Brewster wondered whether the body was that of Lily. But who else could it be?

After he finished examining the body he checked his notebook and repeated his actions of last night, inspecting each segment of the room in turn. Once completed, he turned his attention to the furniture in the room. The sideboard contained some crockery, two cups, some plates and saucers. An empty jam jar and some cutlery. He frowned. Surely it should have held more?

Inside the wardrobe hung a skirt, blouse and coat, along with a cluster of empty hangers in an untidy pile at the bottom. That was odd because he thought Aggie's girls would possess more clothes and dress better than the street doxies. Even his Maggie had more clothes than this wardrobe held.

Avoiding the blood splatter, he knelt on the floor to look under the bed. Pushed right to the back, out of sight, was a suitcase. He pulled it out. Inside, it contained crockery, cutlery and clothing. It looked as if Lily planned to go somewhere.

He sat back on his heels and looked at the body on the bed. 'What were you up to Lily? Where were you planning to go?'

'Davvy's here with the barrow.' Archie's voice interrupted his ruminations.

Cramp shot through Brewster's right leg and he grasped the iron bed end to hoist himself from the floor. He tried to mask the grimace of pain when it intensified and straightened his leg in an attempt to ease it.

'You all right, sir?'

'I'm fine, Archie. Just a spot of cramp because I've been kneeling.' He pointed to the suitcase. 'Get one of the constables to take that to the office.'

'Will do, sir.'

Brewster took a last look around the room to make sure he hadn't missed anything before saying, 'You can send Davvy in now. I think I'm done here.'

'I would if I could but he nobbled a couple of the lads so he didn't have to come upstairs. Said he had to stay with the barrow.'

Brewster grinned. 'Our Davvy doesn't like to exert himself.'

Archie grinned back before beckoning the two young bobbies into the room. They entered carrying the long, narrow length of wood which served as a makeshift stretcher.

'You'll need to get the body onto the stretcher, carry her downstairs and transfer her to Davvy's barrow,' Brewster said.

The men approached the bed. 'How are we going to do this?' They hovered at the edge of the bed looking first at the board and then at the body. By the look on their faces, they weren't looking forward to the task.

Brewster sighed. Some of the younger policemen the force recruited nowadays seemed to lack the ability to think.

'Hold the stretcher level with the bed and keep a tight grip so it doesn't move when the body is transferred. Archie, come and help me slide the body over.'

Archie's face reflected his apprehension which Brewster chose to ignore.

'Grasp the hips and legs and I'll manoeuvre her shoulders.'

Rigor mortis had set in and there was no flexibility in Lily's limbs. Archie nodded to Brewster that he was ready and the two men leaned over to lift her. But she was stiffer than the board which served as a stretcher and they were forced to slide her to the edge of the bed.

Once the body was in position they held it there. 'Ready when you are,' Brewster said and the two of them heaved the body onto the stretcher.

The board wobbled and tilted with the increased weight forcing Brewster to dig his fingers into her shoulder. He glared at the constable nearest to him. 'Drop her,' he hissed, 'and I'll put you on midnight patrol in the Scouringburn for the next year.'

'Yes, sir. I mean no, sir. I won't drop her.'

The two men tightened their hold on the stretcher and turned to leave the room.

'Wait a minute,' Brewster said. 'She'll need to be covered with something. We can't take her out like that.'

He looked around the room. The blood-soaked sheets and blankets on the bed wouldn't do and the tablecloth was threadbare. But the curtains on the window looked more substantial. He grasped the left-hand curtain and tugged it free then wrenched the other one down. After he covered the body he gave the go-ahead for the constables to carry her downstairs.

12

No answer came to Kirsty's knock on the door of number nine. She checked her notebook again to make sure she had the correct address. Then she peered through the window. The room was empty and there was no place for Nancy to hide. Where was she?

'If you're looking for Nancy she isn't there. She took off this morning before it was light. Said she wasn't staying here to be murdered in her bed.'

Kirsty turned to see who was speaking. 'It's Elsie, isn't it? We talked earlier.'

Elsie nodded. 'Us girls talked among ourselves after you left and we decided we want to help. Not everyone agreed because they think the bobbies will cart them off to prison. But I'd rather have prison before getting what Lily got. Anyway, we took a vote and most of us said that when you came back we'd help you all we could. But it has to be you. We don't want any of the bobbies questioning us.'

'That would be helpful,' Kirsty said. She made no comment about the condition that any questioning had to be done by her because that was something she couldn't guarantee.

'We saw you arrive about an hour ago. Everyone's waiting for you.'

Kirsty followed Elsie up the stairs to the next landing. She ignored Brewster, who was outside Lily's door talking to the policeman on duty, and followed Elsie to her flat.

A hush descended on the girls clustered inside when Kirsty entered. Curiosity and resentment showed in their eyes and expressions. These women were more accustomed to avoiding the police than helping them and interviewing them would not be an easy task. Nor could she expect them to tell the truth at all times. She would have to convince them she could be trusted.

Elsie pointed to a chair beside the table. 'I kept that chair for you, Miss Campbell, so you could use the table to lean on when you write your notes.'

'That was thoughtful.' Kirsty laid her notebook and pencil on the table and turned to speak to the girls in the room. 'Thank you for agreeing to help me find Lily's killer. Elsie has informed me you would prefer to talk to me than any of the bobbies and I'll make sure Inspector Brewster understands that.'

'How can you be sure the bobbies won't arrest us?' One of the older women stood up. Her voice was more menacing than worried.

'I can't be sure you'll never be arrested for what you do,' Kirsty said. 'What I can guarantee is that I will make no mention of your profession in my notes. I will only write down what is relevant to Lily's murder and I will refer to you as witnesses and nothing else.'

The woman sat down. She muttered something to the girl next to her.

'That's good enough for me,' Elsie said. 'Now can we get on with it so we can all sleep easy in our beds again.'

Sniggers rippled around the group. 'Sleep would be a good thing,' someone shouted. Laughter echoed through the room.

Kirsty breathed a sigh of relief. They were in a good mood that would make her task easier.

'The first thing I want to ask is about Nancy Allardyce. Does anyone know where I can find her?'

'She's in number nine.'

'She's scarpered.'

'She's long gone.'

Voices merged until the room buzzed with them and Kirsty could only hear the loudest. A group interview was turning out to be impossible.

She beckoned to Elsie. 'It might be better if I talked to each girl on their own.'

'They won't agree to that, they feel safer together. If I ask them to see you on their own most of them will slink back to their rooms.'

Kirsty felt overwhelmed. Women and girls packed the room,

sitting on the bed, every available chair, and crammed together on the floor. If they all talked through each other the information would be jumbled and get lost.

While Kirsty thought how best to handle the interviews the clamour of voices died down although mutterings from some of the girls rumbled on as they spoke quietly together.

'In that case, can they come to the table, one at a time, so I can make sense of what they are saying. But it might be better if you asked them.'

Elsie stood up. 'If you all talk at once Miss Campbell won't be able to understand what you're saying so can each of you come to the table when I ask you and tell Miss Campbell what she wants to know. We'll start with you, Eva.'

A thin girl with her hair tied in pigtails rose from her sitting position on the floor.

'Can we get Eva a chair? It makes me feel like a school marm when she stands in front of me.'

Elsie prodded one of the girls from a chair and brought it to the table. The girl sat and looked at Kirsty with wary eyes.

'I'll need your name first.'

The girl hesitated.

'There's nothing to be afraid of I need it as a witness statement, nothing else.'

'Eva Green, miss.'

'And your age?'

'Old enough.' The girl's voice was defiant and she glared at Kirsty.

Elsie bent and whispered in Kirsty's ear. 'That's not a good question to ask if you want them to talk to you.'

Kirsty nodded and decided, in the interests of gaining as much information as possible, she would not follow that line of inquiry even though some of the girls might be underage.

Eva answered all Kirsty's questions although she didn't know anything about Lily, her clients, or where she came from. And she knew nothing about Nancy Allardyce.

Similar responses were made by most of the women until she came to Daisy Miller.

'What can you tell me about Lily?' Kirsty relaxed her grip

on the pencil and flexed her fingers.

'The men liked her. Sometimes they came to me when she wasn't available.'

'Why you?'

'Because I looked like Lily. But I always knew they preferred her and I was second best.'

'Tell me about the men you shared with her?'

'Well, there's the Laird. But I don't think he is a laird because if he was he'd have had more money and his clothes would have been fancier. He had a real liking for Lily, though. He used to talk about her when he was with me.'

'Do you know where he came from?'

Daisy shook her head. 'In the country someplace. He always came on a Friday night. That's cattle market day. And you could tell by the stink of him.'

'Was there anyone else?'

'The Captain visited me once or twice. I didn't like him. You had to be careful what you said and did or he'd wallop you. He gave Lily a black eye one time.'

'Have you any idea where he might live?'

Again Daisy shook her head. 'I think it's someplace where military men live. He was in the war?'

'Anything else?'

'That's all I know, miss.'

After the interviews were over and the last girl left, Kirsty turned to Elsie. 'I need to find out more about Lily and I think Nancy is the only one who can tell me. If she comes back or you hear anything about where she went, can you keep me informed?'

'Aggie might know, I think she kept records on all us girls.'

Kirsty closed her notebook and put it in her pocket. It was time to look for Brewster because that meant another visit to Freddie on the ground floor.

An icy draught rippled around the room when she opened the door. She paused for a moment in the doorway. 'Thank you for the use of your flat, Elsie and for persuading the others to be interviewed,' she said as she left.

Along the landing, Brewster gesticulated at two young

constables trying to manoeuvre what looked like a stretcher with Lily's body on top.

'Careful,' she heard him shout, 'we don't want to lose her before we get downstairs.'

Freddie grimaced at the taste of the gum as he licked the flaps of the envelopes containing his blackmail letters. Once the job was done he laid them on the table and, with his finger keeping the place in Lily's journal which lay beside them, he carefully copied a name and address on each envelope. After checking there were no mistakes, he thrust the notebook and the letters into the inside pocket of his jacket.

The taste of gum lingered and he crossed the room to the sink. He turned the tap and held his mouth below the gush of water, swilling it around before spitting it out.

Outside the echoing rumble of wheels on the cobbles caused him to peer out the window. He watched Davvy manoeuvre the barrow, a coffin-shaped box on wheels, into the close. Freddie shivered, there was no mistaking that barrow, it was here for Lily's body. The bobbies on guard at the entrance followed it, leaving the street empty apart from a crowd of folks clustered on the opposite pavement.

This was his opportunity to slink away without anyone knowing but he hesitated with his hand on the doorknob, the urge to wait and say his last farewell to Lily beating strong in his heart. Tears pricked his eyes but he dashed them away with angry hands. He had a reputation to protect and it wouldn't do for anyone to know how the death of Lily affected him.

He turned the doorknob with a fierce twist of his hand and sneaked out of the house, not bothering to lock up behind him. What did it matter now?

He pulled the peak of his flat cap downward to shade his eyes and conceal more of his face as he hurried along Scouringburn. Instead of continuing on to the West Port he turned left at Session Street, stepping off the pavement to avoid bumping into two women looking into a shop window. Wind whistled up the road sending dust spiralling upwards, stinging his eyes and skin, and he wished he'd donned a great coat before he came out. Guthrie Street ran at right angles at the end of the road and he breathed more freely once he turned the corner and could escape the biting wind. He carried on, to where it merged with Meadow Street, walking briskly until he reached the Post Office, an imposing building which faced the Howff graveyard. After stopping in front of it he searched his pockets for money, counting out nine pennies, the cost of six stamps.

Several people pushed past him as he stood there and he imagined curious eyes watching him. Anxiety made his heart pound and he pulled his cap lower over his face and turned his collar up before he mounted the steps. Suppressing the urge to hurry, he sauntered into the public room through the double doors on the left side of the lobby. The place buzzed with activity with people everywhere. coming and going about their business. A mailman pushed past him, opening a door at the end of the room to reveal uniformed workers sorting parcels. He kept his head down and joined people waiting to be served but the line moved slowly and the wait seemed interminable. Sweat built on his forehead and his grip on the envelopes tightened. The words written on the paper inside bounced around his mind until he was sure everyone knew what he intended doing. Several times he almost left the queue but he gritted his teeth and clenched his fists until he shuffled in front of the clerk at the counter.

Once he purchased his stamps and posted his letters, he hurried from the building and didn't stop until he was outside. Sweat dripped from his forehead and his shirt stuck to his back. A group of women approached from his left and looked at him askance. He lifted his cap and said, 'Ladies.' They nodded in return but he could see alarm reflected in their faces.

The iron gates of the graveyard opposite were open so he crossed the road and walked through them. He wandered down one of the paths until he came to Jonathan Bogue's grave. This was where he'd told the recipients of his letters to come. The altar tombstone squatted like a morbid table among the ornately carved headstones nearby and was surrounded by grass and weeds which grew in abundance in this neglected part of the cemetery.

He perched on the flat top of the stone and wiped the sweat from his brow. This place was ideal because of its history. Jonathan Bogue had a reputation as a necromancer and it was here, less than a month ago, a young girl had been sacrificed. He'd read all about it in the *Dundee Courier*. He patted the stone. 'Soon,' he said, 'I'll be rich and I won't have to work for Aggie. I'll recruit my own girls and I'll be as important as anyone here.'

13

Daisy heaved a sigh of relief. It hadn't been too bad and she'd managed to avoid talking about the more intimate details of her contact with Lily.

She perched on the edge of the bed beside Elsie. All the others appeared relieved once their interviews were over and seemed glad to escape to their own flats but Daisy didn't want to leave Elsie alone with the policewoman and so she stayed.

They sat in silence, listening to Kirsty's footsteps clattering on the concrete landing. When they stopped, she could tell from the sound the policewoman hadn't continued down the stairs.

Daisy shivered as she thought of Lily's body three doors away. Maybe the policewoman was there now.

Her thoughts whirled. She couldn't stop thinking about Lily lying on her bed all battered and bloody and she wondered if she'd ever sleep again or whether she would lie, cowering in her bed, waiting for her turn.

Everyone thought Aggie killed her, and maybe she had. After all, Aggie wouldn't have taken kindly to Lily leaving before she cleared her debt.

A tear slipped down her cheek and Elsie's hand tightened on hers. At least Elsie understood.

A gust of wind blew the door open. 'I'll get it,' Daisy said, thankful for an excuse to stand up and do something. Otherwise she'd end up crying and that would really mess up her looks.

She walked to the door and glanced outside. The policewoman was standing at the top of the stairwell while two good-looking bobbies manhandled a long wooden board. Daisy guessed the object on the board was Lily's body.

'Quick,' she shouted, 'I think they're taking Lily away now.'

Elsie joined her on the landing and after the bobbies manoeuvred the board down the stairs they peered over the railing watching for them to emerge at the bottom.

The barrow, a coffin-shaped box which was trundled on two large wheels, rested on its shafts waiting for the body to be loaded. Fear fluttered through Daisy's chest when the man standing beside it looked up at them. She gripped Elsie's hand and drew back from the railing.

'I can't abide that man, he's got the evil eye.'

'Don't be daft. He's a simpleton and it's only a squint he has.'

'I can't help it. I'm afeared of him and I don't want him asking for me when he comes aknocking.'

'Let's go inside,' Elsie said, 'we can have a smoke and I'll make us a cuppie. We don't need to watch them take her away.'

Conflicting thoughts forced themselves into Daisy's mind as she watched Elsie place the kettle on the gas ring.

Unwanted visions of Lily tormented her. Lily dancing around her room in her shift. Lily, taunting Daisy, defying her to tell the others they were in love. Lily, looking into her eyes and stroking her face as they lay in bed together. Lily, lying all battered and bloody in that same bed. A tear slid down her cheek.

'It's best we don't watch them put her into the barrow to be taken to the mortuary.' Elsie offered Daisy a cigarette and placed a cup of tea on the table in front of her. She struck a match and held it to Daisy's fag and then her own before sitting down beside her. 'Best we remember her as she was.'

Daisy cradled the cup in her hands. It reminded her of Lily and all their shared confidences. Now she had only Elsie.

A silence descended on the room. Daisy looked over the rim of her cup at Elsie. What was she thinking? Were Elsie's thoughts as troubling as her own?

'D'you think we should have told the policewoman about Angus?' Daisy's voice was troubled.

'Angus didn't know what Lily did for a living,' Elsie said, 'and she never told him she lived here. She always said she was visiting from her parents' home.'

Silence enveloped them again.

'He won't know what's happened.'

'Unless we tell him.'

'D'you think we should?' Daisy looked at Elsie for guidance.

'It would be the decent thing.'

'Yes, but how will we manage to do that? If we go to see him the bobbies will want to know where we're going.'

Daisy's hands shook as she imagined walking past them. What would she do if they interrogated her? Lying had never been something she excelled at and she was sure she would tell them if they asked. She'd been able to hide the information from the policewoman because she didn't ask. A direct question was a different thing and she didn't think she could hold out.

Elsie smiled. 'Don't worry. We aren't going to get any customers tonight with those two bobbies standing guard at the close. When we leave we'll tell them we're going to the *Savoy Picture House* in the Nethergate.'

'Angus doesn't work at the Savoy.'

'I know, silly. He's at the *La Scala* but we don't want them to know that or they'd be able to trace him.'

Daisy frowned. She wished she hadn't mentioned Angus because it was all getting too complicated.

'What if they ask what we're going to see?'

'That's easy. It's a Douglas Fairbanks film tonight. I saw a notice about it in the *Courier*.'

Daisy nodded although she wasn't convinced their plan would work.

14

Muttered curses echoed up the circular stairwell as the two young constables manhandled the makeshift stretcher down the stairs. It banged and bumped off the walls and at one point Kirsty was sure Lily would slip off, but as the body slid dangerously near the edge Brewster leapt forward and grabbed the side of the board.

By the time they emerged at the foot of the stairs, the curtain covering Lily's body had slipped to the side uncovering her mutilated face. Brewster leaned over and pulled the material around her while the two constables manoeuvred the stretcher level with the waiting barrow.

'Good man, Davvy. You managed to get the barrow through the close,' Brewster said.

'Aye, sir. It was a bit of a squeeze but I got it through. Didnae think it right to bring the lassie out on the street.'

Kirsty slipped back into the shadow of the stairwell. Davvy's appearance had an unsettling effect on her, with his squinting eyes, yellowish skin, and the suggestion of a hump on his back. She had last seen him at the underground mortuary, a scary place with flickering lights, and at that time she'd thought he looked like a malevolent gnome. In the daylight, he seemed less threatening and although she felt sorry for him, it did not disperse her fear of being alone in his company. She would endeavour to make sure that never happened.

Davvy opened the lid of the coffin-shaped box. 'Put the lassie in here.'

Once the stretcher holding Lily's body had been placed in the box, Davvy secured the lid shut with the hook attached to it. 'Dinnae want fowk gawping at the poor wee lass.' He placed himself between the shafts, hoisted the end of the barrow up and trundled it down the close. The noise of the wooden wheels on the cobbled street outside echoed back to them long after he'd left.

The men, now relieved of the stretcher, lounged against the wall apparently tired out by their exertions while Brewster stood staring down the close, deep in thought. At last, he looked up.

'You two,' he pointed at the constables, 'can join the search party in the backlands. We need to find the murder weapon.'

He turned to peer into the stairwell. 'Ah, there you are.'

Annoyance at herself for hiding from Davvy, and suspecting Brewster was aware of her antipathy to the mortuary attendant, made Kirsty's voice sharper than usual. 'I intended to interview Lily's friend, Nancy Allardyce, but I couldn't find her, sir. Some of the girls said the murder scared her and she left. But no one knows where she's gone.' She caught her breath and modified her tone. 'My guess would be she's returned home to wherever she came from.'

'What do you intend to do to find out?'

'I thought we might question Freddie again. Then I'll go back and talk to Aggie. I'm positive she must keep records.'

'I'd better be the one to tackle Freddie.'

Kirsty seethed as she followed Brewster down the close to the front of the building. Did he think, because she was a woman, she couldn't handle Freddie? This belittling of women was the kind of attitude that led to the suffragette demonstrations prior to the war. Not much had changed, despite Nancy Astor taking her seat in parliament two weeks ago and women now having the right to vote, although it would be a year before Kirsty could claim that right because she wasn't yet thirty. In spite of all that, men still thought they were superior to women.

When she emerged from the close, Brewster was pounding on the door of the ground floor flat. 'Either he's asleep or he's scarpered.' He walked to the window and peered in. 'No sign of him.'

A woman detached herself from the small crowd at the other side of the road. 'If you're looking for that Freddie Simpson, he's gone. Took out of here like a bat out of hell about half an hour back.' She pulled her shawl tighter around her shoulders with grubby hands and crossed her arms in front of her body as a chill wind whistled down the street. 'What's going on here, anyways. I saw the barrow leave ten minutes ago. Was there a body inside?'

'I'm afraid we can't give out any information,' Brewster said. 'But if you give me your name and address we may want to speak to you later?'

The pointed end of the woman's headscarf billowed in the wind revealing curlers underneath. She peered at him through narrowed eyes while she considered his request.

It made Kirsty wonder if the people in this neighbourhood were wary about providing information to the police. Perhaps afraid it would reflect badly on them with their neighbours.

Eventually, the woman shrugged her shoulders. 'Forbes, my name is. Mrs Forbes to you. I live over there.' She pointed across the street. 'My windows look out on this place.' The disgust in her voice was obvious. 'The things I've seen is nobody's business. Place like that shouldn't be allowed where respectable folks like us live.'

'Does that mean you witnessed someone going into the building in the middle of last night?'

'What d'you take me for? All respectable folks are sleeping when night comes. Anyways, the amount of men that go in and out of there is disgusting.'

She flounced back to join the rest of the observers on the opposite pavement.

'It doesn't look like we're going to get much more out of her,' Brewster said. He took his pocket watch out and checked the time. 'There's a pie shop in the next street, and it's about time we ate something. Then you can have another go at Aggie for permission to access her records and I'll go to see the Sheriff about a warrant.'

15

Hunger pangs twisted in Kirsty's stomach when she entered the small bakery. Food aromas hung in the air, tickling her senses and stirring her appetite. It had been several hours since Kirsty ate the slice of toast, her only meal of the day, and she was now ravenous.

In front of her, a wooden counter spread along the length of the shop and behind that sat a large cast-iron range with pots simmering on top. Flames leapt upwards from the red coals burning in the fire basket, providing heat for the ovens at each side as well as the hot plates.

The stout unsmiling woman behind the counter finished ladling soup into a tin canister, secured the lid and inspected the money handed to her before throwing the coins into a cash drawer. Soup, which she turned to stir, bubbled in the massive pot behind her.

'Next,' she shouted without looking up.

The tired-looking woman who was next in the queue handed her a large pewter jug into which the woman ladled soup. 'I'll pay you tomorrow,' the woman whispered.

'You said that yesterday and the day before.' The shopkeeper poured the soup back into the pot. 'No more tick,' she said handing back the empty pewter jug.

The woman's shoulders slumped and she shuffled out to the street.

Kirsty, watching from the rear of the shop, observed the look of desperation on the woman's face and saw the tear that slipped down her cheeks. Despite the many examples of poverty she witnessed during her time as a policewoman she still couldn't imagine what destitution felt like.

The shopkeeper noticed the way Kirsty's eyes followed the woman. 'I can't afford to prop her up,' she said. 'Takes me all my time to keep the doors open. Times are hard.' She stirred the soup with a vicious turn of her wrist, spattering drops on the stove.

Kirsty would have given anything for a plate of that soup but without a container, it was an idle hope.

'Have you got two hot pies?' Brewster leaned on the counter, at the same time shaking his head at Kirsty when she dug into her pocket for money.

The woman grabbed a brown paper bag and bent over to open the oven door. After sliding two pies into the bag she secured the top and handed it to Brewster.

'Carry this and hop in,' he said, thrusting it at Kirsty, 'while I start the engine. Pies are best eaten hot.'

Grease seeped through the bottom of the paper bag and Kirsty kept her hand underneath it so her skirt wouldn't be soiled, but that meant she couldn't hold on to anything while Brewster steered through the streets. She bounced about in her seat and at one point thought they were going to crash, so it was with a sense of relief that she stepped out of the car at police headquarters.

The canteen was empty and the fire had burned low. Brewster threw more coal on, then placed the kettle on the hob and swung it over the flame. 'You'll find a couple of plates in there.' He nodded towards the cupboard on the opposite wall.

Grease saturated the bag and Kirsty almost dropped the pies on the floor when the paper disintegrated as she sought to transfer them to the tin plates. They didn't look appealing but the smell of the meat inside wafted up to her nostrils stimulating her hunger pangs. She grabbed one and bit into it. The pie tasted better than it looked and she was soon wiping the grease off her chin and wishing there was more.

Brewster spooned tea leaves into the brown earthenware teapot, lifted the kettle from the hob over the fire and poured scalding water on top. He picked up a spoon and stirred the tea before pouring it into two tin mugs, one of which he placed in front of Kirsty.

She watched him as he ate. The sparkle had gone from his eyes and he looked tired. Not surprising given the circumstances. He'd taken her to the crime scene at six o'clock this morning and he must have been called out before that. Something inside her stirred but she pushed it back, ignoring the surge of feeling, not sure whether it was sympathy or something entirely different.

'How is Maggie?' She studied her cup. 'Have you had time to tend to her today?'

Brewster finished chewing and took a gulp of tea. 'I went home this morning and helped her to dress and we had breakfast together. Mrs McCormack, she's a neighbour, will make sure she eats during the day and will see to anything she needs.'

'That's good,' she said for want of anything else to say.

Brewster set his cup on the table. 'I'd better take myself off to the courthouse and get the Sheriff to sign a warrant to search Aggie's premises. You can interview her again but I doubt she'll give her agreement.'

'Do you want a report written on this morning's interviews?' She reached for her hat.

'Of course.' Brewster halted in the doorway. 'But before you do any of that, will you wash the plates and mugs.'

Kirsty's eyes widened. What did he think she was? A skivvy? It was always the same, just when she thought she was getting somewhere with him and he recognized her status, something like this would happen. During her early years as a policewoman in London, she'd suffered many jibes. One of them was being told to get back to the kitchen. How was that any different to what he had asked her to do?

She flung her hat across the room, grabbed the kettle and poured hot water into the enamel basin resting in the sink. Then she scrubbed the plates and the angrier she got the harder she scrubbed.

16

William huddled in the doorway of the ironmonger's shop, underneath The Globe clock tower at the West Port, as Davvy pulled the barrow down the cobbled road. He didn't have to be told what was inside the barrow's coffin-shaped box and a wave of sadness shuddered through him.

He closed his eyes but that didn't remove the image, engraved on his mind, of Lily's bloodied body lying on the bed and Aggie sitting on the floor in hysterics. Despite his best efforts, he had failed to convince her to leave the room.

'You can't be here when the bobbies come,' he'd said.

But she'd sat on the floor with her back pressed against the wall and wouldn't stop screaming. She had still been there when the police arrived although William had removed himself to the office by that time.

He watched from the window as they took her away and then slumped in the armchair in front of the cold fireplace wondering what he should do. It was too much for him. His brain whirled as thoughts raced through his mind. This was a disaster. The police would be crawling all over the building for days to come. Panic seized him and he left the flat and ran next door to fetch Freddie.

He banged on the door.

'Who is it?'

'It's me. William.'

The door opened and Freddie pulled him inside. 'I'm keeping out of the way while the bobbies are here.'

William slumped into a chair. He didn't think his legs would support him much longer. 'You've heard,' he muttered.

'Couldn't avoid it, Aggie screamed loud enough, and I was on the landing below. But I kept my nose out of it when she hollered "bloody murder". I thought that's not something I want to get mixed up with so I scarpered here and locked the door.'

'They've taken Aggie away.' William's breath rasped out of his chest and the walls seemed to be closing in on him.

'I know. I bet they pin it on her.'

William's heart thumped. He liked Aggie and she'd been good to him but she did run a brothel as well as a shebeen and in the bobbies' eyes that made her a criminal. 'Maybe she did do it,' he said but his voice contained doubt.

'Nah! I don't think so. I heard her open the door and then she screamed. There wouldn't have been enough time. Besides, I thought I saw someone slip down the stairs and run off across the backlands about ten minutes before Aggie got there.'

William looked at his brother, suspicion glinting in his eyes. 'What were you doing up there, anyway?'

Freddie laughed. 'Chatting up one of the girls. What else?'

'What else,' William repeated. His head swam, he didn't feel well. 'I've got to get out of here. I need fresh air but I can't leave the office unattended.' He stood, swayed and grasped the back of the chair.

'I suppose you want me to mind it for you.'

'That's what I came to ask,' he said. 'It's only until my head clears.'

Freddie nodded. 'Don't stay away too long.'

That had been seven hours ago and Freddie would be annoyed.

William left the doorway and trudged along Scouringburn until he came to Aggie's tenement. He nodded to the two constables standing guard at the mouth of the close and pushed the office door open.

'Freddie,' he called. 'I'm back.'

He expected his brother to come steaming through from the back room swearing at him for his absence. But the flat was empty.

William slumped into a chair. Freddie shouldn't have gone off, leaving the place unlocked. Anyone could have come in and it was a wonder the bobbies hadn't torn the place to pieces. Panic rushed through him. The money. Was it still here?

He heaved himself up, raced to the back room, pulled out a

drawer in the desk and prised open the lid of the tin box inside. His breath whistled from his chest. The money was safe.

'Did you think I'd run off with it?'

He swung around and glared at Freddie. His brother had a habit of sneaking up on folk and William was sure he did it deliberately to catch them unawares.

'Where were you? I came back to find the office empty and unlocked.'

Freddie shrugged. 'I had to pop out to do something and you stayed away too long.'

William narrowed his eyes. Freddie was doing it again, making him feel guilty as if he was the one in the wrong. But Freddie had always been the one who got up to mischief, the one who wasn't afraid to buck the law, while William avoided trouble. Guilt was something William lived with on a daily basis but he doubted if his brother ever experienced a twinge.

Even as a child Freddie made sure his brother knew who was top dog and he and his gang ridiculed William who preferred the library to roaming the streets. Again and again, they chased after him shouting, 'Wullie, Wullie,' and making rude gestures. Later when he reached the safety of the house he would say to his brother, 'My name's William, not Wullie,' but Freddie only laughed at him.

He thought Freddie was laughing at him now. 'Are you staying or leaving?' he snapped.

'Oh, I'm leaving,' Freddie said. 'I just came back to see if you'd returned.'

Damn, Freddie was making him feel guilty again.

'Close the door when you go.'

Freddie grinned. 'Will do. By the way, the bobbies were here earlier asking to see the records but I refused. They said they'd be back with a search warrant.' He slid out the door banging it shut behind him.

William sighed. He wished he got on better with his brother but they always seemed to rub each other up the wrong way. After replacing the cash box in the desk drawer he returned to the front room and sank into a chair to await the police.

17

'Back again?' The turnkey led Kirsty down the corridor to Aggie's cell. She selected a large iron key from the bunch dangling from her waist and turned it in the lock. 'Someone to see you,' she said as she swung the door open.

Aggie looked up from where she sat on the bench. 'Last time you came here I told you I wasn't going to say any more until I talked to my solicitor.'

'Does that mean you haven't seen him yet?'

'He's in court but he'll be here soon. While you're here you can tell that lazy sod of a turnkey I want my bucket emptied. This place stinks. And while you're at it, tell her this mattress is a disgrace. My girls have better mattresses than this.'

Kirsty perched on the bench beside Aggie. 'I'll see what I can do. But I wanted to ask you something first.'

Aggie leaned back against the tiled wall. 'What would that be?'

'Detective Inspector Brewster is over at the court seeking a warrant to get access to your records but it would be a lot better if you gave permission.'

Aggie snorted. 'Permission is it you're looking for? Well, you can go whistle. You'll get no permission from me, my records are private.'

'Whether or not you agree is immaterial. The warrant will allow us to search, but we thought co-operation with the police would look good for you when this comes to court for trial.'

'There won't be a trial.' Aggie's eyes glittered. 'Because I didn't do it and Simon Harvie will look after me. Besides, why would I harm one of my own girls?'

'Maybe because she was planning to leave you.'

'That's not true. Who told you that?'

'I'm sorry, Aggie, I can't tell you. We never divulge our

sources.' Kirsty watched the changing expressions on Aggie's face. 'Don't you understand, if we can find out about Lily it could help to clear you? If you're innocent, that is.'

'Of course, I'm innocent. You should be out there finding out who killed her instead of badgering me.' Aggie glared at her. 'If you don't find him and he goes after any of my girls, I'll hold you responsible.'

Aggie's threat sent a shiver through Kirsty. What if there were more deaths?

'There are policemen guarding your building. Your girls are safe.'

Aggie snorted. 'They better be.'

Kirsty stood, there was nothing else she could do or say. 'I'll leave you, for now. But we will be searching your records with or without your permission.'

Cold air whispered through the cell block and Kirsty's footsteps sent echoes bouncing off the walls. Were they hers or something more ghostly? These corridors underneath the police station chilled her and set her wondering how many had been incarcerated here in the past. She never felt safe until the iron doors clanged shut behind her and she emerged into the safer confines of the station with its hustle and bustle. Although that seemed to be lacking at the moment. All the constables were either out on the beat or at the murder scene hunting for a weapon Kirsty was sure they weren't going to find.

Kirsty's office, previously a cloakroom, was not the most welcoming place. But the smell of dust, old boots, damp oilskins and floor wax that hung in the air and invaded every corner of the gloomy room didn't seem so bad after the foul odours in Aggie's cell. She squeezed behind her desk and slumped in the chair. Aggie's interview had been a waste of time.

She pulled several sheets of paper out of a drawer, rummaged for a pencil and wondered where to start. Which report would she write first? Her interviews with the girls at the tenement or those with Aggie? Or Brewster's interview with Freddie? Brewster wouldn't be writing that one because he'd instructed her to take the notes.

After consulting her notebook she started to write but she'd barely inscribed the first of her interviews before Brewster bounced into her office waving a sheet of paper.

'We've got the warrant,' he said, 'and I'll need you to help me go through Aggie's records.'

Kirsty gestured towards the paper on her desk. 'The reports...'

'Do them later. It's more important to check the records.' He barged back out the door. 'Come on. What are you waiting for?'

She put her hat on, buttoned her jacket and followed him out. 'What is it you hope to find?'

'We need to know more about Lily. Where she came from? Who her family are? As well as information about any of her contacts and customers.' The words came in short gasps as he cranked the motor's starting handle.

'Does that mean you're not convinced Aggie killed her?' Kirsty hesitated with her hand on the car door.

'I didn't say that but in an investigation, you have to look at all the angles so there is a solid case when it comes to court.'

The engine sputtered several times before it roared into life. 'Hop in,' he said. 'We don't have all day.'

Kirsty slumped in the passenger seat, unconvinced Aggie was responsible for the killing. There was more to this murder than what appeared on the surface.

18

'Well, you caught him yet?' The woman in the headscarf shouted across the street when the car drew up at the kerb.

Kirsty stepped out. It wasn't her place to answer the woman, she would leave that to Brewster but he also seemed intent on ignoring the comment.

The group appeared larger than it was earlier. Heads nodded and fingers pointed as they talked among themselves while the woman who had shouted to them, folded her arms over her chest and muttered something to the woman standing nearest to her.

Brewster joined Kirsty on the pavement and motioned for one of the constables to accompany them to the door of the downstairs flat.

'They're like a bunch of curious cats,' the constable said. 'After the *Courier* reporter came the crowd got bigger. Maybe they're hoping he'll come back and they'll get their names in the paper.'

'When did the reporter come?'

'Just after you left, sir. We gave him nothing and wouldn't let him up the close. He did talk to that lot, though.' He pointed across the street.

'Good lad.' Brewster patted him on the shoulder. 'Be ready to kick the door in if I don't get an answer.'

'Yes, sir. But I think someone is inside. He came back a while ago.'

The man who answered the knock on the door wasn't the one they saw on their earlier visit. Unlike the previous man, this one didn't look like a thug. He was clean-shaven with slicked back hair and was smartly dressed in a navy blue single-breasted serge suit, a white shirt and a grey and blue striped tie. Rimless spectacles perched on his nose, masking the curiosity in his eyes.

His gaze lingered for a moment on Kirsty before he addressed Brewster. 'I've been expecting you.' He motioned for them to enter.

Brewster turned to the constable. 'Stand guard on the door while we're inside.'

The man smiled through tight lips. 'I can assure you I won't be running away.'

'A reporter's been snooping around,' Brewster said as he walked into the front room. 'I wouldn't want him barging in here.'

'My brother mentioned a warrant. Have you got it with you?'

Brewster pulled the sheet of paper from his pocket and laid it on the table. 'Do I assume you are William Simpson?'

The man readjusted the spectacles on his nose while he studied the warrant. 'That is correct,' he said without looking up until he had stopped reading the document. 'Everything seems to be in order. Where would you like to start?'

'The records would be a good place but, before we begin, perhaps you can describe your procedures and what kind of records you keep.'

William removed his spectacles, polished them with a large white handkerchief and replaced them on his nose as he considered their request. 'As you wish, the records are in the next room.' He ushered them through a door.

'There is a file on each girl who rents a room here.'

Kirsty noticed the emphasis on renting. William seemed to be a man who thought about everything he was going to say before he said it and he would be unlikely to incriminate himself voluntarily.

She pulled her notebook from her pocket. 'What about the services they offer. How is that recorded?'

William remained unperturbed. 'We do not monitor what our tenants do in the privacy of their homes. That is a matter for them.'

'But you charge for keys and provide tokens to be given to the girls. You must keep records of those transactions.' Kirsty smiled as she watched his discomfort.

Brewster interrupted. 'There's no use denying what happens in those rooms nor is there any point in ignoring what Aggie's business is. Let's stop evading the issue and just tell us how it works and show us the records.'

William polished his spectacles again but he seemed less confident now. 'You must realize I'm only an employee.'

'Then there should be no problem in connection with your co-operation with this investigation.'

'You seem to know most of it already.' A note of despondency crept into his voice. 'The keys, the tokens, and what the girls do.' He removed a ledger from one of the desk drawers. 'Everyone who wishes to visit one of the girls, reports here first. They pay me for a key after which I inscribe the payment in here as well as the name of which girl they require, but most of the men do not supply their real names. They are given a token which they must give to the girl of their choice. Those tokens are redeemed by me the next day or whenever the girls present them to me.'

'I assume the redeemable rate is less than the selling rate?' Brewster's voice was as smooth as silk.

'Aggie does require a commission on every key sold,' William replied.

'Of course. But that means you are aware of everyone who visits each girl.'

'Naturally.'

'And you were on duty last night?'

'I'm on duty every night. Freddie only fills in for me during the day when there are unlikely to be any customers.'

'In that case, you will know who Lily entertained last night.'

'Lily was indisposed last night and therefore unable to work. Her key is still on its hook.'

'Someone must have visited or she wouldn't be lying in the mortuary,' Brewster said.

'I would assume it was someone she knew well enough to open her door.'

Kirsty finished noting William's comments and closed her notebook. 'Do you want me to start checking the files?'

Brewster nodded and flashed one of his rare smiles at her. 'Yes, you check the files and I'll go through this ledger.'

'You might want to look for any entries referring to the Laird or the Captain. I believe they were among Lily's regulars.'

'I think you will find that Lily's name will be referenced against anyone who wished to see her.' William ran his finger down one of the ledger's pages. 'Here is an entry indicating Lily met with one of the gentlemen concerned.' He handed the ledger to Brewster. 'I will wait in the front room until you are finished.'

Every file was in its own brown envelope with the name of the girl written on the front and they were filed in alphabetical order so Kirsty had no problem locating Lily's file. But, when she opened it, the envelope was empty.

'That's strange,' she said. 'There's nothing inside Lily's file, it's empty.'

Brewster looked up from the ledger. 'Find out from William if anyone other than himself or Freddie has been in here today.'

Kirsty walked through to the front room where William was slumped in an armchair.

'I've been going through the files but Lily's envelope is empty. Have the contents been removed?'

William looked up. 'Let me see.' He opened the envelope and frowned. 'All her information should be in here.'

'That's what I thought. Are you and Freddie the only people who have been in here today?'

'If you're suggesting I removed Lily's information, you're mistaken. I would never tamper with files.' His fists clenched and he pulled himself out of the chair to face her.

'If not you, then Freddie?' Kirsty suggested.

A mixture of expressions flitted over his face. 'Freddie had a soft spot for Lily,' he admitted. 'But why would he want to remove her file?' He thought for a moment. 'The office was empty when I got back and it was unlocked so it could have been anyone.'

'You forget there are two constables at the mouth of the close. They would know if anyone had entered the flat after

Freddie left.'

William slumped back into his chair an expression of defeat on his face.

Kirsty returned to the filing cabinets to check the rest of the files. She riffled through several before she found the one she was looking for. Nancy Allardyce, according to Elsie, was an old school friend of Lily. Maybe she would find something inside this one.

The file was detailed and Kirsty's heart leapt when she found Nancy's home address.

'Brewster.' She turned to him. 'I've found an address for Nancy Allardyce, the girl who ran off after the murder.'

'Good,' he said. 'I think a visit to Nancy might be in order.'

'Her family live in Montrose.'

'Hmm.' He looked up from the ledger. 'Well, we're not going to be able to go there today. First thing tomorrow you can hop on a train and interview her if she's there.'

'Will you be coming with me?'

'I don't think that will be necessary. It is your job to interview women and children, after all. The girls who work for Aggie don't trust the police so I'd be in the way.'

'Yes, sir.'

19

Brewster selected the ledger and Nancy's file. 'I'll take these with me.'

William didn't look pleased but shrugged his shoulders, acknowledging there was nothing he could say or do to prevent him.

Kirsty followed him out of the flat and through the close to the rear of the tenement where he stood for a moment watching the searchers.

'There's not much more you can do here and you still have reports to complete, but I'll stay for a while.' He handed Kirsty the ledger and file. 'Take these to the office and leave them on my desk.'

She stared at him. The streets in this area were a warren and because they'd arrived here by car she wasn't entirely sure she could remember the way back to the police station.

'Don't look at me like that,' Brewster said. 'Trams run at the end of the road. You should be able to catch one to take you back.'

'Will I wait for you to return?'

'No, that won't be necessary. Go home after you finish your reports, you'll need to make an early start tomorrow.'

She left Brewster conferring with Sergeant Brodie, no doubt he would join the search before long because he was intent on finding the murder weapon. Kirsty didn't share his conviction it was hidden somewhere in the backlands behind the tenement.

Outside, the women on the opposite pavement clustered together, watching everything with curious eyes. She ignored them and hurried along the cobbled road. Moments after she reached the main thoroughfare, a tram clanked to a halt and she ran to the stop and jumped on.

When she recognized The Pillars, she alighted. She hadn't

meant to return to the police station this way but in her hurry, she'd hopped on the wrong tram and it deposited her in the High Street. However, she wouldn't have known the murder had hit the papers so soon if she'd taken a shorter route.

'Murder, bloody murder. Buy the Tele and read all about it.' The raucous voice of a newspaper seller soared above the crowds hurrying along the pavement. '*Evening Telegraph*, miss?' He pulled a copy of the newspaper from under the brick which squatted on top of the bundle to prevent them blowing away.

Gusts of wind whistled up Whitehall Street rounding the corner into the High Street and Kirsty grabbed the newspaper he held out to her, tucking it under her arm before the wind claimed it. She dug into her pocket for a penny and handed it over.

'Thanks, miss.' He touched the peak of his cap in a salute to her before turning to another customer.

The newspaper seller's voice, carried by the wind, followed her along the road, bringing visions of Lily lying on her blood-soaked bed. Kirsty doubted if she would be able to rid herself of the image. It would probably haunt her for months to come.

Hamish looked up from behind the charge room counter when she barged into the police station. He was less friendly than Geordie who had been on duty earlier and he simply nodded to her. Geordie would have passed the time of day but that wasn't Hamish's style.

Kirsty nodded back and let the door slam behind her after she passed through to the inner corridor. Her office was even more gloomy than usual and she flicked on the electric light. At least the police station had moved with the times as far as lighting was concerned.

She sat on the wooden chair behind her desk and reminded herself she must buy a cushion. Once she wriggled into a better position she placed the ledger, Nancy's file, and the newspaper, on the edge of the desk and searched around for paper and pencils.

The reports didn't take her long to write and she was careful to stick to the facts. Brewster preferred her not to add her opinions and thoughts although sometimes she couldn't resist doing this. After she laid down the pencil she sorted the sheets of paper into a neat pile and placed them in a cardboard folder on which she wrote Brewster's name followed by 'Murder Reports'. She knew if she didn't label the file it would be swallowed up among all the other files on his desk.

She set the folder to one side and spread the newspaper out, leafing through the pages until she came to the one describing the murder. The details were brief but lurid. It was obvious the reporter had got his information from the bystanders and had managed to find out the murdered woman's name. She closed the newspaper and gathered together the file, the ledger and the folder, before she walked down the corridor to Brewster's office to leave them on his desk.

Hamish was busy writing in a ledger when she returned to the charge room.

She leaned on the counter but Hamish didn't look up. She suspected he ignored her deliberately.

'Have you got the log book?' She drummed her fingers on the counter.

With a sigh of exasperation, he slid the book along to her. She signed off and entered 'Montrose' for her whereabouts the next day. The dressing down she got for omitting to fill the log book in, shortly after her arrival, still stung. No one had told her about it. Another deliberate omission on Hamish's part.

'Goodnight' She left without waiting to hear Hamish's grunt in reply.

The full force of the icy blast didn't hit her until she exited the courtyard. After she walked under the arch the wind took her breath away. It whipped the edges of her skirt and whirled around her body forcing her to turn her collar up to protect her neck. Not that it did much good. Anxious to get home she raced through the dark streets but by the time she got there her fingers and toes were numb and her nose felt like an icicle.

Her feet clattered on the wooden stairs and once she pushed open her door she hurried to the mantel to find the matches. She struck one and turned the gas tap until she heard the familiar hiss, the cue for her to hold the match underneath the mantle.

With a plop, it ignited and the mantle glowed red, spreading light throughout the room.

Shivers consumed her. The room felt as cold as it was outside although no icy wind whistled down her neck. She looked in despair at the fireplace where the ashes of yesterday's fire still lay. With a huge sigh, she grabbed the poker, knelt in front of it and stirred and raked the ash until it fell into the ash pan below. Then, scrunching newspaper into a loose ball she placed it in the grate before piling kindling and small lumps of coal on top. She struck another match and held it to the paper, keeping her fingers crossed the fire would burn and not flicker out.

Food came next and she couldn't remember what she had in her cupboard. Domesticity had never been high on her list of priorities. But she discovered a few potatoes an egg and a sausage. That would have to do.

While she waited for the potatoes to boil, she sat in her chair and thought about Lily. Despite spending all day investigating the murder and interviewing witnesses, she was no further forward in understanding who this girl was and why she was dead.

Who was Lily? Kirsty knew she was a prostitute and she worked for Aggie. Everything else was a mystery.

Maybe tomorrow, if she found Nancy, she might be able to fill in the blanks.

20

Angus Laidlaw strode through the streets of Dundee glad to be escaping the house, his nagging wife, and the baby who never seemed to stop crying. Already there was a queue forming in front of the picture house, Douglas Fairbanks always drew a big crowd.

'Open the doors,' the man at the head of the queue shouted. 'It's bleeding cold out here.'

Angus consulted his pocket watch. 'Another ten minutes.' He nipped the end of his fag between two fingers and tossed it into the gutter, unlocked the door and slipped through locking it behind him. It wouldn't do to let the crowds in before he donned his commissionaire's uniform.

The uniform hung from a hook in the small room he used as his changing room. He brushed the shoulders before donning it and admiring himself in the mirror on the back of the door. He smoothed his hair and placed the peaked cap on his head, adjusting it so he looked his best. He smiled and fingered his pencil-thin moustache. When he wore the uniform he felt like Douglas Fairbanks and although you couldn't tell the colour of the film star's uniform on the cinema screen he was sure it would be scarlet with gold braiding and epaulettes, just like the one he wore.

Impressed with his appearance, he walked to the glass doors and opened them.

'At last,' the man at the head of the queue grumbled.

Angus glared at him ready to deny him entrance to the picture house if he said anything else.

The man looked away and smiled sheepishly. 'Don't mean any harm, sir. But it's perishing cold standing here.'

Angus smirked. He liked exerting his authority and the crowd waiting knew he had the power to deny them entrance.

Satisfied with the man's response, he nodded and stood aside.

The queue of picture-goers filtered past him pushing their way to the ticket kiosk and into the darkness of the auditorium where the usherettes waited to shine their torches to show them to their seats. The front rows were the cheapest ones, known locally as 'the flechers' because many of their previous occupants left fleas behind them. These front stall seats were so near the screen folks got a crick in the neck. The seats stretching from the middle row to the back cost more. While the balcony, which soared over the stalls, was the reserve of the more affluent picture-goer and young men eager to impress a new girlfriend.

Men and women shoved past him, anxious to get into the auditorium. It would be standing room only when the film started. Glancing along the line of people waiting, his heart flipped inside his chest. A girl at the end looked like Lily and for a moment he imagined it was her.

He closed his eyes and remembered Lily as he'd last seen her. It was following Wednesday's matinee after the film finished and the doors secured, prior to the evening performance. She had been waiting for him in the room he used for changing his uniform.

This was where they met and where they consummated their love for each other. After, when it was all over and the guilt pangs consumed him, he knew it couldn't last forever. The thought of Edna finding out terrified him and if she told her father or her brothers. He shuddered at that thought. Fear of what her brothers would do had convinced him marrying Edna was the right thing to do when he got her in the family way. He dreaded to think what they would do to him if they found out about Lily.

Lily had smiled at him when he entered, making his stomach churn. Her smile, innocent and yet knowing, had that effect on him. But he needed to stay firm, tell her it was over and couldn't continue and this must be the last time.

His breathing became erratic as the words he'd rehearsed raced through his mind. 'Lily,' he said, concentrating on unbuttoning his uniform so he didn't have to look at her, 'we need to talk.'

She ran her hands inside his jacket and picked at the buttons on his shirt. 'Later. I have something to tell you.'

Heat spread through his body but he clenched his teeth and maintained his resolve. He pushed her hands away. He had to tell her and he had to tell her now. 'It's over, Lily. I can't see you anymore.'

Her response hadn't been what he expected. She'd leaned back and laughed. 'Don't think you're going to leave me in the lurch. No one gets off with that.' Her face no longer looked like that of an innocent young girl. 'I'm carrying your child in my belly and I'll be seeing the minister to tell him to call the banns and book the church for the wedding. You'll make a respectable woman of me or I'll contact your boss to tell him all about you.'

'You can't do that.'

'Oh, can't I? Just watch me.' She opened the door. 'I'll be back, my bonnie lad. Don't think of running out on me or your name will be mud all over Dundee.'

He slumped on the stool in the corner and watched her storm out of the cinema. Thank goodness he hadn't told her about Edna or she'd be on her way to see his wife. What on earth was he going to do?

'Are you Angus?'

Thoughts of Lily and their last meeting slithered away. 'Pardon?'

'I said, are you Angus?'

Two girls stood in front of him. A tall dark-haired girl and the one who looked like Lily. 'Yes. Do I know you?' He frowned, wondering what they wanted.

'We're friends of Lily,' the tall one said.

His heart thumped so loudly they were bound to hear.

'I don't know any Lily.' Desperation made his voice sound higher than normal.

'Yes, you do. She told us all about you. How she loved you and that you were to wed.'

Heat engulfed him and he ran a finger around his collar to relieve the pressure on his neck.

'Look, we're not here to make trouble but we thought you

should be told.' The girl hesitated and looked at her friend.

'I'm sorry,' the girl who looked like Lily said. 'Lily's dead.'

'What?' His heartbeat quickened even more.

'I'm sorry,' she said again.

'How can she be dead? I saw her last week and she didn't look ill or anything.'

'Somebody killed her. They beat her to death.'

'The police...'

'We haven't told them about you.'

He leaned against the wall. He'd wanted to be rid of Lily but not like this. Never like this.

'I'm sorry,' one of the girls said again, he wasn't sure which one. Then they slipped out the door.

The rest of the evening passed in a haze and he hardly noticed the crowds leaving the cinema at the end of the film. He changed out of his uniform while the usherettes checked everyone had left. Once the place was empty, he locked up.

Sleet battered his face as he walked along the darkened streets. His was a dejected figure, stooped with slumped shoulders, wearing a threadbare, once fashionable, pin-striped suit and a flat cap on top of his slicked-back hair. He'd left the glamour of the film world behind him when he locked the cinema door and he no longer felt like Douglas Fairbanks. He was just Angus Laidlaw with a wife and bairn waiting for him at home.

He should have felt relief now the problem Lily presented was over. She was gone, really gone, and he could move on with his life. He wouldn't have to worry about her anymore. But the excitement seeped out of his life and he couldn't suppress the ache in his heart. All he had left was his humdrum existence with Edna and their squalling brat.

Daisy and Elsie slipped through the cinema doors leaving Angus slumped against the wall. The street outside was empty and they hurried down the marble entrance steps anxious to put space between themselves and the man inside.

Sleet battered their faces. An icy wind threatened to send

their hats spinning off into the night and whipped hair around their heads. Daisy stopped briefly to pull her coat collar up then grasped Elsie's hand. 'Let's run, it's damned cold and besides, I'm not sure we did the right thing coming here.'

The clank of a tram sounded in the distance and they ran along the Murraygate and across another street, speeding past the imposing frontage of St Paul's Cathedral. They raced to the stop, hopped onto the tram and sank into a seat where they could huddle together for warmth.

They didn't speak or discuss their visit to Angus until they were ensconced in Elsie's flat.

Elsie stirred the embers of the fire with the poker and added several lumps of coal. 'We'll soon get the heat up. In the meantime, I'll put the kettle on.' She held it under the tap, filled it with water, and placed it on the gas ring. After that was done she removed her coat.

'Give me your wet coat,' she said to Daisy. 'You'll get your death of cold if you keep it on.'

Daisy shrugged it off and handed it to Elsie who hung it on the hook adjacent to her own coat.

Flames flickered around the coal which stirred and settled in the fireplace. Daisy stared into the red embers while thoughts whirled through her brain. Not for the first time she wondered if they'd done the right thing by informing Angus of Lily's death. His response had been odd, not what she expected.

'A penny for them?' Elsie laid a cup of tea in front of her.

'I was thinking about Angus. Did we do right going to see him?'

'It was the decent thing to do. But he did seem odd.'

'D'you think it strange he denied knowing her?' Daisy whispered. 'If he loved her why would he do that?'

'I thought that funny as well.'

'He looked uncomfortable when he realized we knew about him and Lily.'

'I thought for a moment he might hit us.'

'When we told him she was dead he looked more relieved than upset.'

'I reckon he was more concerned about the police than

Lily's death.'

Daisy looked at Elsie. 'You're right. You don't suppose...' she couldn't finish. The thought was too horrible to contemplate.

'I don't know.'

'D'you think we should tell the police?'

'No,' Elsie said. 'I think we keep it to ourselves because we don't know and we don't want trouble.'

'But what if...'

'We stay out of his way and we don't go near that part of the town.'

'What if he comes here?'

'He'd be daft to do that. Now wouldn't he?'

'I suppose.'

21

Tuesday, 9 December 1919

'How is Kirsty settling in?'

Brewster paused in the middle of peeling a potato. He'd oiled the wheels of Maggie's wheelchair the night before and hadn't heard her enter the kitchen. He turned the question over in his mind. How was she settling in? It wasn't something he ever thought to ask her.

'All right, I suppose,' he said. 'I think the men are finding it difficult.'

Maggie laughed. 'I've no doubt. They've never had to work with a woman before.'

'What about Annie,' Brewster protested. 'They don't mind her.'

'You've always had a woman turnkey for the female prisoners but there's never been a policewoman before. I would imagine they think she's encroaching on male territory.'

'You think too much, Maggie. Kirsty is well able to hold her own with them.'

'No doubt. What about you, Jamie. What do you think of her? Do you like her?'

Brewster peeled another potato. 'I hadn't given that much thought. And whether or not I like her is immaterial. I work with her.'

She laughed. 'But you do like her.'

He popped the last potato into the pot and turned to face his wife. 'You're not jealous, are you?'

Maggie shook her head.

He knelt beside her wheelchair and grasped her hands. 'You know I love you, and would never leave you. As for Kirsty, I find her annoying, opinionated, and argumentative, and she doesn't know her place. At the same time, she's clever, intuitive, and I value her opinion, even when she's telling me I'm wrong.'

'I knew you liked her. And I'm not jealous, I'm just glad you've got someone who reminds you that you're not always right because you can sometimes be overbearing.'

Brewster leaned forward and hugged her. 'I'd better be off. There's a lot to do at the office.'

Brewster stepped out of the house into a chilly dawn where the first glimmers of a winter sun struggled to make an impact. He inhaled the cold air and fastened the top button of his coat. At the gate, he had to wait until a horse clopped past pulling a milk cart along the narrow lane. Empty bottles tinkled and clattered together indicating the deliveries were complete and it was time to return to the stable. The sound of the horse's hooves faded into the distance and, skirting a pile of steaming manure, Brewster hurried, until he reached the archway leading into the police station.

Warmth enveloped him when he pushed open the door to the charge room.

'Good morning, sir,' the duty sergeant said. 'Archie brought in the suitcase from the crime scene. I wasn't sure whether you wanted it in your office so I kept it here.' He pushed the door of the pot-bellied stove shut encasing the glowing red embers inside.

'I'll check the contents here.' Brewster lifted the flap and slipped behind the high counter.

'I thought you might, sir. Not much room in your office.' Brewster glanced at him, uncertain whether he was trying to be funny, but Geordie had a straight face that looked as if he wouldn't know a humorous comment if he tripped over it.

Ledgers and papers littered a table on the back wall. After removing them he hoisted the suitcase on top. Then he clicked open the locks, lifted the lid and inspected the contents.

'Geordie, I need you to record each item as I remove it from the case.'

'Two cups, two saucers, two plates. A bunch of forks,

CHRIS LONGMUIR

knives, and spoons. Why would anyone pack this?' He scratched his head.

'It's beyond me, sir. But looks like she planned to move out.'

A whiff of perfume rose from the silk dress Brewster removed next, the aroma becoming stronger with each additional item of clothing removed. The smell reminded him of Maggie. It was her favourite scent, Lily of the Valley, but now, in his mind, it would be forever associated with Lily who was lying in the mortuary with her face battered out of all recognition. Maybe he should buy Maggie a different perfume for her Christmas this year.

Brewster continued to remove items from the case describing each one so Geordie could document them. Underneath the last item of clothing nestled a large brown envelope. 'What's this?' He turned it over in his hands before untying the cord that fastened the flap.

Inside was a yellow, legal-looking document with an address on the front. The handwritten text was difficult to read and had evidently been written a long time ago but there was no mistaking what he was looking at. Title deeds to a house in the Hawkhill.

'That's interesting,' he said. 'I'll take this along to my office to examine. In the meantime, you can enter all this for evidence.' He gestured at the items piled on the table. 'After that, place everything back inside the case and make sure it's locked in the evidence cupboard.'

Geordie nodded his assent.

For the second day running the corridor seemed empty and quiet. The constables' room was devoid of bodies which meant the fug of smoke was less than usual. Sergeant Brodie hunched over his desk in the sergeants' room.

Brewster stopped at the door. 'Any results from the search of the backlands at the Scouringburn?'

'Nothing so far, sir. I'll go there as soon as I complete next week's rotas. We might finish searching by tonight or tomorrow at the latest.'

'It's essential we find the murder weapon. Keep me posted.'

'Yes, sir.'

Brewster frowned. They should have found the weapon by this time. It couldn't have travelled far when Aggie heaved it over the railing into the backlands after the deed was done. His frown intensified. What if he was wrong? Kirsty didn't believe Aggie killed Lily but he'd refused to listen to her reasons. Aggie was on the spot and covered in blood. Who else could it be? But without a murder weapon, he couldn't prove it.

Still frowning he entered his office, deposited the legal document on the desk and slumped in his chair. Today he needed to examine the ledger and file he'd removed from Aggie's building, and now he had to decipher and make sense of this damned thing as well. This was the part of the job he liked the least, the interminable paperwork.

He sighed and reached out his hand to open Kirsty's reports. No doubt her opinion would be different to the one he had and she never held back in expressing her views. But she was often right, that was what made her irritating. This time, although she believed he was wrong when he arrested Aggie, she had no more of a clue who committed the murder than he did.

22

Kirsty was the only person to alight from the train at Montrose. She crossed the footbridge over the rail tracks, pausing for a moment at the top to survey her surroundings. Behind her, an expanse of water skirted the railway station forming a vast inland lake which she understood formed mud flats when the tide went out. And in front of her, a few streets to her right, a majestic church steeple reached to the sky.

She hurried down the steps leading from the top of the bridge and headed in the direction of the steeple. The smell of animals and dung increased as she approached a low wooden building, evidently the town's cattle market, although no animals occupied the empty stalls today.

Pedestrians thronged the pavements at each side of the wide, cobbled main street and it didn't take her long to get directions to India Lane.

'Down that road.' The man she had stopped, pointed across the road to a narrow street with an arch over it. 'Keep going until you reach the mid links at the bottom, and it's one of the streets at the other side of the park.'

What the passerby hadn't said was that the mid links was a series of parks that stretched the length of the town but she walked down a road dividing two of them and soon found India Lane.

The narrow unpaved lane, flanked at one side by a house and the other side by a shed, gave no indication of being a residential area. Kirsty walked between the shed and house, following the rough dirt track to the right, before the lane straightened out to reveal a row of two-storey houses stretching down the right-hand side. The left side appeared to be uncultivated ground until it reached a cottage and stables a third of the way down. Beyond that lay a section of vegetable plots with a few houses even further down at the end of the lane.

Kirsty checked the house numbers as she walked down the lane but the ones on the right all had even numbers. The odd numbers should have been on the other side and there weren't enough houses on the left to amount to thirty-three, the number she'd been given.

She continued to walk down the lane until she came to the cottages. The first one was numbered thirty-one and the one next to it number thirty-three.

A high wall surrounded the cottage. Access, through a wooden gate, led to a path, bordered by grass and several trees. A curtain in the window of the room to the left of the front door twitched, and she knew her approach was being observed.

Someone must have been behind the door because it opened before her hand released the knocker. She was faced with a shrunken, grey-haired woman wearing an apron over her dress.

'I'm looking for Nancy Allardyce.'

The woman frowned while her eyes examined Kirsty.

'Who might you be?' The woman placed her hands on her hips. 'And what's that strange outfit you're wearing? I've never seen anything like that before.'

'I'm a policewoman and I need to speak to Nancy about her friend Lily.'

'Policewoman? No such thing.'

'Maybe not here, but I assure you there are policewomen in other places. I work in Dundee.'

The woman snorted. 'Den of iniquity, that's what Dundee is. Thank goodness Nancy came home.'

'Granny, I'll speak to the lady. You go back inside the house and sit by the fire.' The girl who appeared behind her put her hand on the older woman's shoulder and waited until she shuffled through the door to the left of the small lobby. She turned to Kirsty. 'Can you wait until I get my coat, I'd prefer she didn't hear.'

A few moments later Nancy joined her outside. 'If you don't mind,' she said, 'we'll walk to where we can't be overheard.'

Kirsty nodded and followed Nancy out the gate. They turned left and walked to the bottom of the lane and through a turnstile which led to an expanse of rough ground and grass. Avoiding a hollow where someone had dumped a feather mattress they stopped when they were no longer in earshot of any of the houses.

'You've come because of Lily,' Nancy said.

'Yes, I looked for you in Dundee but you'd already left.' Kirsty produced her notebook and pencil. 'I'll need to make notes, I hope you don't mind.'

Nancy continued to speak. 'I couldn't stay after what happened to Lily. I didn't want to be the next one found murdered in bed.'

'Did you think you were in danger?'

'We're all in danger. We know the risks involved in what we do and I didn't want to be part of it anymore. Not after Lily was killed.'

'Any idea why she might have been killed?'

Nancy shook her head.

'Had she been involved in anything that might have led to someone wanting to get her out of the way?'

'Lily always had big plans, but she was a fantasist.' Nancy stared into the distance. 'There was a man she'd been seeing. She said he was going to marry her as if that would ever happen, but she was convinced. She talked about living in a fancy house and having a servant. And she said they were going to talk to a minister about reading their banns.'

'Who was the man?'

'I never saw him. She said his name was Angus and he was posh. He owned a cinema.' Nancy paused. 'I think it was all in her mind.'

She bent down and pulled a blade of the long grass, twisting it around her fingers.

'She also said she planned to set up her own house in competition with Aggie and wanted me to go with her. I told her that would never happen but she said she had savings and she had connections.'

'What kind of connections?'

'She said she had her eye on a house and the owner was sweet on her. I also saw her in the Overgate with Freddie

Simpson. He's one of the local pimps. But what she wanted from him is a mystery to me.'

'I see.' Kirsty turned the information over in her mind. 'Do you know the name of the man who owned the house?'

Nancy shook her head. 'She never told me.'

'What about the other men who visited her?'

'We aren't told the real names of the men who visit so we give them nicknames.' Nancy paused to think. 'The Captain and the Laird are the only two I remember who visited Lily.'

'Tell me about them.'

'The Captain liked Lily, didn't want to go with any of the other girls and often he paid extra to stay all night. She used to say he sometimes had nightmares and she thought he'd been in the war. He gave her a black eye once and that made her careful what she said to him and she tried not to make him angry.'

Kirsty made notes. 'What about the Laird?'

'I don't know much about him. Daisy would know more.'

'Is that Daisy Miller?' Kirsty remembered her from previous interviews.

'I suppose. I don't ask their other names.'

'What else can you tell me?'

'Not much. I think Lily planned to leave and the other girls seemed to know something.'

'Did Big Aggie know?'

'Lily wouldn't have told her, but Aggie keeps her ear to the ground and there's not much she doesn't know.'

'I take it Aggie wouldn't approve.'

'You can say that again. The only way out once you're tied to Aggie is either in a box or with a bairn. I got away because you lot clapped her in prison.'

'One of the other girls told me you knew Lily from before you went to Dundee.'

'It was Lily who got me to go to Dundee. She said I'd make my fortune.' Nancy laughed. 'Some fortune.'

'You must have known her well to trust her.'

'I thought I could trust her. We grew up together. We went to school together. We played together. We shared all our secrets. We were friends. Some friend she turned out to be.'

'That means she lived nearby. Does she still have family here?'

Daisy nodded. 'She lived in the next street. There's a wall between the back of her house and mine.'

'Can you give me the address of her family? I'll need to inform them what has happened to her.'

'Good luck with that,' Nancy said. 'They won't want to know.'

'I'll need the address all the same.'

'Can't remember the number we just call it the manse, and it's in Bents Road.'

Kirsty wrote it in her notebook.

'I've told you all I know.' Nancy turned away from her and started to walk back the way they had come.

'Thank you,' Kirsty said. 'If I need anything else I'll be in touch.'

Nancy reached the stile. She climbed over it and vanished up the lane without answering.

23

Bents Road was the next street along from India Lane and as Kirsty turned the corner she wondered what kind of reception she would get from Lily's parents. Nancy's response when she'd asked about them hadn't been encouraging.

Heaps of steaming horse dung littered the road, indicative of stables further down, but she kept to the narrow pavement. None of the cottages she passed seemed large enough to be the house she sought but halfway down, she came to a wall too high for her to see over. When she peered through the wrought-iron gate she glimpsed a large house off to the left, in the shadow of the wall.

The creak of rusty hinges set her nerves on edge when she pushed the heavy iron gate. A sense of foreboding overwhelmed her and an involuntary shiver crept up her spine when she saw the house hidden behind it. Two storeys high with a further attic floor above and overshadowed by the wall at one side and trees at the other, the ominous feeling was impounded by the darkened stone of the building and the flaking paintwork of the window frames. The sense of being watched as she walked up the path, strengthened, although there were no faces at the windows.

A large lion's head knocker stood guard on the front door. It seemed to be daring her to touch it but she lifted the iron ring dangling from its mouth and pounded several times, each knock louder than the previous one. She was getting ready to knock again when the door opened.

'Yes?'

The young woman standing before her didn't look like a minister's wife. Her hair straggled onto her shoulders, lank and lifeless, while her eyes had a definite squint so Kirsty couldn't be sure if she was looking at her or past her.

'I wish to see Reverend Josiah Petrie,' Kirsty said.

'I'll ask if the master is receiving.'

'It is imperative I see him,' she shouted after the vanishing form of the little servant.

'Follow me,' the maid said when she returned. She opened a door leading from the cavernous hall and ushered Kirsty inside the room.

There was something unsettling about the man in front of her. Perhaps it was because he did not look up at her entry, or it might be his appearance. Gaunt and skeletal with only the white of his clerical collar to relieve the black suit he wore.

'Reverend Petrie?' Her tongue stuck to the roof of her mouth and she had trouble pronouncing his name.

The man, sitting at the desk reading a large leather-bound book, looked up. His eyes pierced her with a look that unnerved her. They reminded her of a bird's eyes, probing and curious.

'You may go, Jessie.' He waved his hand at the door and the maid scurried out.

He turned his attention back to Kirsty. 'You do not belong to my congregation, but you asked to see me. If it is your nuptials you wish to discuss you are wasting your time. I only perform wedding ceremonies for church members. I have no time to spare for heathens.'

'I am here on official business, sir.'

The minister frowned. 'I am not in the habit of discussing business, official or otherwise, with women.'

'I am a policewoman, sir, and I am here to inform you of some sad news.'

'There is no such thing as a policewoman.' He made no reference to her statement about the sad news.

Since her return to Scotland, Kirsty had met this reaction many times.

'I assure you I am, sir. I work with the City of Dundee Police and I have business to discuss with you.' She could not resist adding, 'Whether you like it or not.'

He looked her up and down. 'I suppose that explains the strange garb you are wearing but, as I previously said, I do not wish to discuss anything with you. Perhaps you should return with a policeman or your senior officer.'

Kirsty bit her lip to prevent her annoyance becoming obvious.

'As I said, I have sad news to impart first.'

'Well, say your piece and go. I'm a busy man.'

'It might be better if Mrs Petrie was also present as it concerns her as well.'

'I don't see the point of involving my wife. I handle everything that concerns this family.'

Kirsty stiffened. She wasn't going to let this bully have it all his own way.

'Nevertheless, I insist, sir.'

He threw the pencil he was holding onto the desk and slammed the book shut.

'Very well, but I assure you I will be informing your superior officer of your insubordination.' Anger contorted his face. 'Follow me.'

Kirsty hadn't appreciated how tall he was until he rose from his chair, circled the desk, and towered over her. She resisted an urge to shrink back from him.

His annoyance at the lack of fear she displayed seemed to anger him even more and he stomped from the room.

'In here,' he said, opening a door further down the hall.

The woman sitting in an armchair beside the empty fireplace looked up when they entered the room, but the two girls on the sofa never raised their heads from their embroidery.

She shivered. This room felt unwelcoming and seemed colder than the air outside. Reverend Petrie claimed the armchair opposite his wife but did not offer a chair to Kirsty.

'This policewoman,' his voice was thick with sarcasm, 'wishes to discuss something with us. I informed her I speak for all of us, but she insists that you are present.'

'Yes, dear,' the woman murmured with an anxious glance at her husband.

One of the girls on the sofa peeked at Kirsty before concentrating again on her needlework.

'Well, get on with it. I'm a busy man.'

Kirsty ignored the minister's frown and pulled a chair over

to position herself between the woman and the girls.

'I am sorry, to bring you sad news.' She placed her hand on the arm of the chair the woman was sitting in. 'Your daughter, Lily, is dead.'

She bit her lip, the statement sounded so harsh.

'I have no daughter named Lily.' The minister glared at Kirsty.

A tear slid down the woman's face and she laid her embroidery on the small table at the side of her chair.

The elder girl on the sofa put her arms around her sister.

'I have no daughter named Lily.' The minister's voice was louder this time. 'You will not mention that name in my house.'

'I am sorry if I upset you, but Lily was murdered and I do need information about her to enable us to identify her killer.'

'I have told you, and I will not say it again. I have no daughter named Lily. Now, I will be obliged if you would leave my house.'

Kirsty stood. There was nothing to be gained by remaining here.

'My name is Kirsty Campbell and I can be contacted at Police Headquarters in Dundee if you decide you want more information, or if you wish to talk to me.'

The minister tugged the bell pull dangling beside the fireplace. 'The maid will show you out.' He stalked from the room without glancing at Kirsty.

'This way, miss,' Jessie said. She cast a furtive glance over her shoulder as she opened the door. 'The park at the top of the road,' she whispered, 'the one with the drinking well.'

Kirsty turned to ask her what she meant but the door slammed and she was alone on the doorstep.

24

Several grassy parks stretched along the length of the road in front of Kirsty when she reached the top of Bents Road. The one directly in front of her didn't have a drinking fountain nor did the one to the right while the park further along to the left had a structure that looked like a statue or monument in the middle, where the footpaths intersected. She headed for the park with the monument, hoping she'd made the right choice.

Frost glistened on the grass bordering the footpath and gravel crunched under her feet as she walked to the centre of the park. But she was unable to detect a drinking fountain on the monument which faced her. It was a square structure with no obvious purpose, rounded at the top with a dome, cap and ball finial, and it sat on a three-step stone base. She thought she might be in the wrong place until she found the drinking fountain at the front of the monument, facing towards the town. Kirsty climbed the steps to study the memorial plaque in a recess above the fountain and read, 'Erected by subscription in recognition of public improvements initiated and carried out by George Scott, Provost of Montrose 1887-1890.' It meant nothing to her. She had never heard of this man although he was apparently well thought of by the people of the town.

Four benches sat facing each side of the memorial and she chose one which would allow her to see anyone approaching from the Bents Road direction. They appeared to be free of frost but it wasn't long before the cold seeped through her serge skirt. Ignoring it, Kirsty pulled out her notebook and added her observations of the Petrie family while she waited for Jessie.

The interview hadn't gone as well as she'd hoped. The Reverend Josiah Petrie impressed her as a bully who expected to be obeyed by the other members of the household while Mrs Petrie and her two daughters seemed shadowy figures with no will of their own. In retrospect, Kirsty thought she would have gained more from Mrs Petrie if her husband had not been present. But the minister was unlikely to allow that to happen. However, Jessie hadn't made much of an impression either and Kirsty wondered what information the maidservant might provide.

Kirsty stuffed her notebook into her pocket. Where was Jessie? It seemed hours since she'd left the Petrie home. She got up and walked around the memorial. Then she marched along each of the footpaths in turn until her feet felt less numb.

At last, the girl emerged from the top of Bents Road. Kirsty started to walk towards her, but the girl wouldn't want attention to be drawn to their meeting so she stopped halfway and returned to the bench.

Jessie placed her shopping basket on the bench and sat down beside her.

'You wanted to meet me?' Kirsty avoided looking at the girl's eyes.

'Yes, miss. I wanted to ask you about Lily.' Jessie twisted her hands together. 'How did she die?'

'She was murdered, and I want to find out who killed her.'

'Did she suffer?'

'I don't know. Someone beat her about the head. I think she died quickly.' Kirsty wasn't sure about this but there was no point in making the girl feel worse than she did.

'Mrs Petrie was crying when I left the house and the minister locked himself in his study.' Jessie wiped away a tear. 'He doesn't care,' she said. 'All he thinks about is his bible and cursing sinners.'

'What about you, Jessie? Do you care?'

'Of course, I do. Lily was like a sister to me.'

'Does that mean you've been with the family a long time?'

'Ever since I was a baby, miss. You see, I'm Lily's cousin. My ma was Mrs Petrie's sister and she looked after me when my ma died giving birth to me.'

'What about your father?' Kirsty didn't think the Reverend Petrie would countenance an illegitimate child in his household.

'He died in the Boer War and left my ma destitute. I don't

know what would have happened to me if Aunt Mary hadn't taken me in. It wasn't easy for her because she was carrying Lily at the time. I'm three months older than Lily and we were brought up like sisters.'

'But the Reverend Petrie treats you like a servant.'

'Aunt Mary's good to me when he isn't there.'

Kirsty thought for a moment.

'Tell me about Lily.'

'Lovely, miss. Lovely to look at and with a lovely nature as well.'

'What happened to make her father disown her?'

'Lily got herself a boyfriend when she was fifteen. Nice, he was. But he got her in the family way. The minister took her to a goodwife and she got rid of the baby. Then he threw her out and told her she was no longer part of the family. Aunt Mary tried to stop him but it wasn't any use. I didn't know where she went until I saw her one day when I was in Dundee on an errand. I told Aunt Mary and she went to see her anytime she could get away.'

'Do you think your aunt might come to Dundee to see me?'

'I could ask her when the minister isn't in the house. What do you want me to say?'

'Tell her it would be helpful to find out more about Lily and the people she knew. It might lead us to her killer.'

Jessie gathered up her basket. 'I've got to go, miss. I've been here too long and the minister won't be pleased. He'll say I've been dallying.'

Kirsty put a hand on her arm. 'Before you go. Can you give me the names of anyone you think Lily might have known? Her boyfriend's name, for example.'

'I can't quite recall, miss. His first name was Billy, but he joined the army and he's not around here anymore.'

'Is there anyone else?'

'Well, there's her Uncle David, Aunt Mary's brother. He has his own church in Broughty Ferry.'

'Thank you. If I need to talk to you again will that be all right?' Kirsty released her grip on Jessie's arm.

'Yes, miss.' Jessie ran up the footpath in the direction of the town.

Kirsty sat for a few moments mulling over what she had learned before she rose and made her way to the railway station. It hadn't been a wasted journey and the righteous Reverend Petrie wasn't such a good man after all.

25

It was dark when Kirsty stepped off the train at Dundee station shortly after four o'clock.

A chill breeze whipped up Union Street, nipping her cheeks and fingers. She stuffed her hands into her pockets and hurried to the town centre where she would be out of the full force of the wind. When she reached the Nethergate she crossed the road to enter the more sheltered Tally Street which led to the crowded Overgate. Heads turned and fingers pointed as she fought through the crowds to reach Barrack Street. Kirsty, in uniform, was still a curiosity in Dundee. She ignored the interest she aroused as well as any comments which were mild in comparison to those thrown at her in London.

Barrack Street was quieter but just as chilly and she had to pass the Howff graveyard, a place that gave her the shivers which had nothing to do with the cold. But she tucked her head down and hurried on, not stopping until she reached Police Headquarters in West Bell Street.

After the freezing atmosphere outside, the heat in the charge room hit her like a physical blow. Her fingers and face tingled with a burning sensation and she stamped her feet in an effort to bring the feeling back.

'Evening, miss.' The desk sergeant slammed the door of the pot-bellied stove shut and laid the poker down. 'Inspector Brewster was looking for you earlier. Said to report to him when you came in.'

'Thanks, Geordie.' Kirsty headed in the direction of Brewster's office, letting the door of the charge room swing shut behind her.

A buzz of voices seeped out of the constables' room along with the usual fug of smoke. The search of the backlands at Aggie's building had either finished or they'd given up for the day when darkness fell.

Laughter echoed out of the room after she passed and she guessed the constables would be making lewd comments but that didn't trouble her because they weren't brave enough to say these things to her face. They had probably figured out by this time she was capable of giving them short shrift.

Brewster sat hunched over his desk studying a yellow-tinged document. He looked up at Kirsty's entry. 'Ah! There you are,' he said.

'You were looking for me, sir?'

'Sit, sit,' he said.

The other two chairs in Brewster's office were piled high with files. She removed one of the piles and laid them on the floor before pulling the chair in front of his desk.

'What do you make of this?' He tapped the document with his fingers.

Kirsty squinted across the desk but the print looked like squiggles of hieroglyphics.

'It's taken me most of the day to decipher,' he continued. 'This document is the title deed to a property in the Hawkhill made out to Lily Petrie. It's not just a house as I originally thought but an entire building. Much bigger than Aggie's tenement.'

'Where on earth would Lily find the money to buy a building? I wouldn't have thought one of Aggie's girls would be able to make that kind of money.'

'That's what I thought.'

'Lily is turning into a woman of mystery.' Kirsty leaned forward in the chair. 'I'm sure the reason for her murder is connected to her. Something she was involved with, or something from her past.'

Brewster chewed the end of a pencil. 'I'm not so sure about that. I still think Aggie had a hand in it.'

She ignored his comment. 'As a matter of interest where did you find this?'

'In the suitcase I found, hidden under her bed.'

'You didn't tell me about the suitcase. What else did you find inside?'

'Clothing and various bits and pieces. Nothing out of the usual except for this document and some crockery and cutlery. I got Geordie to make a list. Have a look and see what you make of it.' As an afterthought, he added, 'A woman's eye might see something I've missed.'

Kirsty nodded her assent, certain she would interpret the contents of Lily's suitcase much better than any man. He should have asked her to check it in the first place.

Changing the subject, Kirsty said, 'My Montrose trip turned up fresh information.'

'Ah, yes. You were contacting Nancy Allardyce today.'

'Nancy was most informative and told me all about Lily and her family. I also interviewed Lily's parents and their serving girl. Her father is the Reverend Josiah Petrie who preaches at the United Free Church in Montrose. He disowned Lily after she became pregnant but he was the one who arranged for her to have an abortion.' Kirsty paused for breath. 'Hypocrite.'

'Interesting,' Brewster said.

'I think he bullies his wife and two daughters. They appeared subservient and didn't have much to say. I'd like to get them on their own. But I did get a chance to talk to Lily's cousin Jessie, although you would never guess she was related because they treat her like a serving girl.'

'Good work. Put it all in a report and I'll study it in the morning.'

Kirsty would have preferred to discuss her interviews with Brewster but it was evident he had dismissed her. She rose from the chair, muttering, 'Yes, sir.' She wanted to add, 'Three bags full, sir,' but bit her tongue to prevent herself saying the words.

She marched down the corridor to her own office, seething at her dismissal when things were becoming interesting and she had much more to say.

Brewster could be such an annoying person. Every time she thought she made progress with him and he had started to value her contribution, he would slap her down as if reminding her of her place. Typical man, she thought, can't bear the idea a woman could possibly be of value. Well, she would show him.

She squeezed behind her desk and grabbed a pencil which

she stabbed on the paper. 'Blast,' she said when the point broke.

An hour later she gathered her reports together in a cardboard file and took them to Brewster but he had already left. She pushed some papers aside and laid them on his desk where he couldn't fail to see them when he returned.

The yellow legal document perched on top of his in-tray. She stepped outside the office and peered along the corridor. Apart from the buzz of voices emanating from the constables' room, the place appeared empty. She returned to the desk, picked up the document and laid it flat but the ancient handwriting was difficult to decipher. Rather than spending hours trying to read the script, she decided to rely on Brewster's interpretation. After replacing it she scurried along the corridor to the charge room.

Geordie looked up at her entry. 'The inspector's gone for the night.'

'I gathered that.' Kirsty placed her elbows on the counter. 'Did he tell you he asked me to inspect the suitcase taken from the crime scene?'

'He did mention it, miss. The case is on the table over there.' He lifted the flap at the end of the counter. 'The list is sitting beside it.'

'Thanks, Geordie.' She edged through the gap in the counter and walked to the table. After opening the suitcase, she inspected the contents, marking each one off against the list in her hand.

'Why would Lily pack crockery and cutlery?' she mused.

Geordie evidently heard because he came to stand beside her. 'The inspector wondered about that as well. Doesn't make any sense.'

'Perhaps it's a sign her move from Aggie's establishment was imminent,' she murmured, thinking about the title deed sitting in Brewster's in-tray.

'Big Aggie wouldn't like that,' Geordie said.

Kirsty closed the lid of the suitcase. 'That's all I need, Geordie. I'll be off now.'

The courtyard outside was dark and silent and it took a moment for her eyes to adjust. The glimmer of light which shone through the arch leading to the street illuminated a faint sheen on the cobbles, warning her of a frost descending which might make it slippery underfoot.

As she walked home through the deserted streets with only the echo of her footsteps for company her mind buzzed with thoughts of Lily and her murder. Aggie was the obvious choice as the person responsible and Brewster was unshakeable in his belief in her guilt. But Kirsty wasn't so sure.

In her hurry to reach the station earlier in the day, she'd forgotten to take her torch and the entry to her building was in darkness. Once she pushed the outer door open she wrinkled her nose at the smells which always seemed to pervade the building. The smell of cooked cabbage she could tolerate, but the stink of cats was something she would never get used to. She clutched the banister and felt her way up the stairs while praying under her breath no rats or mice lurked in the shadows and she wouldn't step on something foul. A faint sound of music drifted down from one of the upper flats the only sign of anyone else in the building.

The lock on her door was stiff and she had to wiggle the key to open it. She'd been intending to do something about it before it finally seized up altogether. But in her job, time had a habit of being gobbled up leaving nothing spare to do anything else.

The room inside seemed no warmer than the street outside and was as dark as the stairwell. She felt her way around the walls until she came to the mantelpiece. Her fingers crept along it until they reached the box of matches and after striking one she held it to the gas mantle.

She glared at the oil heater. The flame petered out two nights ago when it ran out of paraffin. Blast, she would freeze if she didn't get a fire going. Spurred on by the cold, she soon had a fire laid and flames licking through the sticks and the coal.

Satisfied the fire was burning and in no danger of flickering out, she set about making herself something to eat. She filled the kettle and placed it on the gas ring and went to the cupboard to bring out her cup and saucer. That was when she realized what had been bothering her about the crockery in Lily's suitcase. Lily had two of everything. Kirsty, on the other hand, had one of everything because she lived on her own and had no intention of entertaining anyone in her flat.

If Lily intended to move out why did she need two of everything? Did she have a lover or a partner? Kirsty couldn't imagine Lily would waste time preparing tea for a customer. Another chat with Aggie's girls was indicated. Lily was indeed, a mystery woman.

26

Wednesday, 10 December 1919

Peggy Armstrong set the plate in front of her husband. 'I managed to get bacon from the butcher this week but he slipped it to me without the others seeing. Said he kept it for his special customers and not to go telling folks because he didn't want a riot on his hands.'

'Eggs too?' Gregor laid his cigar in the ashtray and lifted his knife and fork. 'I don't know how you do it with all the shortages. The shops never seem to have enough of anything.'

Gregor knew why the butcher and other traders treated his wife as a special customer and that they would continue to do so as long as he held ownership of their properties. A word from him would see their rents increased. It paid them to keep his wife sweet.

It also paid him to make sure she felt special and valued and he made a point of praising her as often as he could. As a church elder, he needed his wife by his side to enhance his respectability. That would be important when he sought election as a councillor and, later on, when he stood for a parliamentary seat. Nothing must get in the way of that and from now on he had to make sure he didn't transgress.

At least, Lily was out of the way so that solved one problem. Lily had been a moment of madness. She'd cast a spell over him ensuring he stayed besotted enough to meet all her demands. Those demands had been increasing lately. That was over now and he could move on with his life and his ambitions although he would miss her ability to satisfy the passions she aroused, something his wife seemed unable to do. But if he wanted to advance himself and get on in the world, it would be far too dangerous to indulge his passions. He would have to learn to live without them and turn his back on women like Lily.

He laid his knife and fork on the empty plate, leaned back in his chair with a sigh of contentment and patted his lips with a napkin while he listened to his wife clattering about in the kitchen. Before the war, they'd had a cook and a couple of servants but girls and women nowadays didn't want to be skivvies, cleaning up behind their betters. He still found it strange that Peggy was happier doing these tasks herself and no longer as discontented as she had been as a lady of leisure. She said her life now had a purpose which it previously lacked and she enjoyed looking after him and their three daughters and, no thank you, she didn't want a cook or servants.

Perhaps it was for the best and it did lead to a harmonious household.

The noise in the kitchen stopped and Peggy's quiet footsteps came up behind him. She always seemed to sense the moment he finished eating.

He stood, turned towards her and kissed her on the forehead. 'That was lovely,' he said. 'But I need to leave for the office. I'll see you tonight.'

'Yes, dear,' she murmured lifting his empty plate.

Gregor picked up his cigar and filled his mouth with the fragrant smoke. Cigars were one of the pleasures of his life along with good food and a loving family. As he left the breakfast room he wondered if Peggy spent all her time in the kitchen when he was away but if she did and it made her happy that was fine with him.

His overcoat hung in the hall cupboard. He shrugged it on, straining to fasten it around his corpulent body and fearing the buttons might pop off. Time to visit his tailor, everything was becoming too tight. He was no longer able to fasten the top button on his trousers and relied on his braces to keep them up. His waistcoats and jackets were straining at the seams and his shirts were strangling him. Yes, a visit to his tailor was in order. He would make the appointment today.

Would he wear the homburg or the bowler hat today? He tapped a finger on his chin before choosing the homburg and placing it at an angle on his head. Then, after selecting the malacca cane with the ivory handle and pulling on his leather gloves, he opened the door.

He stood for a moment on the top step. Magdalen Green stretched in front of him with the bandstand off to his right and a glimpse of the River Tay in the distance. In the summer the water glittered with the reflection of the sun although today waves broke the surface in a blustery race to the sea. It was one of the things that attracted him to this house which he'd bought at a bargain price during the war after its previous owner went bankrupt.

The steps leading down from the front door to Magdalen Yard Road didn't look icy but the grass on Magdalen Green was silvered with frost so he grasped the iron railing as he descended. He consulted his pocket watch when he reached the road and realized he was late. Kate wouldn't be pleased.

27

Charlie Harris lay awake listening to the sounds of the house, all the little creaks and groans associated with older houses. The sounds were different to those he grew up with, in a Scouringburn tenement where noises might indicate part of the building was in danger of collapse. In this house, they signified the settling of ancient timbers and the movement of the occasional loose floorboard. The mansions on Broughty Ferry Road were built to last. No danger of them falling down.

'*As Joseph was a-walking, there did an angel sing.*' The words of the carol floated upstairs reminding him of the approach of Christmas.

Morag always sang as she polished the oak banisters in the morning. He had been lucky when she took him in.

'It's my Christian duty,' she said. 'It's the least I could do for a friend of Ernest. And I will be eternally grateful you were with him when he died.'

Her husband had been fatally wounded at the Battle of the Somme, and if she wanted to think Charlie held his hand as he lay dying, he certainly wasn't going to tell her any different. If truth be told he met Ernest once and he hadn't gone over the top with him on that awful day when so many were blasted into oblivion. But if Morag wanted to think he fought side by side with Ernest, that was fine with him.

Charlie had never been anywhere near the front lines, he'd made sure of that, although being a conscientious objector brought other risks including imprisonment. But he had always been able to talk himself out of difficult situations and he'd readily agreed to join the Friends Ambulance Unit in France. Ferrying injured prisoners back to England on the ambulance trains was much preferable to fighting on the front. Not that he had any scruples about fighting or killing the enemy, it was simply a way of ensuring his own survival. Survival was something Charlie was good at.

The ambulance trains were easy pickings for him. There were always far more wounded soldiers to tend to than there were nurses and medics and conchies like himself, and it was easy to search pockets when soldiers succumbed to their injuries.

When Ernest died Charlie had no qualms about appropriating his belongings including his wife's letters. They had come in useful.

Morag's singing increased in volume, meaning she'd reached the top of the stairs. Any minute now she would tap on his door. He turned over in bed relishing the last few moments of warmth. *The Evening Telegraph* lay on his tallboy where it had been for the last two days. He rarely bought an evening newspaper but the newspaper seller's cry of 'Bloody Murder' made him dig a penny out of his pocket for a copy. Inside, on page five, the details of Lily's death were lurid and, although he couldn't bear to throw the newspaper away, he knew the words off by heart.

Morag's footsteps stopped outside his door a moment before she knocked. 'You awake, Charlie? There's a good fire in the kitchen and the kettle won't take long to boil.'

'I'll be there as soon as I've shaved.' He pushed the blankets aside and slid out of the bed.

'I filled your shaving mug with hot water and left it in the bathroom.' Her feet shuffled along the corridor as she made her way back to the stairs.

Charlie wriggled his toes. Rugs had been a luxury where he came from but here they were everywhere. All the furniture was solid oak. A massive wardrobe contained his own clothes plus those Ernest no longer had any use for. The tallboy contained more drawers than he would ever need. But his favourite place in the large room was the armchair where he could relax in peace when he grew tired of Morag's company and stare out the window to the river beyond.

This house even had a bathroom. Where he came from it was just a cludgie in the stairwell, shared with seven other houses, and a tin bath on a Saturday night in front of the fire. If you were lucky.

Yes, the day Ernest died had been Charlie's luckiest day.

He stood and pulled on Ernest's dressing gown and slid his feet into Ernest's slippers before walking to the window and looking out. Frost silvered leaves on the fir tree at the end of the garden gave it a festive look while the lawn below glistened with ice crystals. The clear blue sky above held the promise of sun later on. Further out the river looked choppy although he saw a boat in the distance, probably the ferry which sailed from Dundee to Newport and affectionately known as the *Fifie*. A good day for taking the air but he would stay away from Big Aggie's house. He had no love of the police and the place would be swarming with them.

His stomach growled reminding him breakfast awaited him downstairs. It was time to tend to his ablutions and don his mantle of respectability.

A large free-standing tub dominated the bathroom. It squatted on clawed feet at the end of the room. The window above was open a fraction allowing a chilly air to circulate. Charlie shivered. He wouldn't stay in here longer than he had to, just long enough to make himself look respectable.

Steam misted up from the mug of hot water perched on the marble table top next to the pedestal sink. Beside it, sat his shaving brush and bowl of shaving soap. He dipped the brush into the mug, lifted it out again and gently squeezed it to remove excess water. After sprinkling some of the water on the shaving soap he swirled the brush around until it built up a good lather. A soon as he judged it was at the right consistency he wet his face and lathered his chin. He lifted one side of his moustache and then the other side to ensure the area underneath was soaped. Then he clicked open the cut-throat razor and started to shave. When he finished he splashed water over his face, dried it with a towel, and twirled the ends of his moustache before returning to his bedroom to dress.

Downstairs, embers glowed red in the fire basket in the middle of the iron range throwing out heat that made the kitchen the warmest room in the house. This was where he preferred to take his meals although, to begin with, Morag had different ideas.

'It's not proper,' she'd said. 'You're a guest in my house and should eat in the dining room.'

But the dining room was chilly and the table covered with a starched white cloth. Charlie was terrified he would spill food on its sterile surface. The kitchen was a much friendlier place.

'But I'm Ernest's friend,' he'd replied, 'and if Ernest were here I'm sure he wouldn't want to treat me like a guest. We were close and we faced so much together, we considered ourselves family.'

She hadn't taken much convincing and Charlie spent more and more of his time in her company and she'd grown fond of him. He could do worse than settle down with a widow woman who had a nice bank balance even though she wasn't the most attractive woman in town. He could always get his pleasures elsewhere. With Lily out of the way, there was nothing to stop him and Christmas would be a good time to broach the question of marriage.

Morag set a steaming plate on the wooden table. 'Sit yourself down,' she said, 'and sup your porridge.'

He pulled a chair out and sat. 'You're very good to me,' he said, lifting the spoon.

A flush crept up Morag's cheeks. 'Not at all.' She turned back to the range. 'The butcher didn't have any bacon this week but the henwife came round the doors early this morning so I can scramble eggs.'

'That would be lovely.' Charlie sprinkled salt on his porridge and started to eat.

'Oh, I forgot. There's a letter for you.' She fished it out of her apron pocket and laid it on the table beside him.

Charlie turned the envelope over in his hands. He didn't recognize the writing. In any case, who would be writing to him? He slit the top with his thumb and pulled out the single sheet of paper.

His eyes bulged when he read the words, 'I know what you done...'

He choked on a mouthful of porridge and all of a sudden he

wasn't hungry any longer.

'You all right, Charlie?'

'Yes, yes, Morag. The porridge went down the wrong way, that's all.'

He thrust the letter into his pocket. The words were burned into his brain so he would get rid of it in the fire the moment Morag left the room. She mustn't see it.

Continuing to eat, he made an effort to swallow the food which no longer appealed to him.

But he was damned if he knew where he would obtain £20 when Lily had already cleaned him out?

28

Gregor Armstrong stopped outside the door leading to his office, raised his arm and polished the brass plaque with his coat sleeve. After his father passed, this plaque had been one of the first things Gregor ordered.

Vanity he could hear his father say but he was proud to see his name displayed for all to see. The only pity was his sister's name was there as well although he made sure her name was inscribed below his. Not that she cared. She just snorted when she saw it and he was convinced she ignored it when she unlocked the office door each morning. She would be there now because she always made a point of being first. Gregor thought she did it to embarrass him and to prove she was the one who made a success of the business, not him.

Women, with shopping baskets dangling from their hands, clustered outside the butcher's shop door. Trade must be good and he'd noticed a steady increase of customers over the past few months, no doubt due to the prime spot it occupied in the Overgate. He made a mental note to check how much rent the shop brought in and work out how much more he could squeeze out of the butcher.

'Ladies,' Gregor said tipping his hat to the women before he opened the door and climbed the stairs to the first-floor office.

Kate sat behind a massive mahogany desk piled high with files and paper. She looked up when he entered. 'It's about time,' she said. 'I've been trying to find information on that building in the Hawkhill and I can't find the title deeds.'

Gregor struggled to allow sufficient air into his chest to answer her. 'Why are you looking for those?' Even to him, his voice sounded odd. Higher pitched and forced.

'Someone's interested in buying the property. That's why.'

'I'm sure the deeds will turn up.' Gregor struggled for

115

breath. There was no way Kate would understand why he gave them to Lily and he had no desire to acquaint her with that information.

'You're hopeless. It's as well father had the foresight to divide the business between us. Goodness knows where we would be if you had sole control. Probably in the poorhouse.'

Her eyes bored into him and he struggled to gather his thoughts together. She was older than him and had always bossed him, even when they were children. He was sure it made him seem weak to his father and may have been the reason he did the unthinkable and left Kate a half-share in the business when he died. Gregor's resentment of his sister intensified after that. It wasn't normal for a father to include a daughter in his will. Daughters were supposed to remain at home and wait for a suitor. But Kate wasn't the type of woman that men found attractive. She was too tall and scrawny, with a tongue that would clip clouts, as Dundee folk would say.

She turned back to the filing cabinet behind her and rummaged through the files. 'At least do something useful,' she said without looking at him. 'Go through the mail. It's on your desk.'

Gregor walked through to the inner office and sank into the chair behind his desk. Why did Kate always make him feel useless? He puffed his cigar and listened to her banging the file drawers in the outer office. Her hunt for the title deeds of the Hawkhill property would come to nothing because Lily had them. But Lily was dead and he would have to think of a way to regain the deeds before Kate found out.

How foolish he'd been to succumb to Lily's demands. However, it seemed reasonable at the time. He would gift her the property to set up her own bawdy house and she would provide him with a percentage of the profits.

He reached for the pile of envelopes on his desk while his mind still concentrated on how to find out what Lily had done with the deeds. Aggie might know but she was in jail. Maybe he could persuade the milksop she employed to do her paperwork to give him access to Lily's room.

Another bill, more money that needed to be paid out. He

groaned as he stuck it on the spike in front of him to join the other six bills already there. The next envelope looked different, maybe it wouldn't be another invoice.

He sliced the top and slid the sheet of paper out.

'I know what you done...' His eyes glazed and his face drained of colour. He laid his cigar on the edge of the desk and shot a panic-stricken glance towards the outer office before glancing back at the sheet of paper. Kate mustn't see this. She mustn't find out. He screwed the paper and the envelope into a tight ball and shoved them into his pocket.

Tomorrow night! Would he be able to acquire £20 by tomorrow night? If he took it from the cash box here would Kate find out?

He would have to risk it.

29

Geordie, the desk sergeant tapped on Kirsty's door. 'Someone asking for you, miss.'

'Did they give a name?'

'Gave her name as Mrs Petrie and she thought you'd like to see her. She doesn't look like our usual sort of customer and she's not comfortable sitting on the bench in the charge room although she's got a gent with her to keep her company.'

Kirsty's initial elation when she heard Mrs Petrie's name, subsided. If the Reverend Josiah was here with his wife, she wouldn't be able to talk freely.

'Is there somewhere I can take them where we can talk in private, Geordie? My wee office isn't big enough.'

'Usually, we speak to folk in the charge room or one of the interview rooms but they aren't very nice and I'd hesitate to put gentry into one of them. I suppose you could use the meeting room upstairs. Best clear it with the inspector, though.' Geordie turned and walked away. 'I'll tell her you'll be along in a few moments.'

'Geordie,' Kirsty shouted after his retreating back, 'show them up to the meeting room and I'll tell the inspector.'

'If you say so, miss. I hope you know what you're doing.'

Kirsty ran along the corridor to Brewster's room. 'Mrs Petrie is here,' she said, 'and she wants to talk to me. Geordie thought we might be able to use the meeting room if that was all right with you.'

Brewster looked up from the file he'd been studying.

'Who?'

'Mrs Petrie, Lily's mother. She hasn't come alone. I think Lily's father might be with her and I didn't get much of a reception from him when I visited them in Montrose.'

'In that case, I'll join you for the interview.' He shut the file and rose from his chair. 'You can take the lead in the interview but if Mr Petrie becomes obnoxious I'll take over.'

'I've asked Geordie to put them in the meeting room.'

'And I thought you were asking permission.' Brewster sighed and flashed her a quizzical look. 'But that's not your style, is it? Maybe the next time you will ask first.'

'Yes, sir.'

Brewster strode to the end of the corridor and up the stairs. The meeting room was the third room along and he pushed the door open leaving Kirsty to follow him inside.

Kirsty bit her lip. She wanted to remind him he'd said she should take the lead, but he'd been abrupt with her earlier and she thought better of it.

The meeting room was larger than any of the offices, with a large oval table of polished oak in the middle of the room. Eight straight-backed chairs surrounded the table, while a further six chairs were strategically placed against the walls. Two sash windows allowed daylight to filter in and a large fireplace filled most of the wall opposite the door. No fire had been laid in the fireplace and a chill air permeated the room.

Mrs Petrie perched on the edge of one of the chairs. Her handbag lay on the table in front of her and her fingers fidgeted with the clasp clicking it open and shut. Her posture and expression indicated she would rather be anywhere else but here. The man sitting beside her had his arm around her shoulders while he whispered to her.

Kirsty's muscles which had tensed at the thought of meeting the Reverend Josiah again, relaxed, because this was not the minister. This was a man she had never met before. She could not judge his height because he was seated, but he looked far younger than Mrs Petrie's husband although he also wore a clerical collar.

'Mrs Petrie, Mr Petrie, I'm Detective Inspector Brewster I believe you wished to talk to Miss Campbell again.'

A look of confusion spread over Mrs Petrie's face and Kirsty surmised Brewster must think the man was the Reverend Josiah Petrie.

'Sir, this gentleman is not Mr Petrie,' Kirsty said. 'Perhaps

Mrs Petrie can introduce him.'

Mrs Petrie pushed her chair back and stood, clasping her bag to her chest. 'This is my brother David Walker. He kindly offered to accompany me here.'

Brewster shook hands with both of them. He grasped the back of the chair, and said, 'Please sit. You've met Miss Campbell before so I'll just sit at the other side of the table and let you talk to her.'

Kirsty sat in the chair next to Mrs Petrie. 'I'm sorry it's chilly in here but I thought it would be more private than the charge room downstairs.'

Mrs Petrie kept her eyes focused on her handbag. 'That's all right, I am accustomed to cold conditions.'

Kirsty recalled the cheerless room with the empty fireplace where she had first met Mrs Petrie and her dislike of the Reverend Josiah increased. This quiet, unassuming woman deserved better.

'The desk sergeant said you wished to speak to me. How can I help you?' Instinctively, Kirsty knew she would clam up if subjected to a barrage of questions.

'I wondered,' The woman said in a hesitant voice. 'Lily. Would it be possible to see her?'

Kirsty glanced at Brewster and he nodded.

'Lily has been taken to the mortuary, Mrs Petrie. It's not a very nice place for someone like yourself. I'm afraid she won't be as you remember her.'

The woman shuddered. 'Nevertheless, I would like to see her.'

'I can accompany my sister.' The man had remained silent up until now.

Mrs Petrie smiled at him and grasped his hand.

'I'll get something arranged but it might not be until tomorrow or the next day.' Kirsty wondered how much of the damage to Lily's face could be covered up. 'In the meantime, it would help us tremendously if you could tell us about your daughter.'

'Why would that help?'

'Even the smallest thing could lead us to the person who did this terrible thing to her. It might be someone from her past or someone she met recently. Until we know all about her we won't be able to tell.'

'I don't know what to tell you.' Mrs Petrie clicked open the clasp of her handbag and reached inside. 'Josiah burned everything of Lily's. He doesn't know I kept this photograph.' She removed it from the bag and handed it to Kirsty.

It showed the image of a girl with fair curly hair. Lily, as she had been before someone obliterated her beauty with savage blows. Mrs Petrie was bound to be devastated when she saw her daughter now.

'She is lovely,' Kirsty murmured.

'She always was. And she had a lovely nature. She always looked out for her younger sisters. She was generous and always shared her sweets when she was a child. Not that they ever had many sweets. Josiah didn't approve.' She smiled at her brother. 'But David spoiled them. He is their only uncle and they twisted him around their little fingers.'

'How did your husband react to that?'

'Most of the time he didn't know. But I used to visit my father and although Josiah didn't approve, he didn't stop me. David lived at home, which meant we always had fun when we visited. The girls loved to play on the beach and David bought them ice creams.' She lapsed into silence.

Kirsty noted the unsaid comment that there was no fun in the Reverend Josiah Petrie's household.

'What about her friends? Do you know of anyone special?'

'Josiah didn't like the children mixing with the locals but she did have one friend, Nancy Allardyce who lived over the wall from us. I don't recall anyone else.'

'What about Billy?'

A flush crept up through Mrs Petrie's neck and stained her cheeks red. Her fingers grew still on the clasp of her handbag and she raised her head to look Kirsty in the eyes.

'You know about Billy?'

Kirsty nodded. 'I know what happened but I don't know anything else about him. However, we can't discount Billy.'

'He's not here anymore. He joined the army after...', she

hesitated.

'After Lily became pregnant.' Kirsty ended the sentence for her.

Mrs Petrie nodded. 'Billy wasn't a bad lad and he wanted to stand by Lily but Josiah wouldn't hear of it because he was a local and not good enough to wed her.'

'But your husband disowned Lily, so would it have mattered?'

'Josiah thought so. He said if they married and continued to live in the town it would disgrace the family. He gave Lily money to leave the town after... after...' Mrs Petrie's voice faltered.

'After the abortion.'

The woman's expression changed and Kirsty wasn't sure whether her face was reflecting horror or misery. Mrs Petrie would be aware abortion was illegal.

She nodded. 'He thought it for the best.'

Kirsty decided not to push her into saying whether the abortion or Lily's departure was for the best.

'Did he know about Lily's occupation?'

'I don't know. He disowned her and wouldn't even admit to anyone, she had ever existed.' She dabbed her eyes with a handkerchief. 'I didn't approve but she was my daughter. If Josiah hadn't...' Sobs overcame her and she clutched her head, tearing at her hair. 'I should have stopped him. I shouldn't have allowed it.'

'Hush, Mary.' Her brother spoke for the first time. 'Nothing you could have said or done would have changed Josiah's mind.'

A wrenching pain gripped Kirsty's chest and she wanted to cry with Mrs Petrie. She wanted to reach out and comfort her but didn't know how. And she, more than most, knew that losing a child was the worst thing that could happen to a mother.

It was mid-afternoon before Mary arrived home. She composed herself before entering the house, Josiah would not be pleased if he found out where she had been although, unless someone told him differently, he would assume she had spent the day engaged in voluntary work at Dorward House of Refuge. Tiptoeing inside, she closed the door quietly behind her and noticed there were letters in the cage behind the letterbox.

She lifted the lid and picked them out. One of the envelopes was addressed to, The Manse, Bents Road, Montrose. She turned it over in her hand but it was bound to be for Josiah so she added it to the other two letters on the small silver tray. Josiah liked to think himself gentry and better than anyone else.

Jessie was in the living room polishing the oak sideboard. 'Will I light a fire, Aunt Mary?' Jessie let go of the duster and knelt before the fireplace. She grabbed a poker and raked ash from the grate. She leaned back on her haunches and rubbed her eyes leaving a smudge of coal dust on her cheek.

'It's too early. The minister wouldn't like it.'

When she was in the family home Mary always referred to her husband as the minister. Never once did she call him by name in his presence, nor would he want her to. He was a stickler for appearances and she was aware a wife and children were simply appendages to him. Such a pity he couldn't have been more like her brother David, who was also a church minister. He didn't believe in the fire and brimstone version of preaching that Josiah adopted.

Jessie rose from in front of the fireplace. 'I'd best get on with the cleaning.'

Mary sighed as she watched Jessie rise and pick up the duster to continue polishing the furniture. She'd promised her sister she would look after her child and she hadn't been able to keep that promise. Josiah saw to that. He thought he was doing his Christian duty by feeding his niece and providing a roof over her head. Caring and love didn't enter into it and he forbade Mary to treat her as part of the family. As far as he was concerned, Jessie was a servant.

She sighed again and picked up the silver tray to carry through to Josiah's study. She tapped on the door, waiting until he responded.

'Enter,' he snapped.

She handed him the letters. 'I wasn't sure about the one addressed to The Manse, but I thought it must be for you.'

He glared at her and ripped the envelope open.

Mary hovered in the doorway, curiosity overcoming her fear of annoying him.

His bushy eyebrows gathered in a frown and his face paled even more than usual when he read the contents.

He scrunched the paper into a ball and tossed it in the waste bin before looking up at her.

'What are you waiting for.' His voice held more fury than she recalled hearing before. 'Go about your business. I am sure you have things to occupy your time.'

Mary backed out of the room and closed the door. Once the minister left on his pastoral visits she would rescue the letter from the waste bin.

30

'When you going to find my daughter a better place to live than this shit-hole.' Tom Gordon glared up at Angus from the depths of the armchair.

'We were lucky to find this place,' Angus mumbled. He hoped Tom wasn't getting ready to pick a fight because he always got the worst of it.

Tom smiled at him, a hellish smile due to the scar which stretched from his mouth to his ear. 'What about that whisky you've got hidden away under the sink? I could do with a dram.'

How did the old bugger know about that? Angus glared at Edna but she shrugged her shoulders and continued feeding wee Angus who was quiet for a change.

The bleach bottle tipped over when he reached underneath for the whisky. He propped it up again thinking he would rather give Edna's dad a drink of that instead of the whisky. But that would make his life not worth living because the old bugger would be bound to spot the difference before he took the first swallow. The old man was maybe past it but he'd had a fearsome reputation in Glasgow's *Penny Mob* before the war. That was where he'd acquired his trademark scar. Between him and Edna's two brothers who were on the run from *The Redskins*, one of Glasgow's biggest gangs, they struck fear into him. If it hadn't been for them, he would never have married Edna.

He poured a dollop of whisky into a teacup. 'I'm off to work,' he said handing the cup to Tom.

'Leave the bottle.' Tom downed the whisky in one gulp.

Edna looked up. 'Isn't it too early?'

'There's some extra work today. I can't refuse to do it.' He shrugged on his coat and opened the door, slamming it shut as soon as he was outside on the landing.

The bairn started to howl and Tom shouted at Edna to get the wee bugger to stop making a noise. Angus swore under his breath, lit a fag and continued walking away from the flat. There was no extra work he just wanted to get out of the house and away from Edna's dad.

It would be another hour before the picture house opened which meant the street was empty and the building deserted when he arrived but that didn't matter because he had a key. He slotted it into the keyhole, let himself in, scuttled to his small cubbyhole of a room and slumped into the chair in the corner. It was the only place he felt safe.

His life was a mess and it was all Edna's fault, getting her pregnant was the biggest mistake he'd ever made. She'd seemed such a sweet and innocent girl, how was he to know her family were Glasgow gangsters? He put his head in his hands and groaned. As far as they were concerned he would never be good enough for her and they made sure he knew it. That was why Lily's threat of the minister putting up their wedding banns sent fear rippling through him. But Lily was gone now and, although he would miss her, it solved his problem.

A slamming door reminded him of time passing and he stripped off his trousers and jacket and scrambled into his uniform taking less care than usual. He checked his appearance in the mirror on the back of the door and headed for the foyer.

He peered through the glass doors at the line of people outside. A new film was showing tonight, *Stella Maris*, starring Lilian Gish, so the queue was mostly women. Men weren't keen on a weepie.

'Ah, there you are, Angus.' Miss Burke, the cashier handed him an envelope. 'This was in the letterbox.'

'Thanks.' He slipped it into his pocket.

'Give me a moment to get the ticket office sorted before you open the doors,' she said.

One of the women at the head of the queue outside rapped on the glass door and mouthed something to him but he ignored her until he saw Miss Burke nod to him she was ready.

'About time,' the woman said when he opened the door. 'It's

perishing out here.'

People filtered into the cinema and although he stood at attention watching for any troublemakers, his mind remained fixed on the envelope in his pocket.

Invoices and notifications of forthcoming films made up most of the mail arriving here. Nothing ever came for the staff except for notices of dismissal or complaints. Had someone complained about him? Maybe that obnoxious wee man who always headed the queue when a Douglas Fairbanks, or Charlie Chaplin film was showing. Or maybe one of the others he'd threatened to eject from the cinema for causing annoyance. He ran a finger around his collar to relieve his breathing while continuing to worry about who might have complained.

But surely the management wouldn't take anything like that seriously? After all, part of his job was to maintain order. For the sake of all the others in the audience, he couldn't allow a few troublemakers to ruin the film for them.

The temptation to rip open the envelope strengthened after the auditorium doors closed and the film commenced but he had to remain on duty in the foyer to welcome latecomers and to respond to requests from the usherettes to intervene with any member of the audience creating a nuisance. Sneaking off to his cubbyhole of a room was not an option and fear of what might be inside the envelope meant he didn't want to open it while still on duty in the foyer. He would have to contain himself and wait.

Time dragged and it seemed an eternity before the last of the cinema-goers emerged from the second showing of the film. Their chatter swirled around his head making no impact and they seemed to dally longer before exiting through the doors onto the street. Relief seeped through him when he finally turned the key to lock the building for the night.

Back in his room he unbuttoned his scarlet jacket, removed his tie and undid the top button of his shirt so he could breathe more easily. He pulled the envelope from his pocket and turned it over in his hands, suddenly reluctant to open it. Fearing he might no longer have a job. Edna's dad would have something to say about that.

Sweat beaded on his forehead. He placed one finger under the flap of the envelope and ripped it open before he could change his mind. Inside was a single folded sheet of paper.

The words swam before his eyes. This was far, far worse than he had imagined.

He blinked and read the words again. 'I know what you done...'

He slumped into the chair. Edna's dad would kill him if he found out about Lily. But it would be impossible to get £20 before tomorrow night?

31

Neil Young unfastened the knots in the string ties behind his waist allowing the rubber apron which covered him from his collar to the top of his Wellington boots to fall loose in front of him. Blood dripped from the hem and the rubber crackled when he slipped the apron off and hung it on a hook to the left of the slaughterhouse door. He was always the last worker to leave the building so the manager entrusted him with the keys.

Neil was a real worker, the manager was fond of telling the other men. Not like them. Lazy buggers the lot of them.

None of them knew about his sideline supplying cut-price meat to a select few butchers who weren't fussy about the quality or where the meat came from. Most of the cuts, rejects meant for the furnace, were never missed. This arrangement kept Neil solvent and his bank balance had been growing at a satisfactory rate. At least, until Lily found out. Now the money in the bank was gone and he only had a few shillings left.

Lily, he sighed when he thought of her because, despite her mercenary nature, he had been fond of her. He had even dreamed of asking her to marry him. But that was a vain dream. Who would want to marry a man with a harelip? A man that women turned from with disgust.

Last night, when he read the newspaper reporting Lily's death, he had cried. He wasn't sure whether his tears were for his lost love, or whether they signified relief because she would make no more demands. With a final sigh, he reached into his pocket for his packet of Woodbines. A smoke was the only way to remove the stench of the slaughterhouse from his nostrils. He tapped a cigarette out and stuck it between his lips ready to light, before shrugging on his jacket.

Fresh air blew in from the river when he emerged from the slaughterhouse and locked the door behind him, shutting in the pungent metallic odour of blood and meat. East Dock Street was quiet in the darkness with no remnant of the daily turmoil left. Sparks flew from the tip of his cigarette when he turned into Market Street to head in the direction of Arbroath Road where he could catch a tram to take him most of the way home. Passing the auction mart, a whiff of manure from the cattle market drifted to his nose. He didn't mind the smell even though it reminded him the cattle leaving the odour behind were probably hanging from hooks in the slaughterhouse by this time.

After he left Market Street behind him, he followed a warren of lanes and alleys until he came to Arbroath Road and a welcome tram. He jumped off the tram at the top of Princes Street, bought an *Evening Telegraph* from the newspaper seller and hurried up Albert Street to the tenement flat he shared with a scraggy cat.

The candle sputtered when lit. He would have to remember to buy oil for the lamp the next time he was at the shops. Some landlords were installing electric light into their buildings so they could increase the rent but his landlord was too mean to do that. He lifted the candle and inspected the cupboard. Inside, he found the remnants of a loaf of bread and a chunk of cheese. That would have to do.

He placed the bread and cheese on the table and went to look for a knife. As he reached for it he noticed the envelope lying inside the door. He bent to pick it up and laid it alongside the knife on the table.

Strange. Who would be writing to him? He couldn't remember the last time he got a letter. He pulled a chair over to the table and, after sawing a slice of bread from the loaf and cutting the cheese in half, he fingered the envelope while he chewed. He turned it over and over in his hands before finally placing a finger under the flap and ripping it open.

It contained one sheet of paper. He stared at the writing. He choked. A lump of cheese stuck in his throat and he tasted bile.

He rushed to the sink and spat the cheese out before retching until his throat ached.

Spreading the note out on the table he read it again – 'I know what you done. Bring £20 to the Howff graveyard at ten of the night on Thursday. Leave it underneath Jonathan Bogue's stone.'

It was starting again. Lily's death meant nothing. His hand shook when he lighted his cigarette, there was no way he'd be able to get £20 by tomorrow night? What was he going to do?

32

Mary alighted from the train at Broughty Ferry Station but David was not there to meet her. No doubt he had become involved in something at the church and lost track of the time. David had always been the same. Someone who couldn't say no when asked for help. But that had its benefits because he'd never been able to refuse her anything.

She adjusted the fox fur around her neck and, after leaving the station, she turned left to walk over the level crossing and then up Gray Street. At the top of the road where it joined Queen Street, she headed in the direction of the church affectionately known by the locals as the 'Wee Free' despite the free churches amalgamating with the Presbyterian Church a few years earlier.

The church was small and less ostentatious than St Luke's further along Queen Street. The Wee Free churches concentrated on simplicity, frowning on ornamentation and having clear-cut views on sin and sinning. Mary felt that while Josiah was well suited to the austerity of the United Free Church, her brother would have made a better priest.

Inside, the pews were little more than benches with a pulpit at the front, not much different to her husband's church in Montrose. The vestry was at the side and that was where she found David, sitting at a plain wooden desk with a ledger open and his head bowed over a letter resting on top.

'I thought I would find you here,' she said.

David looked up. 'Oh, Mary. Is that the time already. I'm sorry.'

He thrust the letter into his pocket and closed the ledger with a thump. 'A representative of the Moderator is visiting next week and I was getting everything up to date.'

'I'm sure he'll find everything in order. You are a most conscientious minister. The church is lucky to have you.'

He ushered her out of the vestry, closing the door behind him. 'We won't take long to get to Dundee in the motor car.'

'Before we go I need to tell you something.'

'Can't it wait?'

'I suppose it could but I'm worried. I need to talk.'

He raised his eyebrows in a mute question.

'Josiah received a letter this morning.'

'I'm sure Josiah receives many letters.'

Mary's fingers itched to shake him. 'But not like this one. This was a blackmail letter.'

David stared at her. 'Josiah? Blackmail? Who on earth would want to blackmail Josiah?'

'I think someone found out about Lily's abortion. He was the one who made the arrangements and that could mean prison.'

'Would that be so awful? If he went to prison you would be free and you know I would look after you.'

Thoughts whirled in Mary's mind. Freedom? She no longer knew what that was like. But the idea was intoxicating. No doubt the church would evict them from the manse but they could come and live with David.

'You're right,' she said. 'The letter is Josiah's problem and is nothing to do with me.' At least, that's what she hoped.

'I think we should leave for Dundee now.' David guided Mary out of the church and around the side to the Model T parked at the pavement edge.

'I thought we would be catching the train. An automobile is such an extravagance.'

David shrugged. 'Why shouldn't I have a car? I can easily afford it and it makes travelling around a lot easier. Climb in and we'll be in Dundee in no time at all.'

Mary huddled in the passenger seat clutching her coat and sinking her chin into the fox fur. Even the hat pins failed to keep her hat anchored as the wind whistled around her in the open top car. One of her hands held her hat to her head while the other clutched the door.

This was her first journey in a motor car and, unable to stop shaking, she swore it would be her last.

She was still shaking when they drew up outside Dundee Police Station.

Kirsty was in the middle of writing her latest report when Geordie tapped on her door.

'The lady and gent who were here yesterday say they've come to identify our body.'

'I'll come along and meet them. Will you let Inspector Brewster know they're here?'

Mary looked dishevelled and was shivering uncontrollably as she sat beside David on the bench that ran the length of the charge room. They stopped whispering and Kirsty wondered what they had been discussing. Probably the forthcoming visit to the mortuary.

'You're still sure you want to do this?'

Mary nodded and looked at her brother.

'Our mortuary isn't the nicest of places. It's underground and can be scary if you've never been there before.'

'I'll look after my sister,' David said. He put his arm around her shoulder. 'You'll be safe with me,' he whispered to her.

'I know,' she said. Tears filled her eyes but she blinked them away.

Brewster barged into the charge room. 'Mrs Petrie, Mr Walker,' he said.

David Walker responded. 'Are we ready to go?'

'The mortuary isn't far from here,' Brewster said. 'It should only take a few minutes to get there.'

Brewster led the way and Kirsty walked beside Mary and David.

They stopped for a moment before opening the door to the underground mortuary.

'The stairs are steep and they can be slippery. Mrs Petrie will require the support of someone's hand.'

David grasped it. 'I'll make sure she doesn't slip,' he said.

Kirsty had a sense of deja vu as she followed Brewster down. The unlit stairs were as gloomy as she remembered and she clutched the metal handrail to ensure she didn't lose her footing on the uneven steps. Behind her, Mary drew in a breath and she realized the woman was experiencing the same feelings that affected her during her first visit.

The stairs seemed to go on forever and the metallic echo of their footsteps increased her feeling of unease. When she reached the bottom she hesitated beside the iron-barred gate which Brewster opened. If Mary sensed her fear that might make things worse, so she pushed it away and turned to check whether the other woman was all right.

She looked pale and her fingers were white where she clutched onto her brother's arm.

'Do you still want to continue?'

Mary nodded.

David tightened his hold on her hand. 'You're sure?'

Mary nodded again. 'I'm sure,' she whispered.

Brewster waited for them at the other side of the gate. 'I got Davvy to put Lily in a side room that means we can avoid the main area.'

Kirsty let her breath out in a long sigh of relief. She'd been dreading the walk through the mortuary with its rows of white-sheeted trolleys.

'Davvy's not here?' She hoped Brewster wouldn't notice her crossed fingers. There wasn't much that scared her but Davvy, who looked like a malevolent gnome, sent chills running through her body.

'No, I told him I'd take care of this.' He gestured to a door in the wall. 'She's in here.'

Vaulted stone walls glistened with damp and the only thing in the cell-like room was the white-sheeted trolley which stood in the middle.

He gripped the edge of the sheet. 'I'm afraid she's not a pretty sight although Davvy has done his best to clean her up. Are you sure you want to see her?'

David put his arm around Mary and looked at her. She nodded.

Brewster pulled the sheet back as far as Lily's shoulders.

The girl's features were battered beyond recognition and

Kirsty heard Mary's sharp intake of breath. Silence cloaked them although all other sounds seemed to be magnified. The drip of water from the walls. Brewster's feet shuffling. Mary's quiet sobs. Kirsty's own breathing.

'Why did it have to be so violent? Why smash her face like that? Why? Why?' Mary's anguished cry echoed around the room.

David folded Mary into his arms. 'Hush,' he said. He looked over to Kirsty with eyes so bleak they reflected the anguish his sister was experiencing and his own despair at being unable to comfort her.

Mary's distress and the obvious love they had for each other tore at Kirsty's heart and she turned away, reluctant to observe their shared grief.

33

Freddie Simpson shrugged on his coat and wrapped a scarf twice around his neck, tucking the ends inside his jacket.

'You going out?' William poked the glowing embers of the fire and pulled his chair nearer to the blaze.

'No point in hanging around here. The bobbies have scared all the punters away. Besides, I'm restless.'

'Where you off to?'

'Not sure. Probably one of the pubs, or I might go down the Overgate to see if there's any action.'

Freddie opened the door, grabbed his flat cap, and slipped outside before his brother could ask any more questions because he had no intention of explaining his movements.

Darkness had come early and tonight no moon lightened the gloom of the streets. His breath misted in front of him as he hurried along the road and the cobbles under his feet were slippery with the evening frost. Freddie hoped the predicted snow wouldn't arrive until his vigil in the Howff graveyard ended. It would be cold enough without the white stuff to complicate matters.

The Howff gates were closed but not locked because he'd had the foresight to push beeswax into the lock the day after he posted the letters. He slipped through into the graveyard leaving the gate ajar. Faced with several paths he followed the one furthest away from the road on the left-hand side. This was the oldest part of the cemetery where the gravestones were in danger of being swallowed by the overgrowth, and creepers and ivy twined around them in an incestuous embrace. Above him, the tree branches rustled menacingly as if defying him to encroach on their territory, while overgrown shrubbery reached for him with their damp fronds and ghostly fingers.

His heartbeat quickened, flutters of fear churned in his

stomach and, after a moment of hesitation, he stepped off the path onto the grass and into the realm of the dead. Vague shapes loomed up in front of him and he picked his way through them until he came to a tall gravestone near to Jonathan Bogue's tomb, the place designated for the money drop. He slid down and sat behind it, shivering as his body came into contact with the damp earth. Here he could observe anyone approaching without his own presence being obvious. Nothing could go wrong.

Time ticked by as he waited. He'd made a deliberate decision to arrive early to settle into his observation spot without being seen. But the gathering frost and the earth he sat on chilled him through and through. He blew on his fingers but the noise sounded deafening in the silence of the cemetery so he shoved them into his pockets instead.

Worries plagued his mind but he had spent the last three days thinking about his plan and how he would collect the money without being detected. The simplest method would be to wait until the middle of the night before fetching the money from the Howff, but he ruled that out because some of his victims might decide to collect instead of delivering. He couldn't have that. In the end, he decided he would collect each payment after it was made and before the next was due. He also planned to make a note of anyone not responding to his blackmail letter. He had no intention of allowing any of them to ignore him.

He pulled his scarf over his chin and mouth, wrapped his arms around his body and leaned back against the gravestone. It would be a long cold wait.

He arrived as dusk was falling, intent on finding out who was behind the blackmail letter.

Opposite the Howff, the post office lay in darkness. But its recessed door provided him with the ideal spot to observe the graveyard. Tucked into the doorway the shadows concealed his presence and he stood there watching, while his fingers played with the leather pouch which nestled deep within his overcoat pocket. He turned it over and over, hearing the contents clink with each turn. The iron bar was slotted up his sleeve, out of sight of any curious passerby. Everything was in order. All he had to do was wait.

An hour later his patience was rewarded when he saw Freddie Simpson, the muscle-bound oaf who sorted out troublemakers for Big Aggie, scurry along the street, stop at the gate of the Howff, and slip inside the graveyard. If he was to take care of him he'd have to be careful. He didn't fancy fisticuffs with this man and would have to catch him off his guard.

He resisted an overwhelming urge to follow the man into the graveyard. For one thing, he was unsure where Freddie had gone, which reduced his chance to catch the man unawares. Besides, he was sure he wasn't Freddie's only blackmail victim so he would watch and wait until making his own contribution at the allotted time. Freddie wouldn't leave until then.

His fingers toyed with the leather pouch and he laughed to himself as he pictured Freddie's face when he opened it to find stones.

Time passed slowly but he had always been a patient man and his patience was rewarded when the first man arrived at 7 o'clock. Then, on the stroke of every hour, another man and another slipped into the graveyard. Some of the men he recognized and some he didn't. No matter, it would soon be his turn and Freddie would get more than he bargained for.

At last, his time came and he walked up the central path to Jonathan Bogue's tomb. He bent and placed his pouch of stones on the earth underneath the table top of the gravestone. Then he turned and retraced his steps to the main gate but instead of going through, he opened and clanged it shut again before turning to his right and slipping around the edge of the graveyard until he was in a position to watch.

As he suspected, after he left his pouch, Freddie slunk to the stone and felt underneath.

He held his breath while he edged nearer to the man and, raising his arm, he brought the iron bar down on his head continuing to thump him long after Freddie slumped to the ground.

After checking the man had stopped breathing, he wiped his weapon on the grass to remove the blood and brain tissue. Then he strolled out of the cemetery and walked to the river to dispose of the bar in the same way he disposed of the poker which killed Lily.

34

Friday, 12 December 1919
Joe Henderson stopped at the corner of Reform Street and Ward Road to catch his breath. He nipped the glowing end of his cigarette between finger and thumb before flicking the butt into the gutter, where a gust of wind whipped it up to send it rolling over the road. Tears stung his eyes and he pulled the brim of his cap down to protect them from the wintry blast.

A newsboy rounded the corner and dashed past, empty paper sack flapping as he ran. Joe stepped to the side to avoid a collision. 'Aye, lad. Late for school again,' he shouted after him but the newsboy didn't stop. Joe shrugged his shoulders, youngsters nowadays had no respect for rules or for their elders. Not like when he was young when a sharp whack with the leather tawse would ensure obedience. But that had been so long ago he could barely remember.

Joe was a methodical man and took his responsibilities seriously so when he found the front gate of the Howff graveyard hanging open he knew something was amiss. Right enough, it wouldn't lock last night because the lock was gummed up. Tramps, he thought, dossing down for the night, well he'd give them something to think about.

He hurried through the gate, shutting it behind him, and started his morning tour of the graveyard.

'Just as I thought,' he muttered when he found the man lying beside Jonathan Bogue's tomb. 'A bloody tramp.'

He crept up to the man and pushed him with his foot causing the body to turn. Sightless eyes stared up at him from a face that looked like something from a butcher's shop.

'Bloody hell.'

His stomach heaved and he leaned on the stone to vomit on the earth at the other side.

He pulled himself together and raced for the gate. After wrenching it open, he stumbled through and ran to the police station in West Bell Street. By the time he got there his legs were buckling under him and he used the last of his strength to barge through the door. Once inside, he collapsed on the bench.

The desk sergeant leaned over the high counter at the other side of the room. 'What's up, mate. You seen a ghost or something?'

'Bloo... mur... bod...' Joe struggled to regain his breath. Air sliced through his chest like a butcher's knife and his words were gasped and garbled.

'Take your time, mate. Can't understand a word you say.'

'The Howff,' he wheezed clutching his arms around his middle in an attempt to regulate his breathing and stop his stomach doing somersaults. He shook his head to rid himself of the man's image imprinted on his brain. 'I thought it was a tramp sleeping but he's all bloody and I'm sure he's dead.'

'Wait there,' the desk sergeant said, 'and I'll get the inspector.' He lifted the flap at the end of the counter and walked to a door at the rear of the charge room.

Left on his own, Joe leaned back against the wall. Shudders consumed his body and he fought the urge to be sick. He inhaled, breathing air deep into his lungs, and gradually the feeling of nausea subsided. But the memory of the dead man remained. Even when he closed his eyes he could see that face, battered and bloody, and if he lived to a hundred he'd never forget.

Brewster's head thumped from concentrating on the files in front of him. He was no further forward in the investigation. The evidence against Aggie incriminated her although Kirsty didn't seem to think so. But who else could be responsible? Aggie was found with the body. Her clothes were bloodstained. And she had motive if Lily planned to leave her. Why was Kirsty unable to understand that? He drummed his fingers on the desk. All they needed was the murder weapon but the search party hadn't turned anything up yet.

A rap on his office door made him look up. 'What is it?'

'There's a man in the charge room saying he's found a dead body in the Howff, sir. He's in a bit of a state and not able to give me much information.' The desk sergeant shuffled his feet.

Brewster pushed the files aside and stood. 'Who is he?'

The desk sergeant shrugged. 'It took me all my time to get what I did and I thought I'd better fetch you rather than trying to prise more out of him.'

Kirsty looked up when he passed her door but he ignored her and continued along the corridor. He poked his head into the constables' room. 'Don't go anywhere,' he said to the two constables who were attempting to look busy. 'I might need you in a few minutes.'

The man sitting in the charge room kept his head bowed when they entered. Brewster studied him for a moment.

'I'm Detective Inspector Brewster,' he said. 'I believe you have something to report.'

'Yes, sir.' The man struggled to his feet before removing his bonnet to reveal sparse grey hair. 'I'm the keeper at the Howff. I keep the grounds tidy and do anything that's needed. It's my job to open up in the morning and close the gates at night.' The man twisted his cap in his hands and looked down at his knees. 'But last night I couldn't lock the gates because of the jammed lock.' He caught his breath. 'I'll be in trouble for not locking them. But that wasn't my fault.'

'The sergeant said something about a body.' Brewster laid his hand on the man's shoulder to calm him.

'I was getting to that, sir. You see when I got to the Howff this morning the gates were hanging open. That's not right, I thought, they shouldn't be open. I thought scallywags had been in or a tramp was sleeping in there. But it was a dead body, all bashed and bloody.' Joe shuddered.

Brewster stood. 'You've done well. I'll send constables to attend to the matter. Give the sergeant your name and address and then go home.'

'But what about my job, sir? I don't want to lose it.'

'The sergeant will speak to your boss and let him know you won't be allowed inside the Howff until we investigate this death. So, don't worry.'

Brewster wasted no time. 'Constables with me,' he shouted as he marched up the corridor to grab his coat. Slamming doors and scurrying feet heralded his departure.

35

Something was up and Brewster hadn't told her. Kirsty listened to the footsteps and banging doors and her annoyance grew. Why was he excluding her? Despite being accustomed to the belittling attitudes of her male colleagues she'd been convinced Brewster wasn't like that.

She slammed her pencil on the desk and grabbed her jacket and hat. If something required constables, she was a constable as well. So, whether he liked it or not she intended to be part of the activity.

When she reached the charge room she aimed her most winning smile at Geordie. 'Afraid I've been slow off the mark and didn't catch where we're supposed to be and now they've all gone. I wouldn't want to get in trouble by not turning up.' With fingers crossed behind her back, she added, 'You wouldn't happen to know, would you?'

'Tut, tut,' Geordie said. 'Doing lady things were we?'

Kirsty suppressed the retort that rose to her lips, masking it with a smile. 'How did you guess?'

'They're off to the Howff, miss, to investigate the body found there this morning.'

'Thanks, I'd better run and catch up before the inspector notices my absence.'

By the time Kirsty arrived at Ward Road she was out of breath and she slowed to compose herself before she reached the two constables standing guard at the entrance to the graveyard.

They looked at her with suspicion in their eyes when she approached but she was used to this reaction from the men.

'Good morning,' she said, brazening it out. 'I assume Inspector Brewster is in the cemetery examining the body?' She marched past them, relaxing and letting her breath out in a rush once out of their sight.

Her stiff leather boots with their smooth soles slithered on the frosty cobbles and she stepped off them to walk on the grassy border. Trees and bushes overhung the twisty path, reaching out their branches to brush against her as she passed. The gravestones, some overgrown with moss and some with ornate carvings, leaned towards her. Stone skulls grinned at her as if observing her progress. Not for the first time the feeling of evil hanging over this place overwhelmed her.

A rustling noise over to her right caused her to hold her breath. Despite knowing it was probably vermin or a bird she was unable to shake off the ominous impact of this place. She shivered, as she remembered the events of a month ago when she ran for her life among the gravestones.

This burial place had too many bad memories for her and her feet dragged, not wanting to continue. She bit her lip and straightened her back to combat her nervousness about what might be around the next bend in the path.

Silence, and the eerie atmosphere, broken only by furtive rustling in the undergrowth and the branches of trees, pressed in on her but she refused to give in to the menace she sensed around her.

When she rounded a turn in the path and spotted Brewster bent over one of the tombstones, relief swept through her. She quickened her pace, anxious to leave the silence behind her.

'What are you doing here?' He continued his examination of the ground around the body which lay sprawled in front of a table-top tombstone.

With a shudder of recognition, Kirsty saw the stone belonged to Jonathan Bogue. Dread filled her again.

She struggled to control her breathing. 'I heard your request for constables to accompany you, sir. And I'm a constable.'

'Is that a fact,' he said without looking up. 'And here was me thinking you were a statement taker.'

'Chief Constable Carmichael hired me as a policewoman, sir. Despite what the Assistant Chief Constable thinks.' Kirsty was unable to suppress the annoyance in her voice.

Brewster looked up at her, his eyes glittering with

amusement. 'I was just thinking you'll have a hard job getting a statement from this chap.'

She realized he'd been baiting her and grinned. 'If you say so, sir. Do we know who he is?'

'Take a look.' He stood and placed several pouches and knotted handkerchiefs on the flat top of the gravestone.

Kirsty bent over the body. 'He's a bit battered and lost his good looks,' she said, 'but I think it's Freddie Simpson.'

Brewster was busy opening the pouches and untying the handkerchiefs to shake out their contents. 'I reckon Freddie may have had a nice sideline in blackmail. There's a tidy sum of money here. But what do you think about this? One of the pouches contained stones.'

She stood and inspected the items on the gravestone. 'He tried to blackmail the wrong person? Do you think he knew the identity of the killer?'

'That's possible but I would guess not, otherwise, he would have been more careful. I'm guessing the person who left the pouch containing stones is our killer.'

'Are we ruling out two killers, sir?'

'I suppose two killers is a possibility but the method of killing is the same. However, I would hate to think we have two on the loose in Dundee at the same time.'

Kirsty nodded. Two killers seemed unlikely. But they were no further forward in finding Lily's killer and now Freddie's death was part of the equation. She hoped this would give them more clues to follow.

'Well, unless two killers are on the prowl that rules Aggie out because she's still locked up in the cells.' Kirsty, unable to resist the thought she had been right all along and Brewster had been wrong, suppressed a smile.

'I'm not ruling anything out at this stage.' Brewster scowled. 'Aggie can stay where she is for the time being.'

36

Kirsty watched Davvy hitch himself between the shafts of the barrow before trundling off down the cobbled path to the iron gates of the Howff. Once he passed through them to the street outside, she turned to Brewster but he had his back to her.

'What do we do now?'

'You,' he said without turning, 'will return to the office and examine the ledger we took from Aggie's building. You will find it on my desk.'

The sharpness in his voice hadn't been there before and Kirsty guessed it was because she'd attempted to prove him wrong in his belief that Aggie was Lily's killer.

'What am I looking for?'

'Anything that links Freddie and Lily. Or a link to anyone else. We need to find the connection between the two deaths.'

'Yes, sir.' Kirsty tried to hide her resentment at being summarily dismissed from the investigation. 'I presume you are not returning to the office?'

'No. I will be pursuing a line of enquiry elsewhere.'

Kirsty seethed but turned on her heel and marched off. She was still seething when she reached the police station.

Inside, Nancy Allardyce sat on the bench in the charge room beside a young man in shabby clothes. The man twisted and pulled at the cap he held in his hands while Nancy whispered in his ear. She looked up when Kirsty approached them.

'I brought my brother to see you,' she said. Her hands shook and her voice wobbled.

Nancy's nervousness and her brother's red-rimmed eyes didn't escape Kirsty's attention. 'Follow me,' she said. 'We'll go somewhere more private.'

'I'm taking them up to the meeting room, Geordie. If Inspector Brewster is looking for me will you inform him?' She was lucky Geordie was on duty today and not Hamish who always put obstacles in her way.

'I don't want Aggie to know I'm here,' Nancy said as they entered the meeting room.

Kirsty nodded and motioned for them to take a seat.

Nancy tore off her blue woollen cloche and laid it on the table. 'I hate wearing hats.' She shook her hair free and slumped into a chair. The young man sat beside her and she reached out to clutch his hand.

Kirsty sat at the opposite side of the table facing them. Why had Nancy come? Why had she brought her brother? And what was his connection to Lily? Could this be Billy, the boyfriend who left for the army after Lily's abortion? She remembered how vague Jessie, the wee servant girl, had been when she talked about him, surely she would have known who he was if his house was only separated from the manse by a wall. Kirsty turned these questions over and over in her mind but she didn't voice any of them. Nancy would talk when she was ready otherwise she wouldn't be here.

Eventually, the young man lifted his head and looked at her with eyes brimful of tears. 'I asked Nancy to bring me here,' he said in a voice so low Kirsty had to strain to hear. 'She didn't want to come to Dundee but I insisted. She said you might think I done for Lily but I could never do that. I loved her.'

The emotion in his voice made Kirsty want to reach out to hold his hand. Instead, she leaned forward and asked, 'Are you, Billy?'

He nodded and looked away, hiding fresh tears.

'My job is to get to know Lily and how she came to live in Dundee. Talking to people who knew her will help us find her killer.'

Billy flinched. 'From the beginning?'

'Yes, from the beginning.'

'Lily was a quiet girl. Her dad wouldn't allow her to mix so she played on her own in the orchard behind the manse. We lived at the other side of the wall and we used to perch on the top and shout to her. At first, she wouldn't speak to us and if her dad saw us we got chased. But she started school at the same time as Nancy so they were in the same class and we all became pals. That's right, isn't it, Nancy?'

Nancy nodded. 'Lily didn't make any other friends so we got close. Her dad didn't like it, though, and he kept her to the manse grounds after school.'

Billy smiled at his sister. 'It didn't stop us hopping over the wall. If he came out we hid among the trees or jumped back over the wall. I used to feel sorry for Lily, she didn't have the freedom we did. We first kissed when Lily was fourteen and I was fifteen. It was all innocent like but her dad caught us once and I've never seen anyone so angry. I went over that wall so fast I nearly fell off the top. We became more careful after that.' Billy closed his eyes and a smile played on his lips.

'What about Lily's baby?' Kirsty kept her voice gentle as she brought him back to the present.

His expression changed. 'That baby wasn't mine, we never did anything like that. As I said, we were innocents. But I did offer to marry her. Make her respectable like.'

Kirsty frowned. 'If the baby wasn't yours, Billy, whose was it?'

'That I don't know because she never got out. She never mixed with anyone else but us, that's why I got the blame. I would never have put Lily in that situation, I had too much respect for her.'

Nancy gripped his hand so tight her knuckles whitened. 'You did your best, Billy.'

'But it wasn't good enough,' he said. 'I wanted her to run away with me but her dad took her to that filthy Ma Henderson and they killed that bairn. After that, he locked her up and I never saw her again. I should have stayed.' His eyes filled with tears. 'If I'd known he intended to throw her out I could have saved her. But what did I do? I went and joined the army and spent the next two years fighting in France.' He shuddered. 'So many of our lads were killed and I wanted to be one of them. But it wasn't to be.'

Kirsty couldn't help wondering if Billy had been in the house when she went to Montrose to interview Nancy.

'What did you do when you came back home?'

'Jobs were scarce so I went anywhere there was work. I bunked up with one of my mates in Glasgow for a time, then I went to Peterhead but I didn't take to the fishing so I came down the coast to Aberdeen and then I moved around the countryside picking up farming jobs. My last one was a farm near Laurencekirk. I came home yesterday and that's when I learned about Lily.' He lapsed into silence.

'Thanks, Billy. You've been helpful.'

Billy heaved himself out of the chair. 'You better find out who did this to Lily before I do, or I won't be responsible for my actions.'

37

Mystery surrounded Lily and the more Kirsty discovered, the more the mystery deepened. Kirsty's mind buzzed with unanswered questions as she traversed the corridor to her office after Billy and Nancy departed.

Billy's appearance on the scene altered everything and left Kirsty wondering about the implications of Lily's pregnancy for many of those around her. Billy maintained he wasn't the father of the unborn child and according to him, Lily had no other male contacts apart from her family. Fingers of suspicion slithered into Kirsty's brain but she pushed them away as being unthinkable. These things might happen with more deprived families but not in respectable ones.

It didn't bear thinking about.

But there was no compulsion on Billy to tell her he wasn't responsible and she only knew of his return because he persuaded Nancy to bring him to Dundee. Besides, he couldn't fail to know this would add him to the list of suspects. However, his anger with the person who ended Lily's life and his grief at her death appeared genuine.

She slumped into her chair, pulled a piece of paper from her desk drawer, and tried to order her thoughts. After a few moments, she started to jot down what she knew about the dead girl.

Despite leading a secluded life, Lily, a daughter of the manse, became pregnant. So, who was the father?

Her father ejected her from the family home. But was this correct? Or, did she leave of her own accord? And how did she come to be one of Aggie's girls? What about the men she was involved with? Were they all customers or did she have a secret love life?

The issue of the money bothered Kirsty. Lily had enough to

buy a building. Where did that money come from? A wealthy lover? Or was she a blackmailer?

Kirsty sat back. She had far more questions than answers and was no further forward in unravelling Lily's secrets.

She laid her pencil on top of the sheet of paper and sighed. All she could do at the moment was to comply with Brewster's order to examine the ledger left on his desk. Maybe she would find some answers inside although she doubted it. She'd already examined the suitcase but she could do that again. The only other avenue to pursue lay in re-interviewing Aggie's girls, starting with Daisy and Elsie.

Brewster allowed the door from the charge room to slam behind him and strode up the corridor barely able to conceal his excitement. The search of Freddie's rooms had provided the missing link they were looking for.

He'd instructed two policemen to upend everything and tear furniture apart, they'd even inspected inside the chimney breast. The place was a wreck before they discovered the journal, secured by string to the underside of the metal springs of the bed.

He stopped at the door of Kirsty's office. Her head was bowed over the ledger but her posture and the droop of her shoulders told him she'd found nothing.

'Kirsty,' he said.

Her eyes lit up when she saw him. 'I've obtained fresh information about Lily's background.'

'Put it in your report,' he said. 'Something more important has happened. We've had a breakthrough. I located a notebook in Freddie's rooms and it contains names and addresses. Perhaps it's the missing link.'

He threw the journal onto Kirsty's desk. 'I want you to go through this and make a list of everyone including their addresses and any other information about them. We'll start doing the interviews tomorrow.'

'Tomorrow is Saturday, sir.' Her eyes were inscrutable.

'So it is. But we need to begin as soon as possible and it's too late to start tonight.'

'What time should I come in?'

'Nine o'clock will be fine,' he said. 'And I'm sorry to keep you back tonight when you should be finished. I would do it myself but I should get home for Maggie.'

'I understand, sir.' Kirsty opened the journal.

Guilt followed him outside. He'd refused to listen to what Kirsty wanted to tell him and it wasn't fair expecting her to work late when he was heading for home. But Maggie needed him and he couldn't neglect her. However, that didn't stop him feeling he was taking an unfair advantage of Kirsty.

38

Saturday, 13 December 1919

By the time Kirsty finished collating the contents of Lily's journal it had been late and despite being angry because Brewster refused to listen to her information, she had to admit he'd been right. This was the missing link.

After a restless night, she woke with eyes full of grit and a desire to push the investigation forward. And, if Brewster decided to exclude her from the interviews, she would persuade him otherwise.

A greyish gloom pervaded the room giving just enough relief from the night-time darkness for her to see. She pushed the blankets back, leaned over to light a candle and held it up to inspect the floor before sliding out of the bed. Hatred of spiders and mice were never far from her mind and, although she'd never seen a mouse, she knew by the night-time rustling they inhabited the building. Satisfied it was safe to get out of bed she slid her feet onto the chilly linoleum.

Goose pimples erupted on her skin as soon as the cold air struck and she hugged her arms to her body while she wriggled her feet into slippers. An old coat hung from a hook on the back of her bedroom door and she shrugged it on to protect her from the chill until she completed her ablutions.

Shivering, she walked through to the front room which was as cold as her bedroom. Frost patterns decorated the window and ash overflowed from the grate, the relic of last night's fire. She lit the gas ring, holding her hands over the flame for a brief moment before she placed the kettle on top. While she waited for the water to boil, she raked the ash from the grate into the ashcan below and hurriedly set the fire. Moments later, a tiny flame caught hold, licking its way through the paper to the sticks and coal.

Meanwhile, the kettle on the gas ring bubbled and boiled, hissing and spurting hot water from its spout and steaming up the window. She rushed over to turn the gas tap off before seizing the handle with both hands and pouring water into an enamel basin.

Despite the fire which had roared into life, the room was still chilly making her reluctant to shed the coat in order to wash. Gritting her teeth, she let it drop to the floor and, grasping her flannel and a piece of soap, she scrubbed her skin until it glowed with warmth as well as cleanliness.

She scrambled into her clothes and by the time she made her porridge, ate it and washed it down with a cup of tea, the sun had risen and was making a feeble attempt to shine through the frost covered window.

After fastening her jacket she straightened her tie, checked the fire had burned lower and was in no danger of sending out rogue sparks and lastly, pulled on her hat. She was ready to confront Brewster.

Saturday was often the busiest day of the week at the police station. Despite that, there seemed to be fewer constables on duty than usual and those who were, huddled in the constables' room trying to look busy. No doubt the rest of the force was out patrolling.

'Good morning,' Kirsty said as she hurried past the open door, anxious to leave the cloud of cigarette smoke behind her.

A rumble of voices echoed up the corridor followed by laughter. But she was used to that so paid no heed. Perhaps, through time, they would become accustomed to her presence although, no doubt, it would be a lot longer before they accepted her. She didn't care as long as Brewster thought she contributed some value to the team. His acceptance was all that mattered.

Continuing up the corridor she found him in his office with Lily's journal open in front of him. His eyes flitted between the journal and a sheet of paper with the list of extracted names.

'Sit,' he said without looking up.

Kirsty removed files and papers from a chair, pulled it over to the desk and sat. She waited for him to say something but he continued reading.

Unable to bear the silence any longer, she said, 'Most of the entries are in the form of a diary but starting from the back of the notebook there are names, addresses, and notes on each individual. I've listed the names and read through the diary entries trying to find further information on them. Apart from her family members, the other names have no references elsewhere.'

Brewster leaned back in his chair and steepled his fingers. 'What do you deduce from the list you compiled?'

'I think this may be our blackmail list although I did include the family members because it's possible she might have been blackmailing them as well. Her father, for instance, if anyone knew he arranged her abortion it would finish him with the church. I'm not sure about her Uncle David, though, unless he was party to that as well.'

'I see you've written nicknames beside some of the entries.'

'Yes. I think it fair to say we know the identity of the Laird and the Captain. And, if you notice, the Laird's address is not in the country. He lives right here in Dundee.'

'Good work, Kirsty. We'll interview everyone on your list.'

Brewster stood, plucked his hat from the top of the filing cabinet behind him, and thrust it onto his head.

'Let's go,' he said.

'Would it not be better to bring them to the police station for questioning?' Kirsty backed out of the office.

'On what pretext?'

'The list indicates they may be blackmail victims and they are suspects in a murder investigation.'

'We have no proof the names mean anything. It's possible they are only customers.' Brewster removed his coat from a hook on the wall and pulled it on.

Kirsty followed him along the corridor convinced more than ever he was making a mistake. What did he hope to achieve by rushing out today? Far better to plan ahead and bring them in for questioning. But when did he ever listen to her, a mere woman.

157

As usual, the Overgate was busy. Men, women and children thronged the streets dressed in their weekend finery making Kirsty feel out of place in her policewoman's uniform which was usually a source of pride for her. Today, she detected reprobation as well as curiosity in the glances cast her way. However, that might be her imagination at work due to her own guilt feelings about working instead of visiting her parents.

Kirsty ignored the glances and let her mind wander to memories of her childhood. She was always happy then and couldn't imagine a time when that would change. A protective umbrella surrounded her in those days. Everyone she knew loved her and she loved them back. Life was blissful. It never prepared her for the thing that was to change her forever and rip her from the safety of her family causing a rift that was not yet healed.

Guilt consumed her. Since this investigation began she hadn't seen her parents and she had promised to visit them today. More than anything, she missed Ailsa, the sister who wasn't a sister but also her own child. She resolved that the minute this investigation was over she would visit and spend a few days with her parents.

'I think we may have discovered the link to the title deeds in Lily's possession.'

Brewster's voice jolted her back to the present. He had stopped in front of a door sandwiched between a shoe shop and a butcher's. A brass plaque set into the stone at the side of the door drew her attention.

'Look, Kirsty.' Brewster pointed. 'Gregor Armstrong deals in properties. Now, all we need to do is find out why he transferred the deeds of the Hawkhill property to Lily.'

'Payment for services rendered?' Kirsty failed to keep the sarcasm out of her voice.

It didn't matter because Brewster gave no sign of noticing her comment. 'That's a hefty payment but I'm sure Mr Armstrong will be able to clarify the transaction.'

39

Kate pushed Gregor's office door open. 'Someone to see you.'

'I'm busy,' Gregor snapped. Kate should know better than to interrupt him without warning.

'It's the police,' she said.

Unable to mask his alarm, his eyes widened and he stared at her. 'What do they want?' He clenched his fists and took several deep breaths.

'They didn't say. Just said they wanted to talk to you.'

Kate's eyes gleamed and he could swear she was enjoying herself.

'Show them in, then.'

She stood back and a woman wearing something that looked like a female version of a police uniform walked in, followed by a man in a brown tweed overcoat.

'Shall I stay?'

'No, no! I'll attend to this.' The less Kate knew about his business the better.

Kate left, slamming the door behind her.

'Have a seat.' He waved his cigar in the air while hoping they couldn't hear the thump of his heart.

The man pulled a chair in front of the desk but the woman continued to stand. She leaned against the door as if anticipating the return of his sister.

'How may I help you?' Stress made Gregor's voice go up an octave.

'You are Gregor Armstrong?'

'Yes.' The word whistled out between his teeth.

'We have some questions for you. I am Detective Inspector Brewster and this is Policewoman Campbell.'

'A policewoman? I didn't realize there was such a thing.' Gregor's voice went up yet another octave at the thought of the questions that might be asked.

The inspector ignored his comment. 'We believe you know a prostitute by the name of Lily Petrie. Can you confirm that?'

Gregor's thoughts whirled. He wanted to deny knowing her but that would look suspicious if they found out he did know her. He placed his cigar in his mouth and puffed to give himself time to think.

The detective stared at him while the policewoman poised a pencil over her notebook ready to take down his responses.

'Yes.' His voice was even higher now and sweat gathered on his back and under his arms.

'Can you tell us how you know her?'

Gregor wiped his brow. 'She's one of Aggie's girls. I visited her from time to time.' He glanced towards the door. 'Please don't tell my sister.'

'How well did you know her?'

'I didn't know her all that well she was just one of the girls.'

'And yet,' the inspector said, 'you knew her well enough to give her an entire building in the Hawkhill.' The inspector's eyes narrowed.

Gregor gasped. His heart thumped and he stared at the ledgers on his desk. Anything to avoid those eyes boring into his innermost secrets.

'You don't understand.' He forced the words out. 'We had a business arrangement. She agreed to supply girls and run the business and we would share the profits.'

'If that was the case why would you transfer the property to her in its entirety?'

'It was part of our agreement and the way she wanted it.'

'I see.' The inspector's voice became deceptively soft and Gregor sensed the man didn't believe him.

'Before I go, can you tell me where you were between Sunday midnight and Monday morning?'

Gregor felt on safer ground. 'With my wife of course. I was with her all night.'

'And on Thursday evening?'

Bile rose in Gregor's throat. They knew. But how could they?

'At home,' he croaked. 'I'm always at home in the evenings.'

'Except, of course, the evenings you were with Lily,' the inspector said.

Gregor closed his eyes. They must know, why else were they questioning him?

The inspector stood. 'I'll want to speak to you again and I'll want your wife to confirm your whereabouts on both those dates.'

The policewoman inserted her notebook into a pocket before following the detective out of the office.

After they left, Gregor rammed his cigar into his mouth and slumped back in his chair. His heart thumped in his chest and he thought he was going to have a heart attack.

Kirsty heaved a sigh of relief after she left Gregor Armstrong's office. The atmosphere inside had been cloying and claustrophobic making her want to throw a window open. Besides that, the man repelled her. His eyes seemed to slide over her before looking away while even the pores of his body oozed guilt and deception.

The woman in the outer office looked up. 'Will that be all?'

'For the moment,' Brewster replied.

Kirsty's boots clattered on the wooden stairs, echoing upwards like a drummer beating the retreat. She didn't stop until she emerged outside and could breathe fresh air again.

The Overgate was even busier now than it had been when they arrived at Gregor Armstrong's office. Brewster pushed through the queue of customers outside the butcher's shop and Kirsty followed in his wake. Caught in a stream of shoppers heading for the market, she thought they were going to be separated. However, Brewster grabbed her hand to pull her along. He thrust his way between the crowds, stopping when they reached the junction of the Overgate and the High Street.

'Sorry about that.' He let go of her hand.

'That's all right,' she said. But she'd felt safe while he held her hand and now there was something missing.

They stood in silence for a few moments watching the crowds surge into the narrow entrance to the Overgate. Embarrassment overtook Kirsty and she became reluctant to break the silence. What did you say when a man had been holding your hand? Especially when it gave you some degree of pleasure.

At last, Brewster spoke. 'What did you make of Mr Armstrong?'

'Our visit worried him and he wasn't being honest.' She wanted to add that he repelled her and made her flesh creep, but Brewster didn't appreciate comments based on instinct rather than fact.

'I agree. He's hiding something and next time we interview him we'll lean on him a bit harder.'

'What now, sir?'

Brewster pulled Kirsty's list from his pocket and tapped his finger on it.

'Next one is Neil Young, he lives in Albert Street. We can board a tram further along which will take us there.'

'Yes, sir,' Kirsty said already walking to the tram stop.

40

The tram clanked to a stop in Albert Street a few yards from its junction with Lyon Street and Raglan Street. Brewster got off first and Kirsty jumped off after him, ignoring the hand he held out to help her alight. The surge of feeling she experienced when he grasped her hand earlier followed by embarrassment was something she was reluctant to repeat.

Tenements, not dissimilar to Aggie's building, lined each side of the road. Brewster started checking off numbers. 'It seems to be odd numbers at this side of the street so I reckon we need to cross the road,' he said after consulting his list.

Halfway down the section of Albert Street between Raglan Street and the Arbroath Road junction, he came to a stop in front of a close.

'I think we're here.'

Kirsty followed him through the close to the rear of the building. Like most tenements in Dundee, a stairwell shaped like a turret jutted from the back.

They climbed the stairs, checking the numbers as they went. By the time they reached the second landing they realized the flat they wanted was at the top of the four-storey building. Kirsty peered up the final flight of stairs and although the muscles in the back of her legs ached, she resisted the temptation to grasp the banister. She would never admit any weakness to a man and especially not to Brewster.

When there was no response to Brewster's knock on the door Kirsty walked to the window and peered inside. A cat launched itself at the glass and she staggered back with a squeal of surprise.

'What is it?'

'Just a cat, I don't think there's anyone inside.'

A door further along the landing opened and a woman,

wearing a filthy apron and with her hair in curlers, peered out. 'If you're looking for him, he'll be at his work.'

'Can you tell us where he works?'

The smell coming from the house intensified the nearer Kirsty got to the woman.

'What d'you want to know that for?'

'We need to speak to him, we think there is something he could help us with.'

'Ma, Ma, Davy's hitting me,' sounded from inside the house.

'No I'm not. He's telling lies.'

'Will the pair of you shut up,' the woman screamed through the door. 'Or I'll tell yer Faither on ye.' The sounds stopped. 'Bairns,' she said turning to Kirsty. 'That pair will be the death of me with their fighting.'

'You were going to tell me where Mr Young works?' Kirsty reminded the woman.

'Oh, aye. Ye'll find him at the slaughterhouse on the corner of Market Street and East Dock Street. I wouldnae like his job.' The woman turned and went into her flat, slamming the door in Kirsty's face.

'I know where that is,' Brewster said coming up behind Kirsty. 'We can catch a tram to Baxter Park, it's an easy walk from there.'

Icy air blasted up the covered walkway from the holding pens when Neil Young opened the door at the rear of the kill room. The harness, which secured an animal once it reached its final destination, swung in the wind. He pushed it to the side, lifted his bucket and heaved water down the slope. After refilling it a second and a third time he repeated his actions. Satisfied the walkway was reasonably clean, he closed the door and turned his attention to the kill room.

Saturday was cleaning day, the pens outside in the adjacent cattle market were empty and most of the beef in the ice room had already been despatched. Voices, and the sound of scrubbing, issued from every corner of the building as workers tackled the onerous task of removing blood, bone and effluent from their tools, as well as the floors and walls.

The kill room was a smaller area than the rest of the slaughterhouse which meant Neil had sole responsibility for its cleanliness and, in here, the voices from the other sections sounded muted. This room housed one animal at a time and was the place where it was killed before being moved on to the larger skinning and butchery areas in order to be prepared for the market. There would be no carcases hanging from the hooks in the iron rails in these vast areas on this day.

Water splashed over Neil's wellingtons and up his rubber apron as he threw bucketful after bucketful of water over the floor and into every corner. Convinced every inch had been covered, he grabbed a long-handled brush and commenced to sweep the water towards the central draining channel. But that was only the beginning. It would take several more buckets of water and a lot more sweeping before he was satisfied the kill room was clean.

Voices echoing from the adjoining area grew louder and a draught whistled around his ankles. He knew, without looking up from the tap where he was filling his bucket, the door separating him from the skinning room had opened.

'Someone here to see you.'

Neil and the gaffer didn't get on so he didn't look up until the bucket was full of water.

'Bloody well get a move on I don't have all day to stand here.'

'What's so important about someone wanting to see me?' Curiosity got the better of him and he straightened before turning to face the gaffer.

'Because it's the bloody police.' The gaffer glared at him. 'What you been up to?'

Neil splashed water over the bottom of his apron and his boots. 'Nothing as far as I know.' He kept his voice mild although his heart thumped in his chest. If they'd found out about his sideline, selling cut-price beef, he would brazen it out.

Heads turned when he walked through the skinning area to the entrance hall. The men would be curious and talking about him but that was nothing out of the usual. It hadn't taken him long to learn to keep his distance from the others when he first started working here straight from school at the age of fourteen. A figure of fun because of his harelip, many a time he'd gone home in tears because they tormented him and mimicked his speech. But that had been years ago and they wouldn't dare mimic him now, although he was sure they did it out of his hearing.

'They asked for somewhere private to speak to you,' the gaffer said as he led the way to the hut-like structure to the right of the main entrance. Throwing open the door, he announced, 'This is Neil Young.' He hovered in the doorway, an avid look on his face.

The man perched on the edge of the desk said, 'Thank you, shut the door when you leave.'

The gaffer scowled and edged out, slamming the door behind him.

That'll sort the bugger, Neil thought as he sized up the man in front of him. He didn't look like a policeman and wasn't wearing a uniform. His tweed overcoat was unbuttoned revealing a blue pinstriped suit underneath and a shirt that looked slightly grubby. But the most surprising thing in the room was the woman in uniform seated on the chair at the side of the desk.

Kirsty noted the look in Neil Young's eyes and it made her uneasy. She smoothed her skirt over her knees and tucked her legs below the desk before grabbing her pencil and focusing her eyes on her notebook. 'Ready when you are, sir,' she said.

The slaughterman leaned against the door hunching his shoulders as tall men often do but he still towered over Brewster. His eyes remained wary and an aura of menace surrounded him.

Brewster thrust a chair over to Neil. 'Sit,' he said.

Neil grasped the back of the chair and glared at Brewster before he sat.

This was a man who did not like being told what to do and Kirsty sensed his resentment and the unspoken message he was still the stronger of the two even though he complied with Brewster's order.

'I believe you knew a prostitute by the name of Lily Petrie.' The formality in Brewster's voice asserted his authority.

'What if I did?'

'How well did you know her?' Brewster leaned against the desk while he directed his questions at Neil Young.

'Well enough.'

'We are investigating Lily's murder and have questions we wish you to answer.'

'Nothing to tell. Don't know anything about that.'

'Are you saying you didn't know she'd been murdered?' Brewster frowned his disbelief.

'I read the papers.'

'Where were you between Sunday evening and Monday morning?' The brittle tone of Brewster's voice indicated the level of his annoyance with the brevity of the man's replies.

'Home, in my bed.'

'Can anyone confirm that?'

'No.'

'What about Thursday evening?'

The man's eyes narrowed and Kirsty sensed him becoming wary.

'Same thing,' Neil said, 'I was in my bed.'

Brewster's irritation increased with each staccato answer the slaughterman gave.

'Were you being blackmailed?'

Neil's fists clenched. 'Why would anyone want to blackmail me?' He rose from his chair and towered over Brewster. 'If you're trying to say I killed Lily, or anyone else, you're wrong. I kill animals, not people. Now, if you're finished with me I need to get back to work.'

Kirsty laid her pencil down after Neil slammed out the door. 'That man has something to hide.'

'I think you're right, Kirsty. Next time we question him it will be at the police station.'

41

Although the cattle market pens were empty the stench of manure pervaded the area and Kirsty was glad when they left Market Street behind them. They were in sight of Arbroath Road when they heard the familiar clank of an approaching tram.

Brewster grabbed her hand, and said, 'If we run we'll catch it.'

Kirsty had no time to object and they ran hand in hand to the tram stop. After they settled in their seat, Kirsty realized she had experienced no aversion to Brewster's touch. In fact, she'd felt the opposite, a comforting tingle which warmed her.

'Come on,' Brewster said when they reached the High Street, 'there's a bakery near here, we'll buy a loaf of bread and you can come home with me for a plate of soup. Maggie will be pleased to see you.'

Hunger pangs overwhelmed Kirsty when the smell of freshly baked bread assailed her nostrils. It had been a long time since she ate breakfast and she had been unaware of the passage of time. The loaf Brewster bought was still warm from the oven and he thrust the paper package into her hands as they walked through the streets. Despite her hunger, she resisted the temptation to tear the paper off and pull warm chunks of bread from it.

Brewster grew quiet as they neared his cottage and Kirsty found herself wondering about his relationship with his wife. It couldn't be easy for him having to care for an invalid as well as hold down a job and it was something she couldn't imagine herself doing. She considered the number of times she had been less than understanding when he absented himself from his office and resolved to be more considerate in the future.

Kirsty's thoughts made her footsteps hesitant as she

followed him up the path and into the cottage. She had no right to encroach on their privacy. Brewster should not have brought her here and the impulse to turn and run gathered strength.

Maggie wheeled herself into the lobby to greet them when they entered. 'I was looking out the window and saw you coming,' she said. 'And you've brought Kirsty.'

Embarrassment forced Kirsty to apologize. 'He insisted I come home with him for a plate of soup before we go off on our next interviews. I hope you don't mind.'

'Why would I mind? It's about time you came back for a visit.'

'I didn't want to put you to any bother.'

'That's no bother to me. Jamie made the broth last night. It only needs to be heated and Jamie will do that.'

'Oh! I didn't realize...'

'That I could cook?' Brewster laughed. 'There's a lot you don't know about me.'

Kirsty smiled. 'I can see that.'

Brewster bent and kissed Maggie's forehead before wheeling her into the sitting room and positioning her chair at one side of the fireplace. 'I'll leave you and Kirsty to chat while I put the soup on to heat. But don't you be giving away any more of my secrets.'

Kirsty hesitated in the doorway before following them into a room obviously designed to cater for Maggie's wheelchair with its wooden floors and not a rug in sight. Love played no part in Kirsty's life and the open display of affection made her uncomfortable. Growing up, she never wondered if her parents loved each other. No doubt they cared about one another but she wasn't sure whether that was the same as the kind of love she witnessed between Maggie and Brewster.

Maggie nodded at the armchair at the other side of the fireplace. 'Jamie won't mind if you sit in his chair. He'll be too busy getting the broth ready to want to sit down.'

The wingback chair had seen better days. The material on the arms was threadbare and the seat sagged in the middle, suggesting a broken spring. Kirsty wriggled herself into a comfortable position before holding her hands in front of the fire which burned with a steady glow in the fireplace.

'You must find Dundee tame after working in London,' Maggie said, 'but Jamie tells me you've settled in.'

Kirsty laughed. 'I'm not sure the others in the police force think that way. As far as they're concerned I have no right to be there.'

'Give them time. They'll get used to you.'

'I'm not so sure about that,' Kirsty said. In her eyes, Dundee was no different to London where policewomen were struggling for recognition. Maybe someday their service would be valued but that day hadn't yet arrived.

'And Jamie appreciates your help with his investigations. Interviewing women and children was always a problem before you came. He says you have the knack of gaining their confidence and they tell you more.'

Warmth crept up Kirsty's neck into her face. 'That's good to know because he never tells me.'

'I don't suppose he would. Jamie isn't the best at handing out compliments, he expects you to know.' Maggie stared into the fire. 'Your father,' she said. 'Does he still disapprove of your work?'

'Nothing would make him happier than if I decided to give it all up and return home to wait for some man to make me his wife.' Kirsty was unable to keep the bitterness out of her voice. 'He's too stuck in the past to accept the changes that mean women can go out to work instead of remaining at home. And, he'll never accept my choice of career.'

'What about your mother?'

'In a way, she's accepted the fact I've made my mind up although, like my father, she's not happy I'm a policewoman.'

'And Ailsa?'

'When I returned to Dundee she bombarded me with questions about my work and living in a rented flat. She was desperate to visit and was so excited it was difficult to restrain her. She's been quieter since we rescued her from the Howff last month.' Kirsty's mind went back to that terrible time when they were fleeing from Ailsa's abductors in the graveyard when both of them could have been killed.

'That must have been a terrifying experience for a child,' Maggie said. 'How has it affected her?'

'She's quieter and doesn't go out on her own anymore although I'm not sure if that's my parents' decision or hers.'

At the time, Kirsty's decision had been to let Ailsa go, to leave her parents with the task of rearing her. As a result, she kept her distance which meant she had no understanding of how the experience had affected Ailsa. Guilt consumed her. She'd taken the easy way out by standing back and that was wrong. She needed to treat Ailsa as her sister and not as a stranger just because it was easier.

A clatter of dishes resounding from the kitchen interrupted her train of thought and a moment later Brewster entered the room carrying two plates. He laid them on the table, saying, 'Come and get it while it's hot,' before leaving the room and reappearing with his own plate of soup and another one piled high with bread.

'Eat up,' he said. 'We'll be in time to catch the matinee at the *La Scala* where we can conduct our next interview.'

42

Angus hated matinees and always tried to arrive early before the queue built up. But no matter how early he set off there was always a line of excited children squabbling and yelling at each other before they were admitted. Today, he heard them before he rounded the corner and saw the little brats filling the pavement and spilling out onto the road. Damned wonder they weren't mowed down by a car or trampled by a horse.

Cold air, sweeping down the street sending paper and other rubbish swirling aloft didn't seem to dampen their spirits. Most of them were scruffy and dirty and in tattered clothes that provided no protection against the elements. No doubt many of them would be paying for their entry to the film with jam jars or the coins they got for the return of empty bottles. Scavenging for them seemed to be the latest Dundee pastime.

He glared at the worst troublemakers as he walked past them but it made no difference and they carried on regardless.

'When you going to open the doors, mister?'

The call echoed up and down the line, creating a cacophony of noise that assaulted his ears.

Angus ignored them and hurried up the marble steps, unlocked the door, slipped through and locked it behind him. They would have to wait.

The poster in the foyer announced the new cartoon *Feline Follies* was showing followed by *The Knickerbocker Buckaroo*. He suppressed a groan because, although it featured his hero, Douglas Fairbanks, it was a western. That meant the little brats would be galloping out of the cinema after the film, pretending to be cowboys.

It didn't take him long to get into his uniform and he marched back to the foyer. The uniform made all the difference, imparting a semblance of power and authority. He waited until the cashier nodded to him to open the doors and braced himself for the tide of unwashed bodies and defiant brats.

The stream of urchins pushed in and he stood out of their way, heaving a sigh of relief when the last one vanished into the auditorium.

The cashier finished counting the takings and backed out of the kiosk with her arms full of empty jam jars. 'Matinees are the bane of my life with most of the bairns paying with jars. Keep an eye on the cash desk while I cart them to the storeroom,' she shouted to him.

Several journeys later the cashier appeared beside him. 'That's the lot. They'll need to be taken to the scrappie on Monday to get the refunds.'

'Does that mean you want me to do it?' He didn't need to ask the question. They always expected him to take the jars to the scrap merchant.

'Only if you want to keep your job.'

The acid tone of her voice had its desired effect on him and he turned away to study the street, watching curiously when a motor car drew up outside the cinema. His interest aroused, he watched a man extricate himself from the car closely followed by a woman in uniform who joined him on the pavement. They spoke for a few minutes before climbing the stairs leading to the glass entrance doors.

Curiosity consumed Angus but he held the door open for them and touched his cap when they entered. The man's eyes appraised him, sending a shiver of unease along his spine. He didn't know why he felt unnerved by this man's presence or gaze. But this man represented authority. It was visible in his appearance, his stance, and those eyes that seemed to bore right through you.

'I'm looking for Angus Laidlaw. I believe he works here.' The man's voice sounded milder than his appearance suggested.

Angus tried to swallow the lump in his throat. 'I'm Angus,' he said. 'What can I do for you?'

The man pulled off his gloves and stuck them in the pocket of his overcoat. 'I'm Detective Inspector Brewster, and this is Policewoman Campbell. Is there somewhere quiet we can talk?'

Aware of the cashier taking a keen interest in the visitors, Angus said, 'The usherettes' room will be empty until the matinee finishes. We could go there.'

Angus cast a glance at the cashier who instantly studied her cash drawer in an attempt to show lack of interest. Nosy bitch, he thought as he led the way to the room. No doubt she would quiz him later but he had no intention of satisfying her curiosity.

The usherettes' room was larger than his own cubby hole. Coats and women's garments hung from a row of pegs lining one wall. A low bench ran along the wall below them and was likewise littered with scarves, hats and bags, while shoes and boots were crammed underneath. The cinema owners provided the usherettes with their uniforms but they were not allowed to take them out of the building.

'Will this do?' Angus stopped in the middle of the room uncertain what to do. The bare room offered nowhere to sit apart from the bench which was too low for comfort.

'This will do nicely,' the inspector said. He turned and closed the door.

'What's this all about?' Heat built up under Angus's uniform but he resisted the temptation to undo his jacket buttons.

'We are investigating the death of a young lady of your acquaintance. Lily Petrie.'

Angus considered disclaiming all knowledge of Lily, but he wilted under the inspector's scrutiny. Those eyes seemed to see right into him and he thought this man would know if he lied. He wasn't so sure about the woman who now leaned against the wall with her notebook and pencil ready to write down everything he said.

'I heard about Lily,' he said. 'Two of her friends told me what happened.'

The woman looked up. 'Which two friends would that be?'

'I think they gave their names as Elsie and Daisy.'

The woman wrote something in her notebook.

'I understand you had a relationship with Lily.' The man resumed the questioning.

'We knew each other but I wouldn't call it a relationship. Lily used to come to the cinema because she liked watching the films. We talked and joked but that was about all.' Sweat soaked his armpits and trickled down his back.

'I understood it was more than that.'

The detective's eyes bored into him.

'Lily was a romantic.' Angus clamped his mouth shut to prevent himself adding to the statement and incriminating himself.

The woman looked up from her notebook. 'How did you feel when you found out about her death?'

'Wretched.' The word spilled out before he could stop it.

'You were fond of her.'

The woman's voice sounded so sympathetic Angus couldn't prevent a tear trickling down his cheek.

'And yet, you say, you didn't have a relationship.' The man paused and seemed to be thinking. 'Tell me,' he said, 'where were you on the night of Sunday and early Monday morning?'

'At home with my wife and bairn. Was that when Lily was murdered?'

'You have a wife?'

He guessed what the man was thinking. Sweat built up underneath his uniform and he was certain the detective was aware of his discomfort. His heart thumped while he awaited the detective's next question but it wasn't what he expected.

'Where were you on Thursday evening?'

Angus gaped at him. He couldn't know about the blackmail demand? Could he? Recovering himself, he said, 'Here working, then I went home.'

'I'll need your wife's name and your home address in order to confirm your alibi,' the detective said.

After Angus gave the details to the policewoman the detective said, 'I'll probably need to speak to you again and it might be wise to inform your wife to expect a visit.'

Angus, avoiding the cashier's eyes, retreated to his own small room after they left. He slumped in the chair and buried his head in his hands. What was he going to do? His wife's father and her brothers would kill him when they found out.

43

Several turns of the starting handle were needed before the engine sprang into life with a roar before settling down to a steady rumble. Brewster jumped into the driving seat and fiddled with the controls before grasping the steering wheel and setting the motor car in motion.

'What did you think of Angus Laidlaw?' His eyes remained fixed on the road.

'He gave the impression of being a young man with a high opinion of himself as well as an eye for a pretty girl,' she said after turning Brewster's question over in her mind, 'and I don't think he was honest with us. I'm sure his relationship with Lily was not platonic despite what he claims, but I'll check that with Elsie and Daisy. Did you notice, before we started questioning him he seemed full of his own importance? But as the questioning went on he got worried and seemed to deflate. He didn't think he was quite so clever by the time we left.'

'I can't help wondering whether he would have mentioned his wife if he hadn't needed her to confirm his alibi.'

'I doubt it and I'm sure Lily wasn't aware of his wife.'

'We will need to speak to her.'

'He's not going to like that.'

Kirsty stared out of the window as they passed Halley's Mill. It reminded her she should be visiting her parents today. She pushed the thought to the back of her mind, the investigation was more important.

They left the tenements and tall buildings of Dundee behind and the scenery changed to open spaces and the occasional house. Iron gates to a small cemetery on their right hung ajar allowing Kirsty to see beyond the wall into a neglected area with gravestones clustered around a central mausoleum. Further down the road, the motor car rumbled past the Orphan

Institution, an imposing building which housed the orphan children of Dundee.

A few minutes later, Brewster drew to a stop in front of a large house on the left. 'I think this must be the house.'

Set back from the road, the three-storey house built of pink granite, looked impressive. Bow windows at the left of the building added to the grandeur and gave it the appearance of a fairytale tower. They walked up a paved path to where two marble steps led up to the front door situated inside a recessed area, also lined with marble. A curtain twitched at the window to the right.

Brewster grasped the ring dangling from the knocker and rapped on the door. It opened at once, the portly woman in the doorway must have been standing behind the door waiting for them to knock.

He removed his hat. 'Mrs Harris?'

'I'm afraid not,' she said. 'I'm Mrs Hamilton, but I do have a lodger with the name of Harris.'

'Would that be Charles Harris?'

She nodded. 'Perhaps you'd better come in. You can wait in the drawing room and I'll tell him you are here.'

She led them down a corridor and opened the door to a room where she indicated they could wait. Kirsty stepped inside. Weak sunlight penetrated the net curtains on the window glinting off the multitude of china ornaments on the polished oak dresser and mantelpiece. The fireplace was a similar oak with carvings down the side. In the middle of the room, a sumptuous ruby brocade sofa took pride of place. While at each side of the unlit fireplace sat matching wing-backed armchairs. Several ladder back chairs with tapestry seats were ranged along the walls at various points in the room.

She followed them in and said, 'Make yourselves comfortable while I inform Charlie.'

Kirsty picked a framed photograph from the mantelpiece. 'Your husband?'

Mrs Hamilton reached for the photo and, with the suggestion of a tear in her eye, she replied, 'Yes. That's my poor Ernest. He died in the war at the Battle of the Somme. I miss him.' She replaced the photograph on the mantelpiece.

'You have children?'

'I wasn't blessed. But, there's no point in having gloomy thoughts. Life is what it is. I'll go and get Charlie now.'

'An interesting setup,' Kirsty said when Mrs Hamilton left the room.

Most afternoons Charlie sat in his armchair in front of the window watching the river. This gateway to the North Sea was always busy, populated with small yachts whose sails billowed in the breeze and the larger cargo ships that chugged in and out of Dundee docks.

Sometimes the river was calm, at other times, wild and stormy. It was relatively calm today and the only boat in sight was the ferry leaving Newport. He often boarded the *Fifie*, a local nickname for the ferry, to make the crossing to Newport and back. When he stood on deck he imagined himself as the captain of an ocean-going liner. And his fascination with ships encouraged him to adopt the title of Captain although the only ones he'd previously sailed on were the troop carriers between France and Britain.

Charlie heaved a sigh of contentment and bit down on the stem of his pipe while smoke swirled up from the bowl. Dusk was drawing in and soon it would be time for him to move. His gloves and scarf were draped on the fender to warm in front of the coal fire, ready for later when he ventured out. He wondered if Aggie's house was open for business yet. He felt in need of female company.

'Charlie.' Morag's voice echoed up the stairs. 'Someone to see you.'

'I'll be down in a moment,' he shouted back, thinking it was probably the reporter from the *Dundee Courier* who had asked if he would be willing to talk about his war experiences for a special edition of the newspaper.

He laid his pipe in the ashtray on top of the tallboy before brushing ash off his waistcoat. Morag was particular about things like that and this was the only room where she allowed him to smoke.

At the moment he wanted to please her although that wouldn't be so important after they wed. Then, buttoning his jacket and grabbing his walking stick, he left the room and went downstairs.

'I've shown them into the drawing room,' Morag said when he reached the bottom of the stairs.

Two of them waited for him and his footsteps faltered as he registered the police uniform the woman wore. Panic fluttered in his chest. This was bound to be about Lily.

'Shall I bring some tea through?' Morag hovered in the doorway.

'That's a kind thought,' Charlie said, 'but I don't think that will be necessary.'

Morag continued to hover.

'I'll join you in the kitchen after I find out what they want and we can have a nice cup of tea together.' Charlie hoped his anxiety didn't show.

Disappointment showed in the droop of her shoulders and the drag of her slippered feet and Charlie knew he would have to make it up to her. Perhaps if he spent the evening in her company instead of going off to the town she would forget how he excluded her from his meeting with the police.

Satisfied she'd gone to the kitchen, he clicked the door shut and turned to face the man and woman. 'You asked to see me?' His tongue clung to the roof of his mouth and a nervous tick flickered at the corner of his eye.

'Can you confirm you are Charles Harris, otherwise known as the Captain?'

Charlie nodded his assent.

'I am Detective Inspector Brewster and this is Policewoman Campbell. We are here to ask you questions about Lily Petrie. I assume you are aware she has been murdered.'

Charlie's mind whirled. He wanted to deny knowing Lily but they wouldn't be here unless they knew of the connection between them. He licked his lips but his tongue was dry and his mouth parched. Not trusting himself to speak, he nodded again.

'I need to ask you where you were last Sunday evening and

early Monday morning.'

Charlie cleared his throat. 'Here,' he croaked, 'all night.'

'Can Mrs Hamilton vouch for that?'

'Up until the time I retired for the night.'

'What time would that be, sir?'

'About ten o'clock. We're early bedders.'

'So, no one can vouch for you after ten o'clock.'

'Mrs Hamilton is a light sleeper, I'm sure she would hear me if I left the house.' Charlie hesitated. He had been concentrating so hard on answering the detective's questions he never gave any thought to the implications. Now, the full horror of what they were asking, struck him. They were checking his alibi for the time of the murder.

'You can't think I had anything to do with Lily's murder. I could never harm that girl.' Heat rose from his neck to his face.

'But you did harm her, several times.'

The softness of the detective's voice sent shivers coursing through Charlie. How did they know that? He clenched his hand on the top of his walking stick while struggling to dampen the rage building within him.

'Maybe I lose my temper from time to time but that doesn't mean I killed her.' He thumped his stick on the floor. 'I was gassed in the war and it affected my behaviour. I can lash out at times and sometimes Lily landed on the receiving end. But I always made it up to her after and she didn't mind.' He slumped into a chair and buried his head in his hands. 'I didn't kill her. I swear I didn't.'

'Are you saying she didn't mind being bruised and battered? And she liked getting black eyes?' The woman spoke for the first time.

Charlie glared at her. What right did she have to ask him questions? Women should know their place. He expected the detective to remonstrate with her but he stayed quiet.

'No, she didn't mind because I always made it worth her while. In fact, she baited me so I would react. She liked the money I gave her.'

Brewster resumed the questioning. 'How much money did you give her?'

'Quite a lot over a period of time. She was saving to buy her own house.'

'So, this was a form of blackmail.'

'I didn't say that. Blackmail had nothing to do with it. I gave her the money to make up for my bad behaviour.'

Brewster narrowed his eyes. 'One thing more. Where were you between Thursday night and Friday morning?'

The blood rushed to Charlie's face. He didn't want to think about Thursday night. In any case, how did they know about that? He recalled the detective's mention of blackmail. Was that what he meant?

'Thursday night.' Charlie almost choked on the words. 'I was here on Thursday night. Mrs Hamilton can vouch for me.'

'I think you should ask Mrs Hamilton to join us for a moment,' Brewster said, 'and we can clear it up right now.'

Charlie's heart raced. What if Morag heard him creep out after she'd gone to bed? He'd waited until she was asleep and then crept out in his socks, putting his shoes on after he left the house. But what if he was wrong? And how was he going to explain to her why he needed an alibi?

'Must you ask her? I don't want her to get the wrong idea.'

'Yes,' Brewster said, 'It's important.'

For the first time, Charlie needed the support of his walking stick so his legs wouldn't collapse beneath him.

Morag wiped her forehead with a floury hand when he walked into the kitchen. 'I thought I'd make pancakes, I know how much you like them.'

Charlie had never felt less interested in pancakes but he forced a smile to his lips. 'That's kind of you, Morag,' he said. 'But the detective would like a word with you before he leaves.'

'What's it all about, Charlie?'

'Nothing to concern you, my dear. It's something that happened downtown. Apparently, someone thought they saw me there so they thought I might have witnessed something. But I didn't go to the town on Thursday night. So I can't help them.'

'If that's all it is,' Morag said, 'tell them to come through here. I don't want to go into the drawing room with floury hands.'

Charlie didn't relax until Morag confirmed he had been at home all Thursday night and with a feeling of relief, he watched them get in their car and drive off.

Hopefully, that would be the last he would see of them.

44

'That was interesting,' Brewster said when they drove off.

'You could say that.'

Kirsty pulled her jacket collar closer to her neck to prevent the freezing air penetrating too deeply.

'I considered him an obnoxious man.'

'That doesn't make him a killer.'

Kirsty had no time for men who used violence against women and she couldn't resist saying, 'Pity his alibi checked out.'

As far as she was concerned, Morag Hamilton's soft spot for Charlie Harris threw doubt on his alibi.

His attitude changed when they entered the kitchen and the way he spoke to her was full of affection. But Kirsty saw through him.

Someone should warn his landlady of the dangers this man posed.

'And if it hadn't, you'd have locked him up and thrown away the key?'

Brewster's face remained expressionless although she could have sworn he was laughing at her. She glared at him and looked away. There was no point in speaking to Brewster when he started to humour her, so she slumped in her seat and kept her thoughts to herself.

Charlie Harris troubled her.

Whether he killed Lily remained to be seen but she didn't doubt her assessment of him as a violent man who posed a danger to women.

Brewster's questions obviously worried him and when she asked one she thought he might hit her with his stick.

This man's demeanour had been suspicious from the start. The lack of emotion when discussing Lily's death and his assertion she liked to be beaten indicated, to her, a man unable to relate to anyone other than himself unless it was in his interests.

Brewster's voice interrupted her line of thought.

'We're here,' he said as the engine sputtered and stopped. 'We'll make this the last visit for today.'

The manse, set back from the road behind a jungle of overgrown bushes, looked forbidding in the gathering dusk.

David frowned. Tomorrow's sermon needed something more forceful included.

He flicked through several pages of the Bible looking for an apt quote and sighed with pleasure when he found one. Josiah never experienced this problem, he always found quotes to enforce his hell and damnation sermons, but David wasn't that kind of preacher, nor did he have any desire to be.

He dipped his pen in the inkwell and started to write, revising and adding quotes to shape the sermon. He became engrossed in his task and didn't hear the tap on the door. A second louder tap broke his concentration.

'Yes,' he said, laying down his pen.

His housekeeper opened the door. 'Two police persons are here to see you. I have shown them into the sitting room.'

'Thank you, Mrs Watson. I expect they want to ask me about Lily.'

'I expect that's it,' she said. 'So sad what happened to your niece.'

Her comment seemed at odds with the expression of disapproval on her face. But, of course, Mrs Watson would know how Lily made her living. It was in all the newspapers.

'She was such a lovely girl, I was fond of her.'

'I'm sure you were, sir. Will I say you'll be with them in a few minutes, sir?'

'That would be appreciated.'

'You are remembering this is Saturday and you said I could finish early today.'

David looked at the wall clock realizing with a start it was well after four o'clock. 'I'm sorry, Mrs Watson. I didn't intend to delay you. I can attend to my visitors myself.'

He waited until his housekeeper left before rising from his desk to join the police in the sitting room.

'What can I help you with, Inspector?' David said when Brewster and Kirsty entered the room.

'Some progress has been made since we last saw you,' Brewster said. 'But there are a few questions we need to ask.'

Kirsty pulled out her notebook and rested it on the arm of the chair. She scribbled progress at the top followed by a question mark. What progress did Brewster refer to? As far as she could see they were no further forward in identifying the killer than they had been at the start of the investigation although she had her own ideas about that. Ideas Brewster did not share because he could not give up the notion that Aggie was the murderer.

'We are still trying to piece together Lily's life and are encountering difficulties because she had so many secrets.'

'I can't imagine what they would be. She was such a lovely child although her life changed drastically after her father disowned her.'

'But you still maintained contact.' Brewster's voice sharpened.

'Why would you think that?'

'We found a journal with a list of men's names, including yours, and they all seemed to be giving her money. Did you give her money?'

David repositioned himself on his chair. 'She was my niece and I was fond of her so I did give her money from time to time. Any uncle would do the same.'

'I am sure that was generous of you,' Brewster said.

Kirsty noticed his deferential tone and looked up from the notebook to ask a question of her own. 'You are close to your sister and her family?'

David, who had not yet acknowledged Kirsty, glanced in her direction. 'Yes, we are close.'

Brewster frowned at Kirsty before saying, 'We need to

clarify your whereabouts at the time of Lily's death.'

Bowing her head over her notebook to conceal her annoyance at Brewster's unspoken reprimand, she concentrated on taking notes.

'Surely you don't think I had anything to do with that?' David's voice held a hint of amusement.

'We have to ask everyone who has a connection,' Brewster explained, 'it's a formality.'

'I see.'

'In that case where were you between Sunday night and Monday morning?'

'Where I always am. After Sunday services I relax here with a book and then go to bed for an early night.'

'Can anyone confirm that, sir?'

'Not really, Mrs Watson, my housekeeper comes in daily. She doesn't sleep over.'

Kirsty jotted the information in her notebook. Other questions she wanted to ask buzzed in her mind but Brewster was in charge and he'd made that plain.

'Can you also confirm your movements on Thursday evening and the early hours of Friday morning?'

'Why would you want to know that?'

'Just answer the question.'

'Let me think. Ah, yes. I visited a parishioner in the infirmary on Thursday evening during visiting hours.'

'Thank you, sir. We may need to question you again if that's convenient for you.'

Kirsty placed her notebook in her pocket and rose from her chair, ignoring her hat which she left lying on the floor.

'I'll be available anytime you want.' David got up and escorted them to the door.

Kirsty remained standing on the pavement while Brewster cranked the car into life. When the engine caught she shouted over the noise, 'I'll have to dive back inside. I've left my hat. You keep the engine going I won't be long.'

She opened the front door to the manse. Once inside she marched to the sitting room.

David stood in the sitting room looking out the window. It

was obvious he watched her return to the house.

'You've come back?'

She grabbed her hat from the floor. 'I forgot my hat. But while I'm here I wanted to ask you something.'

He raised his eyebrows. 'What did you want to ask?'

'You said you were close to Lily and her family. How close? Did your sister request your help with Lily's pregnancy?'

'Of course, I was aware of the pregnancy but there was nothing I could do.'

'Not even when Josiah threw her out of the house.'

'It was not my place to interfere.'

The hint of amusement in his voice left Kirsty feeling he was humouring her. She sharpened her tone in response.

'Are you aware of who was responsible for Lily's condition?'

'Of course. We all knew Billy Allardyce fathered the child. But he soon took himself off. Joined the army, I believe.'

'The strange thing is,' Kirsty spoke quietly and paused to give her statement more effect, 'Billy Allardyce denies responsibility and says that he and Lily did nothing more than kiss.'

'He's lying. He offered to marry her to legitimize the birth.' David's voice contained a hint of stridency which contrasted with his previously mild tones.

'Yes, he told us that. He said he wanted to support her because he loved her. He also said Lily had no contact with any other males except for her family.'

'What are you suggesting?'

'I'm suggesting the person responsible for making Lily pregnant is much nearer home.'

'That is a preposterous suggestion.' David rose from his chair. 'I think it is time you left.'

'You took your time,' Brewster said when she returned.

Kirsty smiled and stepped into the car. She would explain to Brewster when he was in a less condescending mood.

45

Brewster drove in silence.

Kirsty shifted position in her seat. Did Brewster suspect going back for her hat was a ruse so she could ask questions? But she didn't regret doing it. She couldn't imagine him tackling the questions she put to David. He had a more conventional view of families and family life. However, she had seen everything during her police service in London and she didn't imagine things were any different in Scotland although they were probably more hidden. It must be something to do with the Protestant ethic that pervaded the country.

'I hope you didn't mind me asking a question,' she said.

He didn't take his eyes from the road in front of him. 'Not at all although, as I recall, your job is to question women and girls.'

It felt like the smallest of taps on the wrist. A gentle way of putting her in her place.

Brewster steered the car through the arch and parked at the rear of the courtyard. Kirsty glanced at him before she got out of the car. Was he annoyed with her? Unable to tell from his expression, she marched towards the charge room.

Geordie, the duty sergeant, looked up when she entered. 'I have a letter for you, miss.' He handed her an envelope.

She stuck her finger under the flap and tore it open. The brevity of the message from her father indicated his displeasure. 'Your mother was sorely disappointed you could not keep your promise to visit today. I will send my chauffeur for you tomorrow morning in time for us all to attend church together.'

'Sir.' Kirsty turned to Brewster when he entered the charge room after her. 'One interview remains outstanding. The Reverend Josiah Petrie. When do you plan to do it?'

She hoped he wouldn't say tomorrow or she would incite her

father's anger and disappoint her mother.

Perhaps Brewster saw something in her expression because he replied, 'I think that can wait until Monday morning. Once you've written up today's interviews you can finish up until then.'

Kirsty's shoulders relaxed as relief swept through her. She would be able to keep her promise to her mother and father.

Brewster hovered in the doorway of Kirsty's office. 'I'm off home,' he said, 'and it's time you finished up as well.'

'Almost finished, sir. Just completing the last report.'

'Right. Leave them on my desk and I'll look at them tomorrow.'

'Yes, sir.' Kirsty waited until she heard the charge room door slam before laying her pencil on the desk and gathering the reports together. She had finished writing them half an hour ago but had been waiting for Brewster to leave because she wanted to check something out.

A clock somewhere to her left struck seven o'clock as she strode in the direction of the Scouringburn. She'd never ventured into this part of the town on her own before but she felt safe despite its fearsome reputation. It was too early for the rowdy element to be abroad and as long as she didn't linger with Elsie and Daisy she should not come to any harm.

She hesitated for a moment when she reached Aggie's building. The police guard had been stood down and the opening of the close, leading to the rear of the tenement, appeared darker and more forbidding than usual. Bracing her shoulders, she entered the passageway and hurried through. The sound of her footsteps echoed after her, eerie and menacing in the darkness, and she heaved a sigh of relief when she emerged into the open air and the gloom lessened.

The backlands loomed in front of her and with each rustle in the lank grass images of a killer on the prowl surfaced in her mind. But she repressed them and hastily climbed the stairs.

Elsie answered the door after her first knock.

'More questions?'

'Yes, I wanted to check something with you and Daisy.'

Elsie stubbed her cigarette on the doorpost. 'I'll go and get her.'

She left the door open and, after a moment's hesitation, Kirsty walked into the flat. The last time she visited, on the morning after Lily's murder, girls filled every corner of the room. Now empty, it allowed her to appreciate Elsie's home-making skills which were obviously far better than Kirsty's. The clean and tidy room with a cheery fire burning in the grate contained a table, covered with a linen tablecloth, on which the remains of Elsie's evening meal rested. And the patchwork quilt covering the bed was hand sewn. There was nothing tawdry about the room and it was as unlike a doxy's bedroom as it was possible to be.

Voices echoed along the landing outside, heralding the arrival of Elsie and Daisy. Elsie burst through the door and dashed over to the fire to warm her hands. 'Bleeding cold outside,' she said.

Daisy sidled in behind her and stood front of the window. 'You wanted to see us?' Her voice was quiet and hesitant.

Kirsty consulted the notebook she'd pulled out of her pocket. 'Yes. We've been investigating Lily and her background and something puzzles us. She seems to have acquired a lot of money as well as property and we wondered about that. I thought you might know whether she had a source of income other than what she earned here.'

'That's news to me,' Elsie said. 'What about you, Daisy?'

Daisy shook her head. 'I knew she was making plans to start her own house but I thought it was a dream. One of Lily's big ideas.'

'There has been a suggestion she blackmailed some of her customers.'

Elsie laughed. 'Fat chance of that. If she had been, Aggie would have sorted it. She doesn't put up with any shenanigans does our Aggie, otherwise, we'd all be filthy rich.'

'Maybe a wealthy lover?'

'Not many of them going around,' Daisy said. 'And if there were, we'd all be fighting over him.'

'I see. What about Angus Laidlaw?'

Daisy and Elsie exchanged glances. 'What about him?'

'We interviewed Angus Laidlaw and we understand he was having a relationship with Lily. You never mentioned that the last time we talked.'

'We didn't think it important. He wasn't a customer, just someone she fancied.' Elsie paused. 'He didn't have money if that's what you're thinking.'

'But you warned him about the investigation.'

'That's a bit steep, miss. It wasn't a warning. But he needed to be told Lily was dead. It was the Christian thing to do.'

Daisy cut in. 'We've told you everything we know, miss.' Tears filled her eyes. 'I miss Lily and if I knew anything I'd tell you.' Her voice shook. 'I want her killer caught. It wasn't right what he did to her.'

Elsie put her arm around Daisy's shoulder. 'I think you should go now, miss. If we think of anything we'll come to you.'

Kirsty slipped her notebook into her pocket. She would get nothing more from them. 'Make sure you stay safe,' she said as she left. 'Until we catch him, a killer remains on the loose.'

46

Sunday, 14 December 1919

The engine sputtered twice before lapsing into silence.

'The police station is further along,' David said. 'When you come to the arch, walk through into the courtyard and the door is on your left.'

Jessie's grip tightened on the envelope in her hand. 'Are you sure this is the right thing to do?'

'Yes,' he said. 'Mary wants to see her and this is the quickest way.'

Jessie thought of the note which David dictated and doubts percolated through her mind. She wasn't comfortable with lies, no matter how white they were.

'But it seems dishonest.'

'Not at all. It's simply a way of ensuring the policewoman visits today instead of waiting until tomorrow.'

She looked at him but David turned his head away which made her more self-conscious than ever about her squint. Her heart ached because she knew he loved the rest of the family but not her. If only he would love her, couldn't he understand she would do anything for him?

'Hurry,' he said, 'we don't want the girls to be on their own too long.'

Jessie hesitated with her hand on the door handle.

'What if the policewoman's there? What do I say?'

'It's Sunday, she won't be there. You leave the note and then come back here. We need to get back as quick as we can.'

Jessie's mind continued to be troubled as she scurried up the road and through the arch into the courtyard. She halted in front of the closed door to the police station and thought it might be locked, but it opened as soon as she touched the handle.

'Yes, miss. Is there something I can do for you?'

The man behind the counter looked huge in his police uniform and his eyes bored into her sending fear pulsating through her.

Jessie took a step back. Heat rose from her legs up through her body to her face.

'I have a message for the policewoman.' She forced the words from her lips.

'The policewoman, is it?' The man leaned on the top of the long counter making her take another step backwards. 'She isn't here on a Sunday.'

'Can you give her this?'

He turned and placed the envelope in a pigeonhole at his back.

'No!' Panic made her voice stronger. 'She has to get it today. It's important.'

'Too important to wait until tomorrow?'

'It's about my Aunt Mary,' Jessie whispered. 'She's Lily's mum, the girl who was murdered. And it can't wait, not less you want another one on your hands.'

Jessie turned and fled the office. She didn't stop running until she reached the car.

Kirsty's wardrobe of civilian clothes was sparse because she preferred to wear her police uniform. But she wanted to keep her promise to her parents that she would return to the family home today and attend church with them.

She wavered between a blue ensemble or a brown one, eventually selecting a midnight blue skirt and a fuchsia high-necked blouse which she pulled on before she changed her mind.

The knock on the door startled her. She opened it expecting to see her father's chauffeur but instead, it was a young fresh-faced police constable who stood on the threshold.

'Sorry to disturb you, miss, but a young lady left this envelope for you at the police station.'

Kirsty took the envelope he handed her. 'It's been opened,' she said.

'Yes, miss. The duty sergeant needed to check whether it was as important as the young lady said.' He shuffled his feet. 'If that's all, miss?'

'Yes. You can go.'

After the constable clattered down the stairs, Kirsty removed the note from the envelope. Jessie's words left her in no doubt Mary Petrie was in danger. She recalled her suspicions about Josiah. Now, with this letter in her hand, she knew she had not been mistaken and if she did nothing, Mary could end up as dead as her daughter.

Kirsty grabbed her coat, and her blue cloche hat, and bolted from the room.

She ran most of the way to the police station and burst through the door gasping for breath. 'Brewster,' she wheezed. 'Is he in today?'

'No, miss. He takes his wife to church on a Sunday. He's never here in the morning. Sometimes he looks in during the afternoon. Just checking like.'

'I can't wait until afternoon.' She slammed the letter on the counter. 'If he comes in you can tell him I've gone to Montrose.'

'Would you like a constable to accompany you, miss?'

Kirsty thought she detected a sneer in Hamish's voice. He would love her to admit she couldn't cope on her own.

'I think I'll manage,' she snapped and slammed out of the office.

Troubled thoughts flitted through Jessie's mind on the drive back to Broughty Ferry. What was so important her Aunt Mary needed to see the policewoman today? Why couldn't it wait until tomorrow? And the lie about the Reverend Petrie being mad plagued her. Uncle Josiah was strict but not mad. He shouted a lot but he never hit anyone no matter how much they aggravated him.

She shouldn't have agreed to write and deliver the note. But she would do anything for David so when he asked her, she couldn't refuse. Now, she regretted it. What would the policewoman think of her when she found out?

David brought the motor car to a stop outside the manse. 'I'll leave you here,' he said. 'You can look after the girls until I get back.'

Jessie swivelled in her seat to stare at him. 'Aren't you coming in?'

'No, I need to do something first.'

'But, the church service...'

'The curate will take it.' He gave her a push. 'Out you go, I need to hurry.'

Jessie stood on the pavement watching as the car pulled away. What was David up to?

Rose met her at the door of the manse. 'I heard the car stop,' she said, 'and I wanted to speak to Uncle David.'

'He's gone, I'm afraid.'

'When will he be back?'

'I don't know. He didn't say.'

She put her arm around Rose's shoulders. At fifteen she was a beauty already, a younger version of Lily. Jessie hoped she would be luckier than Lily.

'Where is Iris?' Jessie guided Rose inside the manse and closed the door.

'She's in the bedroom and she's been crying ever since he left with you this morning.'

'We'd better find out what's ailing her.'

Iris lay sobbing on the bed. Jessie had never seen her so upset and she walked over to the child and put her arm around her shoulders. 'What's wrong?'

'I love Uncle David and he said he loved me but he took you in the car and left me here.' She glared at Jessie with hate-filled eyes and pushed her away. 'You took him away and he hasn't come back.'

Jessie looked at her with dismay. What on earth was going through the child's mind? She was only twelve, a slight waif-like child who should be playing with dolls not thinking about how much anyone loved her.

'I'm sure we all love you.'

'I don't want your love and neither does Uncle David. He

said you were a freak with your squinty eyes.'

Jessie froze. She drew back from Iris. 'I'm sure he said no such thing.'

'Yes, he did.' Iris's voice sounded petulant. The voice of a child lashing out at an enemy or rival.

Pain gripped Jessie's heart. Had David really said that? She didn't want to believe it but she'd known the child since birth. Iris never lied.

Rose, stood in the doorway. How much did she hear?

Jessie shrugged and patted Rose's shoulder before leaving the bedroom. 'I can't do anything,' she said, 'maybe you can calm her down.'

She walked downstairs and through to the sitting room. After collapsing into an armchair she allowed tears to roll down her cheeks. David had never loved her but to be told he thought her a freak was more than she could bear.

When she stopped crying she started to think about the note David made her leave for Kirsty. It was a lie but he persuaded her and told her it was for the best. But what if it wasn't? Snippets of things overheard surfaced in her mind and her previous doubts returned. Her misgivings convinced her she should never have complied with his wishes.

It might not be too late to rectify the situation. She would go to Dundee and explain and maybe the policewoman wouldn't think badly of her.

Without thinking it through, she jumped out of the chair and sped to the hall. 'I'm going out, Rose,' she shouted up the stairs but didn't wait for an answer. She grabbed her hat and jacket from the coat stand, pulling them on as she ran out the door.

She kept running until she was out of breath and then slowed to a walk. When she reached the tram terminus she searched her pockets for coins but found nothing. With no money, boarding a tram was out of the question and meant walking to the police station.

She hoped she wouldn't be too late to prevent the policewoman going to Montrose.

47

The words from Jessie's note were engraved on Kirsty's mind as she cranked the starting handle of Brewster's car. 'Aunt Mary is in trouble. She thinks the minister's gone mad.'

The engine roared to life and Kirsty jumped into the driver's seat. First gear engaged, with a nerve-jangling crunch. It wasn't meant to make a noise like that but her hand tightened on the steering wheel and she guided the car through the archway that led to the street outside.

A horse pulling a cart clopped towards her and she waited for it to pass before she turned right on to West Bell Street. When she arrived at the junction with the main road she had to wait again for a tram to clank past and, gritting her teeth, she turned left to follow it. She'd never driven a car in a town centre before which made her uncertain whether to pass the tram on the inside or pull out to the middle of the road. However, she didn't want to take any chances so she stopped each time the tram did. It eventually reached the end of the line and she came to a halt behind it. Considering her options she decided she either had to pull out to the middle of the road or stay here forever.

Taking a deep breath she grabbed the steering wheel, closed her eyes and steered towards the middle of the road. Opening them again she drove past the tram and only when she pulled in to her own side of the road did she breathe more easily.

The rest of the drive to Montrose was uneventful although she might have enjoyed it more had she not been worrying about Mary Petrie. But, at last, she drew in outside the gate leading to the manse. After pulling on the handbrake she wiped her sweaty hands on her coat before alighting from the car.

The gate creaked open and Kirsty hesitated before entering. The house, cloaked in shadow from the height of the wall and the trees in the orchard behind, sent out a menacing aura that struck a chill through her. She wiped her hands on her coat again and ached for the comfort of her uniform. Without it, she felt vulnerable.

But this was silly. She was Kirsty Campbell, policewoman, whether or not she wore her uniform. Taking a deep breath, she straightened her shoulders, clanged the gate shut behind her and marched up the path.

Mary Petrie answered the door to Kirsty's knock. 'Thank goodness you're here,' she said. 'Josiah has been raving. He seems to blame me for Lily's death.'

'Why would he blame you?'

A tear rolled down Mary's cheek. 'I don't know. But I think he may have had a brainstorm. He cursed and shouted and threw things around and his face was so red it looked fit to burst. I feared he would strike me.'

She placed her hand on Mary's arm. 'Perhaps if I talked to him?'

'Would you?'

'Of course. Is he in his study?'

Kirsty stepped over the threshold meaning to confront the Reverend Josiah in his lair but Mary blocked her path.

'No, miss. He's gone out to make pastoral visits but I'm scared of what he'll do when he comes back.'

'I'll stay here with you,' Kirsty said, 'and I won't let him assault you. Where can we wait?'

'The sitting room, miss. It's quiet in there.'

Mary led the way. 'I sent the children to their Uncle David. I thought it best until Josiah calms down.'

Kirsty perched on the sofa. 'The last time I came here your husband claimed Lily was no longer part of the family. He went so far as to say she was no daughter of his. What has happened for him to become so angry?'

'Before he disowned Lily, she was his favourite daughter. He never paid much heed to Rose or Iris but he treated Lily different. Anything she wanted he made sure she got and when he went on his pastoral visits he often took her with him. I think her death hit him hard although he would never admit that.'

The suspicion Kirsty had been harbouring ever since the interview with Billy Allardyce, hardened, and she wondered how she would broach it with Mary.

'When you came to see me you indicated Billy Allardyce was responsible for Lily's pregnancy.'

'That's right. Josiah should have allowed them to marry and if he had, Lily would still be alive.' Mary scrubbed at her face with a handkerchief.

'I don't want to cause you any distress but I've interviewed Billy and he denied being the father even though he would have married her.'

'He's lying. He was the one responsible.' Mary's posture changed. Her body stiffened and she clamped her hands on the arms of the chair. Her eyes flashed defiance.

At that moment, Kirsty became convinced Mary knew the identity of the father and it was much nearer home than Billy Allardyce.

'Perhaps,' Kirsty hesitated before continuing, 'your husband may have been responsible.'

Mary's face crumpled and her body slumped. 'That's not possible,' she said, her voice no more than a whisper.

'Perhaps he's been keeping secrets from you.'

'He always kept secrets from us.' Mary's voice strengthened. 'He keeps a private room at the top of the house which the rest of us are not allowed to enter. But, in his hurry this morning he left the door ajar.'

'Did you look inside?'

'No. I was on the point of doing that when you knocked at the door.'

'I think we need to find out what your husband is hiding.'

Mary rose from her chair. 'Follow me,' she said, 'we'll do it before he comes back.'

Pale light from a window on the stair landing illuminated their way to the first floor. Kirsty guessed there were bedrooms behind the closed doors apart from one that clearly led to the attic stairs. Mary opened this door and beckoned to her to go ahead. Her footsteps clattered on the steep wooden steps leading to a door at the top which Kirsty pushed open. She hesitated in the doorway, waiting for Mary to join her.

A blow to her back sent her stumbling into the room. Then the door crashed shut and a key grated in the lock.

'I'm sorry,' Mary whispered through the door.

Lower down in the house a door slammed and the sound of Mary's feet thumping down the stairs indicated Kirsty was alone.

She rattled the handle and thumped on the door but it didn't budge and there was no response although she could hear the murmur of voices down below.

Kirsty was trapped.

48

The church bells were ringing when Jessie left Broughty Ferry. A cacophony of noise echoed all over the city as church after church joined in. She plodded on after the bells fell silent but by the time she reached Dundee the services were over and communicants thronged the streets making their way to their respective homes. When she arrived at the police station she was out of breath and her feet were sore.

She staggered into the charge room and leaned on the counter. 'The note I left for the policewoman,' she gasped.

'Yes, miss. You said it was urgent so I sent one of our constables to deliver it.' The large policeman looked at her with concern in his eyes. 'Are you all right, miss? You look out of sorts.'

'I have to stop her going to Montrose.'

'I'm afraid Miss Campbell has already left. The note said it was urgent.'

'But I made a mistake. She might be in danger. You have to stop her.' The mouthful of air Jessie gasped in, sliced through her chest. She was too late.

'I'm sure it will be all right, miss. Sit down and get your breath back.'

Jessie slumped on the wooden bench that stretched the length of the wall.

'Stay as long as you like and when Miss Campbell returns I'll tell her you want to see her.' The policeman picked up a pen and returned to his ledgers where he busied himself writing entries.

She stared at him but he ignored her. Gradually, her breathing became less laboured and the pain in her chest decreased. But that was replaced by a myriad of thoughts bombarding her mind.

Her agitation increased. The policeman brushed her concerns away as if they were unimportant. Why would he not listen to her? She lowered her head into her hands and groaned.

Foremost in her thoughts was David. Why did he want the policewoman to go to Montrose? And why arrange for his curate to take the church services? Had David gone to Montrose? And, if so, why?

Fragmented images and memories circled through her mind. Lily's death. Aunt Mary's grief. Rose and Iris's curiosity. And Uncle Josiah's strange behaviour. Everything changed when Lily died.

Odd snippets of conversation came back to plague her. Jessie wasn't proud of her eavesdropping but she couldn't help overhearing things. She remembered Uncle Josiah's vehemence Lily got no more than she deserved and Aunt Mary saying Lily didn't deserve to die no matter her sins.

Uncle David visited more often as well and she recalled overhearing him say to Aunt Mary, 'It was an accident,' and Aunt Mary had been crying while he tried to console her. But how did he know it had been an accident? Is that what the police told him?

Jessie caught her breath as she remembered another conversation where Uncle David said, 'I'm sorry. I didn't mean it. I wanted to teach her a lesson.' Then, a few days later she overheard him tell Aunt Mary the policewoman had been poking around and he thought she knew. None of this meant anything at the time. But now, as the connection with Lily's death hit her, a shudder travelled through her body. Did that mean he'd killed Lily? And if that was true, would he do the same to the policewoman? But how could she convince the policeman?

A cold air whistled through the charge room when the door opened. The tall man who entered removed his hat to reveal unruly reddish-brown hair. 'I wish to speak to Detective Inspector Brewster,' he said laying his hat on the counter.

'I'm afraid the detective inspector is not available, sir. Can I help you with anything?'

'I'm trying to find my daughter, she didn't turn up for

church today and she's not at home.'

'I'm sure she'll turn up, sir.'

'I thought she might be working,' the man said. 'My daughter is Miss Campbell who works here.'

'Ah! I think I might know where she is.'

Jessie had heard enough. Maybe the policeman wasn't interested but she was sure this gentleman would listen to her.

She jumped off the bench and thumped on the counter. 'This bobby won't listen to me but he'll listen to you.' She thumped the counter again and glared at the desk sergeant. 'You have to listen to me now,' she shouted. 'Else the policewoman's death will be on your conscience.'

'You know where Kirsty is?' The man gripped her shoulder.

'Yes, she's gone off to Montrose and Lily's killer is waiting for her there. But the bobby wouldn't listen to me.'

The man straightened. 'Get Detective Inspector Brewster immediately,' he said.

Jessie slumped back onto the bench. At last, someone had listened to her. But would they be in time?

49

'You're getting to be quite the cook,' Maggie said as Brewster placed a second slice of roast beef on her plate.

'Maybe you'd better taste it first before you say things like that.' He poured gravy over the meat which nestled beside mashed potatoes and cabbage. 'It's nice being able to spend a day together.'

He laid down his knife and fork when the sound of knocking echoed up the hallway into the living room.

'I think you may have spoken too soon.' Maggie turned her wheelchair sideways.

Brewster pushed it back into position. 'You keep on eating. Just because I've only had two mouthfuls doesn't mean you stop.'

A tall man accompanied by a police constable stood on the doorstep. 'Mr Campbell,' Brewster said. 'What brings you here?'

Words poured out of the man. 'Kirsty is missing and there's a girl at the police station who thinks she might be in danger.'

Kirsty's father didn't appear to be the type of man who panicked easily but Brewster could hear the anxiety in his voice, as well as see it in his eyes. His habitual stoop was gone, replaced by rigidity, and he clenched and unclenched his fists as he spoke.

'I'll get my coat.' Brewster grabbed it before looking into the living room where Maggie sat in her wheelchair. 'Sorry, my love, duty calls.'

He didn't wait for her reply but stalked back to the front door while wrestling his arms into the coat sleeves. The door slammed behind him and he strode down the garden path to join Kirsty's father who was holding the gate open. The police constable trotted behind them.

'I left the car on Constitution Road.' The older man had no trouble keeping up with Brewster as they hurried along the lane.

When they emerged from the lane the chauffeur jumped out of the driver's seat to open the car door for them. Within a few minutes, Brewster was striding into the police station, followed by Robert Campbell.

The girl, huddled on the bench, in the corner of the charge room, looked up when they entered. She reminded him of the waifs who frequented the Overgate. The expression on her face was the same but she was better dressed.

'Jessie wanted to leave,' the duty sergeant said, 'but Mr Campbell said she was to stay here and talk to you first.'

She looked up at him and he noted her squint as well as the tears on her cheeks. The girl seemed terrified.

Brewster sat down beside her. The girl edged away from him, tucking herself further into the corner. 'You have nothing to be afraid of,' he said, 'you are safe here.' He paused for a moment, reluctant to pressure her into telling him what he wanted to know.

'But I did something wrong,' she whispered. Her eyes widened and she stared into Brewster's face. 'I didn't mean for the policewoman to be hurt.' She looked away again, fixing her gaze on the floor.

'Why do you think she will be hurt?' He resisted the urge to hurry the girl. If she took fright and stopped speaking he would be unable to get to the bottom of this.

'My letter to her was a lie.' Jessie's eyes were anguished as she looked up at him. 'I didn't mean to send her into danger.'

'I have the letter here, sir.' The duty sergeant slid it across the counter.

Brewster rose, picked it up and returned to the bench where he unfolded the sheet of paper.

'What I don't understand is why you wrote it,' he said after reading the words.

'Uncle David said I should. He said Aunt Mary wanted to talk to her but the policewoman wouldn't go there today without a reason and if I said Uncle Josiah was having a brainstorm she would want to help Aunt Mary.'

Brewster pondered on her explanation. 'So, the part saying Josiah had lost his reason isn't true and your aunt is not in any danger.'

'That's right, sir.'

He still couldn't understand why that put Kirsty in danger. 'In that case, Kirsty can't be walking into a dangerous situation.'

'You don't understand, sir. The danger isn't Uncle Josiah, it's Uncle David.'

'I think you need to explain.'

Jessie twisted her hands together. 'I didn't want to believe it because Uncle David is nice. But I started thinking about why he wanted me to write the letter to the policewoman and why he was keen to send her to Montrose to see Aunt Mary. Then I started to remember things I'd overheard when he was talking to my aunt but it was only when I pieced them together I realized what they meant.'

Tears trickled down her cheeks.

Brewster waited for her to continue although worry niggled at him and his anxiety for Kirsty mounted.

'I love Uncle David and I don't want to be disloyal to him but if he's done what I think he's done...' Jessie broke down, sobbing loudly.

'What do you think he's done?' Brewster felt like shaking the information out of her but he restrained himself.

'I think he killed Lily. I heard him tell Aunt Mary it was an accident and I also heard him tell her the policewoman knew and they'd have to do something about her.' Jessie gulped and dashed tears from her face with the back of her hands. 'That's why I think the policewoman is in danger.' She buried her face in her hands and sobbed.

Brewster grasped her shoulder and shook her. 'The address, Jessie? Where has Kirsty gone?'

Jessie stuttered out the address.

He let go of her shoulder. 'Stay here until I return.'

'I can't,' she said. 'My cousins are at Uncle David's manse and they're children. I must get back to them.'

The duty sergeant came out from behind the counter. 'I'll

arrange something for Jessie.'

Brewster turned to him. 'I need you to telephone Montrose Police Station. Inform the sergeant there of the situation and order him to go to the Bents Road address to check on Kirsty's safety. After that, contact Sergeant Brodie and tell him to arrange a police escort to take Jessie back to the manse to collect the children.'

Jessie rose from the bench and plucked at his sleeve. 'The girls won't want to leave until their mother comes.'

'Very well. A squad of policemen will be required to remain there until further notice in case David Walker turns up.'

He placed a hand on Jessie's arm. 'If you are to be believed, your uncle could be dangerous.'

Turning to the duty sergeant he ordered, 'Tell Sergeant Brodie that when Walker arrives he must be detained and allowed no contact with Jessie or the children.'

'We'll take my car.' Robert Campbell headed for the door, holding it open for Brewster who followed them out. Kirsty's father gestured to the chauffeur to start the engine. When they were on the point of getting in, the charge room door opened and the duty sergeant shouted to them. 'The Montrose office is not answering the telephone.'

Brewster paused with his foot on the running board. 'Send a telegram and keep on telephoning until you do get an answer.' He jumped into the Arrol-Johnstone Tourer and said, 'I hope your chauffeur knows how to drive fast.'

50

Mary hesitated a moment after turning the key in the lock. 'I'm sorry,' she whispered leaning her brow on the door.

Downstairs a door slammed. He was back. Mary clattered down the attic stairs, closing her ears to the sound of Kirsty's voice and the thumps on the locked door.

He raised his eyebrows in a silent question when she joined him on the ground floor.

'She's locked in,' she said. 'The attic door is too sturdy for her to break down.'

He smiled his approval. 'You know what you have to do now.'

'Must I?'

'Yes, if you want us to be safe.'

'Very well,' she said.

The box of matches sat on the hall table. She shook it, listening to the matches rattling inside.

'Start with the bedrooms,' he said.

The sound of Kirsty's voice and her attempts to force open the door became louder when she reached the first floor. Mary glanced at the attic stairs, drawn by Kirsty's pleas, but having gone this far she couldn't afford to respond. Resolutely, she walked into Rose's bedroom and held a lighted match to the curtains. Then she repeated the process in all the other bedrooms.

She scurried back downstairs and entering each room, in turn, she set fire to the curtains. Flames licked upwards, at first slowly and then with gathering speed until they became a fireball. Smoke blackened the window glass and billowed back into the room, catching in Mary's throat, compelling her to run.

'It's done,' she said when she returned to the hall.

He dropped a kiss on her forehead, grasped her hand and

pulled her out of the house.

'We must make haste,' he said, 'the girls are waiting.'

Mary took one final look at the house where she'd spent all her married life before following him through the gate to the road outside.

Kirsty rattled the doorknob and pounded on the door until her hands became numb with the force of the blows. The house was silent although earlier the sound of a slamming door had sent Mary scuttling downstairs. The slam and the rumble of voices indicated someone else was in the house.

Had Josiah returned? Was Mary safe? And was that why she had imprisoned Kirsty in the attic? It didn't make sense. Kirsty couldn't protect her if she couldn't get out.

After one final thump and rattle of the knob, Kirsty gave up. The solid oak door would never budge no matter how much she hammered.

She turned to survey her prison, a long room with sloping eaves which spanned the length of the house with small windows recessed into the eaves. Two of these windows faced the front of the house and the other two looked out to the orchard at the back. Chimney breasts protruded into the room at either end. Apart from an ancient trunk and a broken chair, the attic room was empty and contained nothing she could use to help her escape.

In desperation, Kirsty opened the trunk hoping to find something she could use to break the door down but it only held old clothes. She slammed the lid down and hurried to the windows overlooking the street outside. She glimpsed two women at the other side of the wall. Their hats, the only thing she could see of them, swayed and bounced as they chatted. Banging the window to attract their attention produced no result and eventually, the women parted company and walked off.

The windows opposite looked out to the orchard where massive apple trees stretched bare branches out to each other in a leafless embrace. A ladder perched against one of them was too far away to be of any use. In any case, no matter how hard

Kirsty pushed at the window frames they refused to slide up and open.

She returned to the door but it still wouldn't budge.

'Mary,' she shouted, over and over again but received no response. Next, she placed her ear against it, hoping to detect some sound from the silent house. It was a vain hope. Bending down, she peered through the keyhole to find out whether Mary had left the key in the lock but she had a clear line of sight down the stairs to the closed door at the bottom.

A faint whiff of smoke reached her nostrils before she stood up. She bent down again to the keyhole and sniffed. Yes, that was smoke she smelled. Maybe it was coming from the chimney breasts at each end of the room. She walked to each of them in turn but the stone was cold when she placed her hands on them.

The smell intensified when she returned to the door and when she looked through the keyhole she saw tentacles of smoke drifting underneath the door at the bottom of the attic stairs.

Wind whistled under the canvas top of the automobile. Shivering, Brewster rested his arm on the top of the rear door and leaned forward to speak to the chauffeur. 'Can't you drive any faster,' he demanded, clutching the door as the car veered around a corner.

'I'm going as fast as I can, sir.' The driver's words were whipped away by the wind.

Kirsty's father sat in silence beside him although Brewster noted his clenched hands and tight lips.

'I'm sure it will be all right,' Brewster shouted, over the noise of the car engine, trying hard to convince himself.

'Kirsty has always been headstrong. Even as a child she was defiant and would go her own way.' Robert Campbell pulled the travelling rug closer to his body.

'I've noticed,' Brewster said.

Kirsty's insubordination was the most aggravating aspect of her personality. He had thought she was settling into her role as a Dundee policewoman and statement taker. But she always wanted more. She wanted to conduct the investigations and when he didn't agree with her she went off and did it anyway. If she would tell him what she was up to he could protect her from the dangerous situations she attracted.

He sighed and tucked his share of the rug around his shoulders. He would never understand Kirsty. He leaned back against the leather upholstery and tried to suppress his anxiety as the car sped out of Dundee.

51

Nancy Allardyce stumbled over the ruts in India Lane in her anxiety to get home. Gran would be looking for her dinner. She could swear the old woman had an alarm clock inside her stomach, dictating when she would eat, and she got fractious when meals weren't on time.

A smell of smoke hung in the air which even the aroma of horse manure emanating from the stables failed to disguise. She hoped the chimney wasn't on fire again. Ever since her dad passed away last year there had been no one to climb on the roof and put the flue brushes down. Maybe now Billy was home he'd do it.

Her eyes scanned the roof as she pushed the gate open but there was only the usual wisp of smoke. If there was a fire it must be somewhere else.

Gran sat at the table dipping her spoon into a bowl of soup which she slurped with gusto while Billy lounged in a chair beside the fireplace.

'Our Billy heated soup for me.' The old woman waved her spoon in the air. 'Couldn't wait for you to come back from your gallivanting.'

Billy looked up. 'She was moaning that much I had to do something.'

Nancy was still thinking about the smoke. She cast an anxious glance at the fire. Their chimney must be in sore need of cleaning. What if it caught fire?

'Billy, there's a fire somewhere near and it set me wondering about our chimney. D'you think you could go on the roof and have a look?'

'I won't be able to put the flue brushes down it while the fire's lit,' he said, 'but I'll have a look if you want although I don't know what good it will do.'

'It will put my mind at rest.'

She followed him along the narrow path at the left of the cottage which led round to the back of the building. This was where a coal cellar, the lavatory, the wash-house, and a shed had been built against the dividing wall between their house and the manse grounds. Inside the shed, hooks shackled the ladder to the rear wall.

Billy unhooked it, carried it to the path and propped it against the cottage before climbing up and onto the roof.

'The chimney looks fine, but the smell of smoke is stronger up here. I think it may be coming from the manse.'

He clambered down and positioned it against the wash-house. He climbed up and vanished out of sight. A moment later he peered down from the roof. 'I was right the manse is on fire. Push the ladder up and I'll go over the wall to check whether anyone is in the house. They might need help.'

'I'll come as well.'

'No, you stay here. Gran might need you.'

'Gran's capable of looking after herself.' Nancy clambered onto the wash-house roof. She turned and grasped the top of the ladder. 'Come on, it'll need the two of us to hoist this thing up.'

They were both out of breath by the time it rested on the roof and it needed all their remaining strength to slide it across and angle it down the other side of the wall.

Nancy sat on the edge of the wash-house roof, where it joined onto the wall, while Billy clambered down. As soon as he reached the ground she turned and followed in his wake.

Billy was already dashing through the orchard trees. So far, she couldn't see any flames but a dense cloud of smoke hovered over the lower part of the house. As she drew nearer a faint crackling sound grew louder and a red glow appeared in the windows.

'I tried thumping on the door,' Billy said, 'but it's red hot. The front of the house is a furnace.'

He darted around the house, peering into windows. Stopping at one near the back of the house, he shouted to Nancy, 'Someone's in here.' Without giving a thought to the danger he shattered the glass with his elbow and slid the window up.

'Don't go in,' she shouted. But she was too late, he had already vanished over the windowsill.

Nancy ran and peered in. Billy was bent over the prone shape of a man and was dragging him to the window. Without releasing his hold he clambered over the sill. 'Help me get him out.'

Between them, they hauled the man out and laid him on the grass underneath one of the apple trees. Billy sank down beside him, gasping for breath.

Nancy bent over the man and put her fingers on his neck to feel for a pulse. She felt nothing but she noticed something strange about his appearance. His soot-streaked face stared up at her with blank eyes but his head lay at an awkward angle and blood trickled over his ear. Fear made her heart beat faster but that did not stop her reaching out and turning his head to see where the blood came from. Then she wished she hadn't. An involuntary gasp escaped her lips and she had a sudden desire to vomit.

'This is no accident,' she said to Billy after she regained her equilibrium. 'He's had a blow to the head.'

'Maybe I knocked it when I hauled him out of the house.' Billy sat up.

'It looks worse than that,' Nancy said. 'I think he's been beaten to death, like Lily.'

The two of them stared at the minister. The Reverend Josiah Petrie didn't look so forbidding in death.

A faint cry echoed through the trees. 'I thought I heard something.' Nancy grasped Billy's arm. 'There it is again.'

52

Smoke caught the back of Kirsty's throat and she doubled over coughing and retching. She couldn't stay in the attic any longer.

She removed her shoe and used it to batter the window until the glass shattered. Then she picked out the rest of the glass and stuck her head out to gulp air into her lungs. It was a tight squeeze but she crawled through the window and perched on the roof slates even though she could see no way to get down to the ground.

Out here, the crackle of the fire down below sounded louder. She panicked and thought about throwing herself off the roof rather than die in the flames. But the ground seemed a long way down.

Tears sprang to Kirsty's eyes and, just when she accepted the hopelessness of her situation, she saw two people drop over the rear wall and sprint through the orchard to the house. She tried shouting but they never looked up at the roof. Instead, they pulled someone out of the house through one of the windows.

When they eventually heard her she didn't know whether to laugh or cry. At least, they knew she was stuck on the roof with no means of getting down to safety. But only a miracle could save her now and Kirsty didn't believe in miracles.

Billy waved and shouted something but she couldn't hear over the crackle of flames. They ran back to the wall and reappeared with a ladder. But even before they propped it against the house Kirsty could see it was too short.

She sat back on the roof tiles. This was one mess she wasn't going to get out of.

They carried the ladder back to the orchard and Billy set it against the apple tree nearest to the house. He hoisted himself into it and climbed up to a higher branch before gesturing to Nancy. She shouted something before grasping a lower one and scrabbling up to join him.

What were they doing? The tree was too far away for him to reach her at the edge of the roof. But now, both of them seemed to be trying to hoist the ladder into it.

An inkling of what they were attempting, struck her. But would it work?

She watched as they manoeuvred it higher and higher up into the tree, using the branches to stabilize its progress. The ladder swayed into position on a strong branch midway up. Billy and Nancy retained their hold and sat on adjoining branches to wedge it into place against the trunk before swinging it towards the house and angling it upwards in her direction.

Kirsty held her breath and thought about the strength needed to do that. She was sure the ladder would slip out of their grasp before it reached her.

Whether by luck or good judgement, it fell into position at the edge of the roof resting on the iron gutter and sloping down to the tree where it was supported by a thick branch and wedged against the trunk.

'Crawl across,' Billy shouted. 'I can't come for you because it won't hold the weight of two people.'

Kirsty knelt and grasped both sides. The ladder felt secure although it only rested on the iron guttering. But what if the guttering gave way? The ground was a long way down.

She sat back on her heels to consider her options. Stay here and wait for the fire brigade? But there was no sign of them yet and the flames had crept dangerously close to the attic. Billowing smoke nipped her eyes and caught in her throat. If she waited too long she would die although it was a toss-up whether the flames or the smoke would get her first.

Her other option was to crawl along the ladder to the safety of the tree but if it gave way she would plunge to her death on the stone path below.

Smoke enveloped her and, choking and spluttering, she leaned forward and started to crawl. But when she reached the second rung her skirt snagged under her legs and refused to move at the same time as her knees. The ladder swayed as she sat back on her heels in an attempt to release it. Grasping the sides she waited a moment until the swaying stopped, then she inched the skirt from below her knees. Once she freed the material from under her legs she tucked it into her waistband. This was no time for modesty. Now her legs moved without any constraints, she crawled along the ladder, counting each rung she came to and keeping her eyes off the ground below.

'Come along, miss. You need to hurry.'

Billy's anxious voice floated to her from the tree. She looked over to him. The smoke, thicker now, made her eyes stream and caught in her throat. But she saw enough to notice he had averted his eyes. Not that this mattered when her life was at stake.

Her chest ached and her breath rasped in her ears, but she continued to crawl, one rung at a time, although moving faster made the ladder sway more beneath her weight. She had no idea how far she had crawled or how far she still had to go. More smoke billowed up, searing into her lungs in choking mouthfuls. Her head spun.

She wasn't going to make it.

But, at least she'd tried.

53

Billy leaned all his weight on the end of the ladder in an effort to control the swaying when Kirsty commenced her precarious downward descent.

At one point he thought she would fall off when she hooked her skirt up out of her way. A brief flash of her undergarments made him look away for a moment but the swaying of the ladder convinced him he had to remain observant and he concentrated on encouraging her to keep moving.

'I'm afraid to look.' Nancy perched below him on a lower branch.

'It's her only chance,' Billy said.

The ladder swayed but Kirsty continued to crawl along it, one rung at a time. Behind her, the flames had reached the attic and were shooting out of the window behind her.

'Come along miss, you need to hurry.' Billy tried to keep the panic out of his voice but his eyes streamed with the smoke drifting towards them as he watched the flames creep nearer to the other end of the ladder.

'I don't think she's going to make it,' Nancy said. 'The smoke's getting thicker and she's slowing down.'

'She's almost here.' Billy stared at Kirsty willing her to keep going. His eyes widened and his heart leapt when she collapsed, just out of his reach.

'You're almost there,' he shouted but she didn't move.

'Look.' Nancy pointed to the roof.

Flames licked out of the attic window and down the slates it would be seconds before they reached the ladder.

Billy's heart thumped. Kirsty was near but not near enough.

'Hold my feet, Nancy. I'll try to reach her.'

He stretched his body along the rungs without waiting to see if his sister complied. But still, he couldn't reach her.

He wriggled further along until he could grasp her wrists. The ladder swayed under their weight.

'Pull my feet back,' he yelled and at the same time slid backwards pulling Kirsty with him.

Billy reached the safety of the tree before the ladder crashed to the ground but Kirsty was still on the end and her body dangled below him.

He hung on to her wrists. 'Grab her body, Nancy. Between us, we can try to lower her to the ground.'

Minutes later, they laid Kirsty on the grass although Billy couldn't understand how they'd managed it.

The clang of the fire engine bell penetrated the fug in Kirsty's brain.

Where was she? The last thing she remembered was struggling to reach the end of the ladder with the smoke affecting her balance and her conviction she was dying.

She opened her eyes but couldn't focus on the face hovering over her and tears dripped down her cheeks. A hand grabbed hers when she tried to wipe them away.

'Don't,' the voice said, 'you'll rub soot into your eyes and make them worse.'

Something hard pressed against her back and when she placed her hands on the ground she felt grass between her fingers.

'Where am I?' Her voice rasped from her chest in knife-sharp croaks.

'You're in the orchard. We've carried you as far away from the fire as possible. There's not as much smoke here.'

Kirsty struggled to sit up and shook her head to clear the mist inside.

A hand went around her shoulders. 'Lean on me until you get your balance back.' It was a woman's voice this time.

Gradually her vision cleared and she saw Nancy and Billy kneeling in front of her.

'How did I get here? I was on the ladder and everything went black.'

'Billy crawled along and pulled you towards the tree. After that, we lowered you to the ground and carried you here.'

A paroxysm of coughing overtook Kirsty and she leaned her head on Nancy's shoulder.

'Then I have you both to thank for my life.' She flinched with the pain of talking.

Billy stood. 'The fire engine has arrived at last but the house is beyond saving. Part of the roof caved in a few minutes ago.'

Kirsty blinked and through the haze of smoke observed firemen, congregating in front of the house, directing water jets on the building in a vain attempt to quench the flames.

Billy strode off in their direction but returned within a short time with a burly man in police uniform. 'Sergeant McPhee tells me he is in charge. He wants to know how the fire started.' A look of concern crossed his face and he placed his hand on Kirsty's arm. 'Are you recovered enough to answer his questions, miss?'

Kirsty lifted her head off Nancy's shoulder and smiled at him. 'I'm fine.'

McPhee squared his shoulders and twitched his mouth, making his walrus moustache waggle. He pulled a notebook from his pocket and brandished a pencil at them. 'I'll need to take witness statements.' His gaze lingered on Kirsty. 'Billy has already told me his version of how he and Nancy came to be involved and, although I know them, I can't say I know you, miss.'

Kirsty met the policeman's stare but felt at a disadvantage sitting on the ground while he towered over her.

'Help me up,' she said to Nancy. 'I feel stupid sitting here.'

Sergeant McPhee tapped his pencil on his notebook while she struggled to her feet. 'When you're ready, miss.'

Despite the wobble in her legs, Kirsty stood erect. She was almost as tall as the policeman in front of her. 'I am Kirsty Campbell. I'm a policewoman with Dundee City Police.' Each word was an effort and she had to suppress the desire to cough.

'And what might someone like you be doing in Montrose?'

Kirsty ignored the mixture of disbelief and curiosity that crossed McPhee's face.

'Dundee City Police have been investigating the murder of Lily Petrie and I received a message that her mother, Mary Petrie, was in danger because her husband, the Reverend Josiah Petrie was having a brainstorm.' A coughing fit shook Kirsty and she stopped speaking until it passed. 'I felt it incumbent on me to investigate.'

'I see.' McPhee studied his notes.

Kirsty leaned against Nancy. The coughing fit had weakened her.

'I do not see any other policemen here. Why would that be?'

'I came alone.' She stared into his eyes. 'It was an emergency.'

'I'm afraid I find all this hard to believe.' The walrus moustache waggled. 'I have known the minister for a long time and he is not the type of person to suffer a brainstorm.'

Overcome with exasperation Kirsty straightened to her full height and adopted her most official tone. 'It is immaterial to me what you believe or don't believe. Dundee City Police have reason to suspect Josiah Petrie is responsible for his daughter's murder, therefore, I gave credence to the letter suggesting his wife was in danger.' Her rant was spoiled by the coughing fit that followed.

A triumphant expression crossed McPhee's face. 'Then perhaps you can explain why the minister's body is lying over there with his head beaten to a pulp.'

Kirsty collapsed against Nancy. It wasn't possible. She had been sure he murdered Lily. But if he had also been killed who could have been responsible? She hardly thought it could be Mary Petrie. She was such a gentle woman. On the other hand, Mary locked her in the attic and set fire to the house. And whose voice had she heard? She had assumed it was Josiah's voice but Josiah was dead.

Her head swam and nausea churned in her stomach. She leaned over and retched into the grass.

54

The motor car rumbled over a suspension bridge and followed the road at the other side of the river until they reached the town centre, dominated by a church steeple. Apart from a group of men clustered beneath one of the arches of a building adjacent to the church, the street was empty.

Robert Campbell leaned forward and tapped his chauffeur on the shoulder. 'Dougal, stop here and ask these men how we get to Bents Road.'

'Yes, sir.' The chauffeur guided the car into the side of the road, got out and crossed to the men. After talking to them he jumped into the driver's seat. 'The arch is where we turn off,' he said.

They travelled down the narrow street under the arch, following it until it widened and led them to an area of grassland and parks beyond which were more houses and streets.

Brewster smelled the smoke as they drove between the parks.

'Drive faster,' he shouted above the noise of the engine. A premonition the fire was connected to Kirsty filled him with dread and he leaned forward as if that would make the automobile go faster.

'We're almost there, sir,' the chauffeur said as he turned into Bents Road.

Halfway down the road, a fire engine occupied most of the road. Brewster's heart thumped and he leapt out of the car before it came to a halt. He barged through the gate and stared aghast at the blazing building behind the wall.

He grabbed a fireman by the arm and demanded, 'Is anyone still inside?'

The fireman shook his hand off. 'Don't know. But so far

there is one survivor and one deceased,' he said. 'Sergeant McPhee is taking care of it.' He pointed to the rear of the house. 'Now, if you don't mind I have a job to do.'

He strode to where the man pointed. Voices filtered through the trees and the glimpse of a blue uniform indicated the presence of Sergeant McPhee. The policeman's burly frame blocked Brewster's view as he hurried towards him but he recognized the young man next to him. He couldn't recall his name although he remembered his visit to the police station in Dundee.

'Sergeant McPhee?'

The policeman turned and Brewster's heart lurched as Kirsty came into view.

'Kirsty!' Robert Campbell dashed forward and wrapped his arms around his daughter.

Brewster restrained himself. His concern for Kirsty had filled his mind and he'd been unaware of her father following him after he jumped out of the car and rushed through the gate.

He reached into his jacket and pulled out his warrant card. 'I'm Detective Inspector Brewster, I'm glad you're here. You got my message from Dundee?'

'Message from Dundee?' McPhee looked puzzled.

'Yes, we telephoned to alert you that our policewoman might be heading for a dangerous situation.'

'Ah! She is a policewoman. But I got no message. I came here when we got the alarm about the house being on fire. It's a strange business and there's a body over there.'

He led Brewster to the edge of the orchard where the minister's body lay.

Brewster bent over and examined the injuries. 'This is no fire death. He's been savagely beaten around the head.'

'Yes, sir. That's what I thought.'

'Are there no other survivors?'

'No, sir. And no sign of anyone else in the house although we won't know for sure until the fire is out.'

'Someone will need to identify the body,' Brewster said.

'I can do that for you, sir. I've known him most of my life. He is the Reverend Josiah Petrie. Well respected hereabouts.'

Brewster had suspected as much but the identification made it official.

'I'll be taking responsibility for the investigation,' Brewster said. 'It's connected to one we are conducting in Dundee.'

'Yes, sir. The young lady told me about that.'

McPhee looked relieved, Brewster reckoned he was thankful he didn't have to follow it up.

'We can't leave the body lying here so I will need you to take responsibility for it to be transported to the local mortuary to be kept on ice until the investigation is complete.'

'Yes, sir. I'll arrange for the reverend to be transported to the mortuary at Montrose Infirmary.'

The sound of a gasp made Brewster turn. Kirsty stood behind him supported by her father.

'I had to see for myself,' she said. 'I was certain he was the person we were looking for. But I was mistaken.'

Brewster took no satisfaction from Kirsty's admission and felt sorry for her. Her professionalism and pride suffered a knock by being proved wrong and it revealed the vulnerability which he had always sensed lurking beneath her prickly exterior.

No sign of professionalism remained in the woman standing before him. Kirsty looked beaten. Her clothes were dishevelled and her hair stuck up in spikes while white tear tracks ran down her sooty face. The hand clutching her father's sleeve was grimy and Brewster was convinced that if her father removed his arm she would fall down.

He led her back to the rear of the orchard where the smoke was less intense. 'Sit down, before you collapse.' For a moment, he thought she would argue, but with a shrug of her shoulders, she lowered herself to the grass.

He flopped down beside her. 'Now, tell me what happened?'

Her story was garbled but from what he could gather, Mary had locked her in the attic and set fire to the house. She'd heard a man's voice and assumed it to be Josiah Petrie. Then Billy and Nancy had rescued her.

'I think you should leave,' Brewster said after she finished talking, 'while I finish up things here. Let your father take you home.' He nodded to Robert Campbell. 'Look after her.'

'I would prefer to remain here,' she rasped as a hint of the old Kirsty surfaced.

'That's an order, Campbell.'

'Yes, sir.' Her tone sounded sullen.

A thought struck him as he turned back to the orchard and he shouted after her, 'Where did you leave my motor car?'

Without looking back she answered, 'Outside, on the street, sir. I left the key in the ignition.' Her slumped shoulders and subdued posture reflected an air of defeat.

Brewster watched as she shuffled off and for a moment yearned for a return of the stubborn Kirsty he knew so well.

With a sigh, he turned to Sergeant McPhee. 'Have you taken statements from everyone?'

'Yes, sir, except for the young lady. I was in the middle of that when you arrived.'

Brewster pulled out his notebook. 'If you read out the statements, I'll note them down and don't worry about Miss Campbell. I've taken her statement.'

He started to scribble while McPhee read from his notebook. But his thoughts were elsewhere, worrying about Kirsty and how the recent events and the fire might have affected her.

55

Relief poured through Kirsty when she saw Brewster striding through the orchard.

When her father wrapped his arms around her, for a moment, she wished they had been Brewster's. She dismissed the thought before it took root and relaxed into the safety of the arms holding her.

But the shock of the Reverend Josiah Petrie's murder, combined with Brewster's order which banished her from the scene of the crime, diminished her. These factors stripped her of her professionalism and left her weak and vulnerable and she was thankful for her father's arm around her waist as he walked her out of the orchard.

Memories of her childhood surged through her and, although her parents had never been demonstrative, she recalled the pleasure she felt when he held her hand.

Firemen in yellow jackets and helmets clustered around the front and sides of the house aiming their water hoses on the building. Workmen in dungarees and men in their Sunday suits ran back and forth with buckets, all to little effect. Most of the roof had already caved in with nothing left of the attics.

A whiff of smoke hit her nostrils and Kirsty looked up and shuddered. That's where she would have been if Billy and Nancy hadn't come to her rescue.

The smoke grew denser when they passed the front of the building to reach the gate and she doubled over coughing and retching again. Her father tightened his grip on her waist and hoisted her off her feet in his hurry to get to the street outside. He lifted her into the car and wrapped the travel rug around her.

Kirsty slumped in the seat and closed her eyes because the houses bordering the road wouldn't stay still and everything seemed to be revolving. Tremors ran through her body and she drew the rug tighter, tucking it under her chin, oblivious to her father's arm around her. She didn't hear the engine start, nor did she feel the vibration of the automobile as it rumbled up the street.

'We're home.'

Kirsty woke with a start. The last thing she remembered was being placed in the car by her father. Her breath rasped out through her mouth and spasms of coughing racked her body.

Her father reached into the car, lifted her into his arms and walked towards the house. The door opened before they got there. Ellen stood on the doorstep.

'What's happened?' Her voice rose in a scream. 'What's wrong with Kirsty?'

Kirsty turned her head to look at her mother. She wanted to tell her she was fine and not to worry but her voice betrayed her and all that issued from her lips was a croak.

'It's all right, Ellen. What Kirsty needs is a warm bath, nourishing food, and a check over by the doctor.' But despite his reassuring tone, worry was etched on her father's face.

'Tell Parker to prepare Kirsty's bedroom and run a bath for her. I think Kirsty will be staying with us for a while.'

Kirsty tried to croak her objections but the effort took up too much energy and she lapsed into a reluctant silence.

56

Billy and Nancy Allardyce confirmed the statements they'd already provided to Sergeant McPhee and Brewster reckoned there was no need for him to remain.

'If there are any further developments send your report to Dundee Central Police Station,' he instructed McPhee before he left.

A rumble followed by the sound of crashing timbers added to the sense of chaos. Sparks floated in the air and the smoke thickened, forcing Brewster to hold a handkerchief over his mouth and nose.

'That's the rest of the roof gone,' one of the firemen shouted. 'Best not linger,' he said. 'It's not safe here.'

Brewster nodded and hurried to the gate in the wall.

'If I have to tell you lot to keep this gate clear one more time I'll be banging heads together.'

He sidled past the irate fireman issuing the threat to the crowd of onlookers jostling each other on the pavement.

'Buggers stood on the hose and cut the water off,' he muttered to Brewster.

'Back off,' Brewster roared, 'or you'll all be spending a night in the local nick.'

'Who says?'

'Aye, what right do you have to order us about.'

Mutters and grumbles circulated through the crowd as they pushed nearer and craned their necks for a better view of the blaze.

The fireman pulled his hose from beneath their feet. 'This lot's uncontrollable,' he said. 'How do they expect us to put the fire out when they keep on obstructing us and getting in our way?'

Brewster glared at the men in front of him before turning and striding back to where McPhee was leaning on a tree. The man quickly hid his cigarette in the palm of his hand.

'Sergeant,' Brewster snapped.

McPhee stood to attention.

'You'd be more gainfully employed controlling that crowd outside the gate than standing here watching the fire.'

'Yes, sir.'

They strode to the front of the building where the crowd had once again clustered outside and inside the gate.

'Clear out of there,' McPhee bellowed in a voice any sergeant major in the army might envy.

'Bloody hell, it's the bobby.' The scruffy looking man who had sidled up the path for a better look at the fire turned and ran through the gate. 'McPhee's on the warpath,' he said as he battled through the scrum.

McPhee grinned at Brewster. 'I have a bit of a reputation hereabouts,' he said. 'I don't think we'll have much more bother.'

'Well, if you do, you have my full permission to lock them up.'

'You hear that, lads. I've got some nice empty cells waiting for any of you lot that get in the way of the firemen.'

Several more men melted away from the crowd and shuffled off down the road.

'I'll take myself back to Dundee now but I want you to stay on the gate and don't let this rabble get out of hand.'

Brewster pushed past the remaining men and walked to the front of the fire engine to where his Ford Model T was sitting. It needed several cranks of the starting handle before it started and he was able to jump into the driving seat. He pulled out but was unable to turn because of the narrowness of the road and he doubted his ability to reverse past the fire engine. But he couldn't wait until the fire was extinguished and he couldn't ask the firemen to move the fire engine.

With a huge sigh, he steered the car down the road in the direction of the rough grass and dunes at the end of the road. Maybe he could drive onto the grass to turn the car but he could become stuck and that would be even worse. However, he had no other option.

Before he reached the dunes he came to large wooden gates which enclosed a yard in front of a stable block. He hopped out of the car, opened them and reversed into the yard. Once the manoeuvre was completed he closed the gates behind him and drove up Bents Road until he came to the fire engine. His heart thumped as he edged the car past and he breathed a sigh of relief when it was a success.

Now, there was no time to be lost. He had to get back to Dundee. He had a murderer to interview.

Darkness had fallen before Brewster drove through the arch into the police courtyard. His feet slid on ice-covered cobbles and he grabbed the car door to regain his balance.

Hamish looked up from the log book on the desk in front of him, laid his pencil in the groove beside the inkwell and pushed his glasses up until they lodged at his hairline. 'I heard about the fire at Montrose,' he said. 'Is Miss Campbell all right?'

Brewster thought he detected a note of worry in the man's voice which surprised him because Hamish made his disapproval of Kirsty obvious.

'Miss Campbell suffered some smoke inhalation and she has gone home with her parents to recover.'

Hamish cleared his throat and leaned on the counter separating them. 'Sergeant Brodie stayed on at the end of his shift. Said he'd wait until you returned to make his report.'

Cigarette smoke wafted into the corridor as Brewster passed the constables' room and the rumble of voices indicated a shift change. They would be getting ready for their evening patrol duties. He pushed open the door to the sergeants' room which was next door, to find Brodie leaning back in his chair puffing his pipe and with his feet up on the desk.

Brewster perched on the corner of the desk. 'Update me on what's been happening,' he said.

Brodie removed his feet so fast his chair rocked on its back legs before righting itself. He tamped the bowl of his pipe with his finger and laid it in the ashtray. 'I took the lass to Broughty

Ferry as ordered, sir. But she and the other two girls refused to return to Dundee. David Walker and Mary Petrie arrived about an hour later. I read David Walker his rights and arrested him but both he and Mary Petrie claimed Lily Petrie's death was an accident and he also claimed to know nothing about Freddie Simpson's murder. That was when Mary Petrie chimed in to tell me she had killed her husband, the Reverend Josiah Petrie. So I arrested her as well. I have them both in the cells and the section sergeant is currently processing the details.'

'I take it you've written your report.'

'Yes, sir. I left it on your desk but I stayed back until you returned.'

'I appreciate that, Ian. You can go off duty now and I'll take it from here.'

'Yes, sir.'

Brewster returned to his office, read the report and headed for the cells. It was time to hear what David Walker had to say for himself.

57

The turnkey slid open the cover of the peephole and peered through. He stepped back and motioned for Brewster to look into the cell.

'Is he praying?' Brewster gestured for him to open the door.

'He's been in that position since I came on duty this morning.' The turnkey said, swinging the door wide. 'I don't think he'll give you any trouble, but I'll be outside if you need me.'

The man inside the cell remained on his knees with his elbows leaning on the mattress-covered bench and his chin resting on his clasped hands. He kept his eyes closed and his lips moved although no sound issued through them.

Brewster waited until the door clanged shut before saying, 'David Walker?'

The man opened his eyes and turned his head.

'Yes.'

'I presume you are aware of the reason for your detention and why you were brought here.'

David Walker stood. He was as tall Brewster and greeted him with a benign expression which made him look harmless.

'The police sergeant who arrested me did explain,' he said. 'But I think there must be some mistake.'

'There is no mistake,' Brewster said. 'You are charged with the murder of your niece, Lily Petrie, on Monday 8th December, at an address in the Scouringburn. Further, you are charged with the murder of Freddie Simpson on the evening of Thursday 11th December, in the Howff cemetery.'

'I don't understand why you think that is murder. They were sinners, all of them. How can you accuse me of murder when I am doing the Lord's work?' Walker's face remained passive and he looked up to the small window set high in the cell wall.

'God sees everything we do.' He lapsed into silence.

'Are you saying that killing Lily and Freddie is God's will?' Brewster couldn't keep the note of scepticism out of his voice.

'We come into this world as sinners but we leave it with our sins absolved.'

'I don't believe that.' Brewster stared at him in disbelief. Did this man really believe he was doing God's work when he murdered two people?

'Tell me about Lily and why you killed her.'

'Why did I release her from her mortal soul?' David Walker looked pensive.

Was that a confession of sorts? Brewster pressed on. 'Why did you?'

'Lily was born into a Christian family. Her father is a minister of the church. And the daughter of any priest, if she profane herself by playing the whore, she profaneth her father: she shall be burnt with fire.'

'But she wasn't burned with fire.' Brewster gritted his teeth. 'You bludgeoned her to death.'

'She was a harlot. I gave her the chance to repent but she refused to take it. For a whore is a deep ditch; and a strange woman is a narrow pit. She was beyond saving.'

'Lily was a young woman who died before her time. You have blood on your hands.'

David Walker sank to his knees and clasped his hands. 'I will pray for Lily's immortal soul.'

'Pray all you like, that won't bring her back nor will it bring Freddie back.'

No response came from the kneeling man and Brewster turned away in disgust. He banged on the door to be let out.

'I doubt whether your God will see things in the same way you do. Nor will a court of law,' he said, before leaving.

The female prison block was a level higher than the male cells. Brewster, familiar with the twisting passages below the police station, never got used to the echoes that bounced along the walls as his footsteps resounded on the flagged stone floors.

Annie Baxter, the turnkey met him at the barred door. 'I thought someone would come to interview the prisoner,' she said, 'but I expected Kirsty Campbell.'

'Kirsty is indisposed.' Brewster waited for her to unlock the gate. He passed through and waited until it clanged shut behind him.

'She's been no bother,' Annie said, 'not like that other one.'

He slapped his forehead. 'Big Aggie. I forgot about her. There is no reason to hold her now. I'll contact the procurator fiscal tomorrow to arrange for her release.'

'Reckon that can wait until morning, sir. She'll scratch your eyes out if you're on your own.'

Brewster shuddered. 'You have a point, Annie. In any case, I need approval from the fiscal first and his office isn't open on a Sunday. Now, what about the new prisoner, Mary Petrie.'

'She's been real quiet since they brought her in, sir. Keeps saying it was all an accident.' She stopped at one of the iron doors and inserted a key.

Brewster hesitated in the doorway. 'You'd best come in with me Annie. It won't look good in court if I question her with no one else present.'

'Yes, sir.' Annie closed the cell door and leaned against it with her arms folded.

Mary Petrie perched on the edge of the mattress-covered bench, a forlorn figure who looked out of place in the bare confines of the cell. She glanced at them, then looked down at her hands.

'I gather you know why you are here?'

A tear slipped down the woman's face and she nodded.

'Do you want to tell me about it?'

'Not really, except that it was an accident.'

'Whether you want to or not, you are going to have to tell us why you killed your husband.'

'I told you it was an accident and I don't want to talk about it.'

Questions buzzed in Brewster's mind. Why did she confess to killing her husband? Did she kill him or was she covering for her brother? And why did she lock Kirsty in the attic and start the fire? If it had been a man sitting before him he would have had no compunction in applying pressure but she looked so forlorn, he didn't have the heart.

He turned away in despair. 'I'll come back tomorrow and I'll expect answers,' he said before he followed Annie out of the cell.

'It's at times like this I wish Kirsty were here,' he said, 'she's good at getting information from the women.'

'I never thought I'd hear you say that.' Annie unlocked the gate leading to the passage beyond.

As he marched through the corridors to the echo of his footsteps, he realized he'd never before voiced his appreciation of Kirsty nor had he admitted to himself how much he depended on her when it came to handling women witnesses and prisoners.

58

Kirsty woke the next morning to find her mother holding her hand.

A candle glimmered on the mantelpiece while the glowing embers in the grate below struggled to maintain the dying flame flickering around the coal. She wriggled her hand free to avoid waking her mother but as she withdrew it from her grasp, Ellen Campbell awoke with a start.

'Have you been here all night?' The effort of speaking caused Kirsty to cough but after several attempts to clear her throat, she thought her voice sounded more normal when she repeated her question.

'I feared for you. Your breathing was laboured and I wanted to stay with you to make sure you were all right.'

'But the doctor examined me last night. He said there was nothing to worry about and I should take honey and lemon to ease my throat.'

'I know. But that didn't stop me worrying.'

Kirsty leaned out of the bed and hugged her mother. She had been so long on her own she'd forgotten what it was like to be cared for and cosseted. And, although a part of her wanted to fight off anything that reduced her independence, another part wanted to lie back and enjoy being spoiled.

'There's no need to worry.' Kirsty pushed the blankets aside, swung herself out of the bed and wriggled her toes in appreciation of the rug under her feet.

'The doctor said you should rest.'

'I am rested. I never woke once during the night.'

'That was because of the potion the doctor prescribed. He said it would help you sleep.'

'Potion? I don't recall taking a potion.'

Ellen Campbell's face reddened.

She grasped her mother's hand. 'Was it in the hot milk? I thought it tasted strange but you said it was honey which would ease my throat.'

'It was for your own good.' Tears welled up in her mother's eyes.

Anger seeped through her but she didn't have the energy to argue and her shoulders slumped.

'I'll get dressed and come down to breakfast.'

'Parker has taken your clothes to be cleaned. They were splotched with soot and smelled of smoke.'

'I'll need something to wear.' Exasperation overtook her. 'I refuse to stay in bed until Parker brings them back.'

'I kept all your clothes after you left, I'm sure you'll find something.'

Kirsty sighed. Fashions had changed drastically since her separation from her parents ten years ago but she supposed her old clothes would suffice.

She selected several items. Underwear that would serve the purpose. A blouse that would pass muster. But the skirt was far too long. No one wore skirts at ankle-length anymore.

'Will I be able to see Ailsa today?' That was the one benefit of being in her parents' house. Access to her child.

'I'm afraid not until later this afternoon. I sent her home with Aunt Bea to avoid upsetting her.'

Kirsty concentrated on dressing to hide her disappointment but her mother had probably done the right thing. After the horrific events last month, Ailsa had been through too much to worry about Kirsty.

Downstairs in the breakfast room, her father looked up from his newspaper when she entered. 'I thought you would be staying in bed to recover from your experience.'

Kirsty helped herself to a bowl of porridge from the tureen on the sideboard. 'I have things to do today.'

'Does that mean you do not intend to remain here until you are fully recovered?'

She noted the disappointment in her father's voice. 'I will return for a short time when I finish what I need to do but you must understand I have my own life and I value my independence.'

'As you are no doubt aware I have found that difficult to accept but I respect your decision. All we want to do is offer to look after you until you are back to your full strength. Your mother would worry about you alone in that flat when you are debilitated.'

'You will not attempt to stop me going to Dundee today?'

'I couldn't stop you even if I wanted to,' Robert Campbell said with a note of regret in his voice. 'But I do ask you to return for a few weeks until you are fully recovered. Will you promise me that?'

Kirsty stirred more milk into her porridge to make swallowing easier. At last, she looked up to find her father watching her as he waited for her answer. 'Yes, father. It will be Christmas in ten days. I will stay until then but after that, I will return to my own home. However, today, there are things that require my attention.'

'Drop me off at the mill,' Robert Campbell instructed his chauffeur, 'then take Kirsty to her flat and remain with her all day in case she needs transport.'

Wind whistled under the top and in the sides of the Arrol-Johnstone automobile and Kirsty tightened the rug which was wrapped around her legs.

'There's no need for Dougal to wait all day,' she said. 'He can wait long enough for me to pack some clothes. After that, I'll manage to find my own way.'

'Nonsense,' her father said. 'Dougal will be at your service all day. I expect you'll be glad of him before the day is out.'

'I'm not a baby.' Kirsty regretted her promise to return to her parents' house. It was bound to end in disaster if he continued to impose his will on her.

The car bounced over the cobbles and stopped at the mill gates. 'I'll see you when I return home tonight,' her father said as he dismounted.

A few minutes later they drew up in front of her tenement.

Kirsty hopped out. 'I won't be long.' Ice on the pavement caught her unawares, her feet slipped and her heel snagged in the hem of her skirt. She sat down with a thump.

'Are you all right, miss?' Dougal helped her up.

'It's this damned skirt.' She yanked it away from her feet. 'I haven't worn skirts as long as this for over ten years. How on earth we suffered them at that time, I'll never know.'

She stamped into the building, sidled past the bicycle and pram which permanently occupied the space at the bottom of the stairs and grabbed the handrail. Halfway up, she stopped to regain her strength. Her legs quivered and her breath rasped out of her throat, sounding like a rusty engine. She was not as fit as she thought and she was glad her father wasn't here to observe her weakness. After what seemed an eternity she finished the climb to her flat.

Once inside she flopped into an armchair until her legs stopped shaking. But the room felt cold and she had to move to keep warm.

Her uniform hung on a hook at the back of the bedroom door and it didn't take her long to discard the dated clothes she wore for the more familiar garb of her police uniform. Satisfied with her appearance, she pulled her battered suitcase from below the bed and packed a selection of clothes. After snapping the clasps shut she hauled it to the door and hoisted it downstairs.

Dougal came hurrying to meet her. 'You should have called me.' He grabbed the suitcase and stowed it in the car.

Kirsty climbed into the back seat. 'Take me to Central Police Station and then you can go.'

'Master said I should wait for you, miss.'

She shrugged. 'Please yourself but it will be a long wait and probably a cold one at that.'

Geordie stared when Kirsty entered the charge room. 'Should you be here, miss?' His brow wrinkled with worry. 'I heard you were not too well after your experience yesterday.'

'I have some jobs to finish before I take time off.' Kirsty smiled at him. She was glad it was Geordie on duty today and not Hamish who was always disapproving. 'Is Inspector Brewster in this morning?'

'You'll find him in his office, miss.'

'Thanks, Geordie.'

She pushed through the inner door and walked down the corridor to Brewster's office. His head was bent over a file and he didn't look up right away. When he did, his eyes lit up as if he was glad to see her.

'What are you doing here?' His voice was gruff and less welcoming. 'I told you to take time off to recover.'

'I can't take time off until I finish what I have to do.'

'And what would that be?'

'To speak to Mary Petrie and make sure Jessie and the two girls are all right. Before I do that I need to be updated on what's happening.'

Brewster sighed. 'Sit down, Kirsty.' He shuffled papers into the file and closed it. 'Both David Walker and Mary Petrie were arrested yesterday and are currently in the cells. David Walker is charged with the murder of Lily Petrie and Freddie Simpson, and Mary Petrie confessed to the murder of her husband.'

'What about Jessie and the girls. Who is caring for them?'

'They remained at David Walker's manse. Jessie is caring for the girls.'

Kirsty turned the information over in her mind.

'You didn't mention Big Aggie. If David Walker killed Lily that means she didn't.'

'I know. I intend to contact the procurator fiscal today to secure her release.'

'Has anyone informed Aggie?'

'Not yet.'

'In that case, I'll talk to her after I interview Mary. Then I'll go out to see Jessie and the girls to work something out for them.'

Brewster sighed. 'You do realize you're impossible. You disobey orders and you follow your own agenda. If I dismissed you it would give me a far easier life.'

'But you won't because you need me.' Kirsty held her breath wondering if she'd gone too far.

'All right. If I allow you to complete these tasks will you take time off and go home to rest?'

'Yes, sir. I promised my parents I will stay with them until Christmas. After that, I expect to be back on duty.'

59

Kirsty's footsteps echoed along the corridor as she strode to the female cell area. The last time she had been here it was to question Big Aggie. She'd never expected Mary Petrie to be incarcerated here. Mary, a minister's wife, meek and respectable, the last person anyone would expect to occupy a prison cell.

Annie, the turnkey, opened the cell door. 'She's as quiet as a lamb. I don't think she knows what's happening to her.'

'How could she not know?' Kirsty peered in. Mary perched on the end of the mattress-covered bench with a bewildered look on her face.

'What's happening to David?' Mary picked at the material of her skirt.

Kirsty sat on the bench beside her. 'David is locked up in a prison cell,' she said. 'He has been charged with Lily's murder as well as the murder of Freddie Simpson.'

At the mention of Lily, tears rolled down Mary's cheeks. 'It was an accident,' she whispered. 'He didn't mean it.'

Kirsty wondered whether she should allow Mary the solace of believing that. But what good would that do? Everything would come out at the trial.

'The attack was too violent to be an accident,' she said. 'Lily's face and head were so badly beaten she was unrecognizable. Surely you noticed when you viewed the body?'

'I closed my eyes.' Mary shuddered. 'David looked for me.'

Kirsty knew that wasn't true. She remembered Mary's anguished cry when she saw Lily. In hindsight, had her questions about the violence of the attack been directed at David Walker?

'He is also charged with the murder of Freddie Simpson.'

'How can that be? I don't know any Freddie Simpson,' Mary said.

'Freddie tried to blackmail David. He was beaten to death.'

Mary huddled on the bench, appearing smaller than when Kirsty entered the cell. Kirsty reached out a hand to her but Mary shrank away.

'Why did you lock me in the attic and set the fire?' Kirsty wanted to understand. It seemed such an unusual thing for Mary to have done.

'David said you knew too much and if I didn't we would land in prison.' She twisted her hands together in a wringing motion. 'I'm sorry, I didn't mean you any harm.'

'What about Josiah? Why did he have to be killed?'

'That was an accident. He came back from church early and heard David telling me to take care of you.' Mary paused before continuing. 'If Josiah hadn't attempted to interfere it wouldn't have happened. But after David left, Josiah told me he would wait for you at the top of the road and warn you off. I couldn't allow that.'

'What did you do?'

'I hit Josiah with the poker when he turned to leave the room. But I didn't mean to kill him.'

'And yet, you set fire to the house. How could that be an accident?'

'I only meant the fire to give us time to get away and it didn't kill anyone.'

Kirsty sighed. Mary seemed intent on deluding herself.

'Tell me about David,' she said. 'Why do you do everything he says?'

Mary looked up to where a chink of daylight shone through the window high in the wall.

'David is the only person who loves me and looks after me. He protects me. I owe him my loyalty.' Her face brightened when she talked about her brother.

'What about your daughters, surely you owe them a duty as well?'

'A mother's duty is different.' Mary lapsed into silence.

Kirsty let the silence continue while she pondered Mary's

relationship with her brother. As far as she knew, few mothers considered their siblings to be more important than their children.

Mary gave no indication of continuing to talk, so Kirsty said, 'I'm not sure I understand why you became so dependent on David.'

'When you are brought up in a family like mine you take your support where you find it. My mother died when I was a child and my father was like Josiah. He didn't let me mix with other children so there was only my older sister, David and me. David and I were the babies of the family, my sister was a lot older which meant that David and I became inseparable. He is the only person I ever truly loved.'

'But you married Josiah.'

'My father arranged the marriage. We were never alone together until our wedding night. I worried about that but I needn't have. Josiah had no interest in me as a woman. All he wanted was my dowry.' Her expression darkened. 'I didn't love him.'

'You had three daughters by him.'

Mary twisted the material in her skirt so hard the bones showed through her fingers. 'He is not the father of my daughters.' Her fingers twisted the material even tighter. 'Josiah was impotent. We never had relations.'

Kirsty blinked. She hadn't expected that. Josiah seemed to her to be a fire and brimstone preacher who enjoyed his status as a minister of the cloth. Not a man who would accept his wife being unfaithful nor enjoy being cuckolded. Neither would he welcome sinners into his family.

'Josiah must have known the girls were not his daughters.' Even to her own ears, Kirsty's voice sounded tentative. 'Why did he accept the situation?'

'I told you.' Mary glared at her. 'He was interested in my dowry, not me. He got the dowry when we married and when my father died his fortune was split between me and David. The money kept us together.'

'That leaves me with another question. If Josiah wasn't the father of your girls, who was?' Kirsty thought she knew but the answer circulating in her mind was so horrific she didn't want to believe it.

Mary confirmed what she was thinking. 'David, of course.' Mary's voice was quiet, matter of fact.

Jumbled thoughts raced through Kirsty's brain but they kept coming to the same conclusion. David murdered his own daughter. But more than that, if Billy was not the father of Lily's aborted child and she had no contact with any other male other than her family, it was a strong possibility David was responsible for her pregnancy.

Kirsty stood. Nausea churned in her stomach. She had to get out of this cell. She couldn't stay here with Mary any longer.

She rapped on the door for Annie to let her out.

Kirsty's footsteps echoed along the corridor leading from the cell area, bombarding her ears with the noise and adding to the confusion inside her head. She had been accustomed to all sorts of depravity when she worked in London. But Mary's calm acceptance of the incestuous relationships within her family shocked her more than anything she encountered during her time as a policewoman.

Nausea churned in the pit of her stomach and her head spun. She quickened her pace. Without thinking about it she left the lower corridor levels behind and ran to Brewster's office. He would know how to handle this.

Brewster looked up when she launched herself into his office and collapsed into the only chair which didn't hold files. 'Are you all right?' His frown held concern.

Kirsty gripped the side of the chair and concentrated on regaining control of her breathing.

He rose. 'I'll get you some water.' He vanished out of the room, returning moments later with a tin cup which he handed to Kirsty.

'Thanks.' She took a sip.

All of a sudden she felt foolish. What must Brewster think of her? Ever since she arrived in Dundee she had been at pains to impress on everyone that she could cope with anything. Now, after a simple interview, she was exhibiting the type of behaviour a new recruit might show.

'Are you all right now?' Brewster hovered at her side.

'Yes,' she said. 'It was nothing.'

Brewster raised his eyebrows but did not comment. After a moment he circled his desk and sat in the chair behind it.

'I've interviewed Mary Petrie. And I believe the information she gave me provides the motive behind the killings.' Kirsty took another sip of water. 'We thought we'd discovered most of Lily's secrets but the ones involving her family are far worse.'

Brewster leaned forward, placing his elbows on the desk. 'Go on.'

'Mary Petrie had an incestuous relationship with her brother David Walker. Her husband, Josiah Petrie knew about it but did nothing. Apparently, their marriage was an arranged one with Mary's fortune being the dominating factor. David is the father of Mary's three daughters. This means he murdered his own daughter, Lily. Further, the father of Lily's aborted child has never been established, apart from the fact it was not Billy Allardyce's child. Given that Lily had no contact with any other male, I believe David Walker was responsible for her pregnancy. We both know Lily had a nice little sideline of blackmail and David Walker's name was listed in her journal. My belief is that Lily blackmailed David and he killed her to prevent that knowledge being made public. He killed Freddie for the same reason and Mary killed Josiah after he overheard them plotting against me.'

'I see. And Mary Petrie told you this?'

'Yes, and she seemed to think there was nothing wrong with all of that.'

'Hmm! David Walker has been less forthcoming with me.'

'Perhaps if you let me interview him. I could confront him with what we know.' Even as she suggested it, Kirsty knew Brewster would never agree. As far as he was concerned her job was to interview and take statements from women and children. He would never allow her to question a man.

'I think he should be confronted with this information but I would be lacking in my duty if I let you do it.' Brewster stood and buttoned his jacket. 'I'll do it now.'

'At least, let me accompany you,' Kirsty said, unable to keep a pleading note out of her voice.

He hesitated.

'I could back you up because I'm the one Mary Petrie told.'

'Very well. I suppose it can do no harm.'

60

Today would be Kirsty's first visit to the male cell block although she didn't imagine it would differ from the female one.

'This way,' Brewster said when they reached a junction in the corridor and instead of turning right they veered left into a passage that sloped down to a lower level.

Kirsty guessed the male cells must be immediately below the female ones. Their footsteps rebounded with an eerie echo and the temperature dropped. Drips of water ran down the walls and the air smelled musty. They must be at least two levels under the police station.

At last, they came to the iron gate which guarded the entrance to the male cells. Brewster rattled the bars and a man in a warder's uniform shuffled along the passage. His shoulders, bent under an invisible weight, gave the impression he was smaller than his frame suggested.

'Forbes was injured in the line of duty,' he whispered to her while they waited for his arrival at the gate. 'He used to be one of the best bobbies in the force.'

The warder shuffled nearer and fumbled with the keys dangling from his belt. Selecting one, he unlocked the gate and motioned for them to enter the inner corridor.

'It's the minister mannie you want to see, is it?' He shuffled in front of them. 'He's been on his knees praying since you left him this morning. Hasn't looked up and ignored the porridge I took into him. What with his muttering and mumbling I can't make sense of anything he says. If you ask me, he's mad.'

He stopped at one of the iron doors, unlocked it and swung it open. 'Good luck in getting any sense out of him,' he said.

The man kneeling in front of the mattress-covered bench did not look up but kept his head pressed to his clasped hands while he muttered something indistinguishable.

Brewster marched to where the man knelt and stood over him. 'David Walker, fresh information has come into my possession which means I need to question you again.'

The man did not look up. It was as if Brewster hadn't spoken.

'I require you to rise and answer my questions.' Brewster's voice sharpened.

Still, the man remained on his knees although his muttering increased in intensity.

Brewster glanced at Kirsty and sighed.

'You do realize there is enough evidence to convict you of the murder of your niece, or should I say, your daughter.'

David Walker grew still and the muttering stopped for a moment before starting again.

'Your refusal to cooperate will not be in your favour when you come to court. But I have a duty to inform you of what we know.'

Kirsty stared at David Walker. She sensed he was listening although his posture didn't alter nor did his muttering stop.

'We have information you conducted a relationship with your sister, Mary Petrie, and that Lily was your daughter. This information will be presented to the court when you are tried for the murder of Lily Petrie, your own daughter, and for the murder of Freddie Simpson who was blackmailing you. There is sufficient evidence to detain you until your trial. Have you anything to say in your defence?'

No response came from the kneeling man although Kirsty noticed his clasped hands tightening until his knuckles turned white.

Frustration showed in Brewster's expression as he banged on the door to be let out.

'Well, that was a waste of time,' Brewster said when they reached his office. He threw himself into his chair and thumped the desk with his fist. 'If you ask me, he's trying to work an insanity plea so he doesn't hang. But I'm damned if I'll let him get off with it.'

Unused to seeing Brewster vent his feelings, Kirsty sat in silence although her mind churned with everything she'd learned from Mary Petrie.

Maybe if yesterday's experience hadn't weakened her she would have handled the interview better and wouldn't have rushed out when the information became upsetting. She cringed at the thought. She was Kirsty Campbell, a professional policewoman, who prided herself on taking everything in her stride. By allowing herself to be affected by Mary's interview she had failed herself. But worse than that she missed an opportunity to discuss what would happen to Mary's daughters now their mother was imprisoned.

Despair washed over her and without realizing what she was doing, she groaned.

'Are you all right, Kirsty?'

She looked up at Brewster who was bent over her with concern in his eyes.

'I was thinking,' she said. 'I didn't ask Mary Petrie how she would provide for her daughters while she was incarcerated, nor did I inform Big Aggie about her release.'

'You are not yourself. I think you should go home. I will tie up all the loose ends.'

'No, I need to ensure Jessie and the two girls are provided for. They will not even have a roof over their heads when the church appoints a new minister. Then, there's Aggie. She doesn't know about her release yet.'

'At least you needn't worry about Aggie. It is my duty to arrange for her release with the procurator fiscal. I will attend to that.' He paused, considering. 'I'll agree for you to visit Jessie and the girls to assess what options there are for their future provided you promise to return home once that is completed.'

Kirsty sighed. The promises were piling up. Would she be able to honour them all? But she forced a smile to her lips as she said, 'Yes, sir.'

Despite telling Dougal she did not need his services, Kirsty was pleased to find him sitting in the charge room chatting with the duty sergeant.

'It got cold outside, miss, so I came in here and I've been

having a rare old chin wag with Geordie.' Dougal stood and handed his empty mug to the sergeant. 'Are you ready to go home now, miss?'

'Not yet. But I do need you to take me to Broughty Ferry.'

Twenty minutes later the motor car pulled up outside the manse. Dougal helped Kirsty out and she strode up the path to the door which opened before she reached it.

'I saw you coming, miss.' Jessie beckoned her inside. 'I don't know what to do now the bobbies have taken Uncle David and Aunt Mary away. What's happening?'

'I'm sorry, Jesse. I'm afraid both your uncle and aunt are in prison.'

'It's all my fault.' Jessie twisted her hands together.

Kirsty placed her hands over Jessie's. 'You did the right thing and you saved my life.'

'Did I?' Jessie's eyes widened making her squint more noticeable.

'Now I want to help you find a place to stay because I expect the church will want this house for the next minister. And the manse at Montrose is gone, consumed by the fire your Aunt Mary set.'

'Why would she set the house on fire? It doesn't make sense.'

Kirsty looked around. 'Is there somewhere we can sit while we talk?'

'I'm sorry, miss. I'm not thinking. The sitting room is through here.'

Jessie perched on the edge of one of the armchairs and Kirsty sat in the other.

'How are the girls coping now their mother is gone.'

'They haven't said but I do most of the looking after in any case so that's no different. They're upstairs where it's warmer. But I thought we'd be more private in here.'

'Is there anyone else in the house?'

'No, miss. Just me and Rose and Iris. Uncle David's housekeeper left this morning and said she wasn't coming back.'

'How old are you, Jessie?'

'I'm nineteen, miss. Same age as Lily was.' A single tear rolled down Jessie's cheek. 'Me and Lily were close, like sisters. She didn't deserve to be killed.'

'No, she didn't.' Kirsty waited for a moment before she continued. 'Had you given any thought about what you want to do now?'

'I could get a job where I could live in but I won't leave Rose and Iris. We're a family.'

'What about any relatives who might be willing to help?'

'Uncle Josiah I suppose but he always left everything to Aunt Mary and never took much interest in us. When do you think the police will let Aunt Mary go? I'm sure she didn't mean to set the manse on fire.'

'You don't know?' Kirsty stared at Jessie. But how could she? Jessie wasn't at the manse yesterday. She tried to choose her words carefully but could find no easy way to tell her. 'I'm afraid Uncle Josiah is not an option because a neighbour pulled his body from the burning house.'

'Is that why they arrested Aunt Mary? Is it because he died in the fire?'

'It's more serious than that. Your Uncle Josiah was killed before the fire started and your Aunt Mary has confessed to his murder.'

Jessie remained calmer than Kirsty expected but it was difficult to tell what she was thinking.

'Is there anyone else you can think of who might help you and the girls?'

Jessie thought for a moment. 'The only one I can think of is a great aunt who lives hereabouts. Aunt Mary used to speak about her sometimes but she never visited and I never met her.'

'What do you know about her?'

'All I know is her name is the same as my mother's, Elizabeth. I think my mother was named after her.'

'You said she lives hereabouts. Do you know where?'

'Aunt Mary pointed it out to me once. It's a big house not far from here. It sits between Fort Street and Camphill Road but you can't see the house behind the wall.'

Kirsty rose from the chair. 'You stay here with the girls and

I'll go along and talk to your great aunt. She might be able to provide some help.'

'You be wasting your time, miss. Aunt Mary said she never had any time for the rest of the family. Seemed to think she was a bit of a hermit.'

'Nevertheless, I have to try. I won't be long.'

61

Hidden behind a high wall and with a spacious garden stretching all the way to Queen Street, Elizabeth Walker's mansion was within walking distance of the church where her nephew David preached.

Kirsty straightened her uniform jacket, took a deep breath, and grasped the brass knocker to rap on the door. She had no idea how she would be received nor did she know how sympathetic Miss Walker would be to the plight of her great nieces.

The door creaked open and a young girl in an over-sized maid's uniform stood before her.

'Milly?' Kirsty's eyes widened. 'I thought you were taken to the Barnhill Orphanage with the other children when you all left the Orphan Institute.' Even now, she couldn't bear to think about what happened that terrible night, nor the events that led up to it.

The girl shuffled her feet. 'I couldn't stay at Barnhill because I'm not a child. But Mr Bogue instructed the matron to look out for me so she found me a job here.'

'Do you like working here?'

Milly nodded. 'Miss Walker is kind to me although cook can be bossy. But she means well.'

'That's good, I'm pleased for you. Now, if you can announce me to Miss Walker I would like to speak to her.'

'Yes, miss. If you wait in the hall I'll inform her.'

Kirsty looked around her while she waited. The hall was as large as the one in her parents' house with a floor of Venetian tiles. A large stained glass window overlooked the landing where the curved stairs met. In the alcove beneath the arc of the stairs, an Italian marble sculpture of the Three Graces stared out. This house was far grander than she anticipated and she wondered how its owner would react to her suggestion.

'Miss Walker will see you now.' Milly escorted her through a door, at the right-hand side of the stairs, into a large but cosy room furnished with sofas, occasional tables and armchairs. An elderly lady sat in an armchair at one side of the glowing fire which burned in an Adams style fireplace.

'Come in and sit down, Miss Campbell.' The woman waved to the armchair opposite her. 'Milly told me all about you and how you rescued her and the children from that awful Orphan Institute.'

Miss Walker peered at Kirsty with bird-like eyes full of curiosity. Instead of the black or brown clothing most elderly women favoured, Miss Walker wore a lush purple dress with a white trim on the collar and cuffs and styled her grey hair into a chignon held in place with a butterfly barrette. Kirsty reckoned the woman must be in her seventies but she showed little signs of the effects of ageing.

'I think we should offer Miss Campbell some tea, Milly, and I smelled something delicious baking earlier. I think some scones if there are any, or perhaps cook's fairy cakes. Run off and see what you can find.'

Miss Walker rearranged her skirt over her knees and peered at Kirsty. 'There must be a reason for you to come here,' she said. 'I'm curious.'

'I came to ask you a favour.' Kirsty hesitated, unsure how to explain everything but felt an explanation necessary to justify what she was about to ask of the older woman.

'Go on.'

'Since yesterday there has been an escalation of events which has left your great nieces, homeless. I was hoping to ask for your help in putting a roof over their heads until their situation is clarified.'

'I read about Lily's murder in the *Dundee Courier*. So, I'm assuming you mean Rose and Iris. And of course poor Jessie.'

'That is correct.'

'They do have parents. Well, at least Rose and Iris do. You are going to have to be more explicit.'

Kirsty wriggled in her chair unable to find an easy way to

provide her with information.

She sat up straight and clasped her hands in front of her. 'I'm afraid your nephew and niece, David, and Mary Petrie, were arrested yesterday. They are waiting for trial and Josiah Petrie is no longer with us. He is dead. This leaves no one else the girls can turn to for help.'

Instead of recoiling in shock as Kirsty expected, Miss Walker leaned back in her chair with a pensive look on her face. 'I see,' she said. 'I must say anything David did would not surprise me but I am somewhat taken aback by Mary's arrest.' She stared into the fireplace as if seeking answers among the glowing coals. 'Where are the girls at the moment?'

'They spent last night at David's manse but I am sure the church will require the manse for a future minister. I do not anticipate the post will be held open for David Walker and even if it was, I would have serious reservations about the girls remaining.'

At the sound of the door opening, Miss Walker turned and beckoned to Milly. 'Ah, you've found a lovely sponge cake for us. Cut a slice for Miss Campbell and pour the tea before you leave us. And make sure no one disturbs us. Miss Campbell and I have a lot to discuss.'

Kirsty poured a large dollop of milk into the cup and sipped the tea, thankful for the respite. Yesterday's fire had left her throat dry and raw which made talking painful.

Miss Walker broke the silence in the room. 'Can I ask what the charges are against David and Mary?'

'David has been charged with the murder of Lily as well as that of an unrelated man. And Mary admitted she killed her husband.' Kirsty did not elaborate further. She did not want to tell Miss Walker of Mary's attempt to kill her by locking her in and setting fire to the manse.

Miss Walker sighed. 'So sad,' she said, 'but David was a strange child. He looked like an angel with his fair hair and blue eyes but even as a child he had a cruel streak. My brother and his wife thought he could do no wrong.'

'When I discussed approaching you, Jessie expressed doubts because of your lack of contact with her aunt and uncle.'

'It was not through lack of interest.'

Kirsty thought she saw the glimmer of a tear in the older woman's eye although she couldn't be sure.

She looked up and fixed her dark eyes on Kirsty. 'David and Mary's father was my brother. We were twins and like most twins, we were inseparable as children.'

She paused.

'I suppose we started to drift apart after Richard met and married Marion. She was a minister's daughter and fanatical about religion and she indoctrinated Richard. Our father possessed no firm beliefs and, during his travels, he'd mixed with people who worshipped different gods. Richard accused him of being a heathen and that, I think, was where the trouble started. I know that doesn't sound like a reason for a father to discriminate against his son but it didn't stop there. I expect you noticed the marble statue in the hall. Well, that wasn't always there. The alcove used to house a large Buddha which Richard took exception to as a symbol of pagan beliefs, so he took a sledgehammer to it. And that is only one example, there were many more incidents. If Richard had not acted in the way he did, our father would not have changed his will and Richard would not have felt cheated. This house belonged to my father and it should have passed to Richard instead of me. I expect you can understand how a grudge can develop in such circumstances.'

'You mentioned earlier that David had a cruel streak.'

'Richard and Marion had three children but they favoured their second born, David, the only boy. I was fond of his older sister, Elizabeth, who was a lovely child. But something about David, the way he looked at you and a coldness in his eyes, made me suspect he was not as angelic as he looked. Mary was the youngest and she doted on David. As I said, I sensed something amiss with David but nothing I could put my finger on, until the day I caught him pulling the legs off a grasshopper. Of course, Richard and Marion didn't believe me because in their eyes he could do no wrong. My cat, that was the final straw. During one of their visits to me, my cat went missing. After they left I hunted for her and found her lying under one of the bushes at the end of the garden. Her tail had been cut off and she'd been beaten over the head with a large stone. She didn't survive.' Miss Walker stopped speaking to draw breath. 'I could never prove David mutilated and killed her but I had my suspicions.'

Miss Walker seemed to shrink in her chair as she recalled her memories of David as a child although it enabled Kirsty to understand the man currently locked up in a prison cell. It also went some way to explain Mary's involvement. But her job at the moment was ensuring a safe place to bring the young girls.

'I am sorry you had to relive some of your past and I am grateful for the information. I think there is little doubt Mary and David will be found guilty and may pay the ultimate penalty for their crimes.' Although she did not say it both of them knew the ultimate penalty was a date with the hangman. 'But that leaves me with my original request about the girls.'

'Of course, they can come here and they can stay as long as they like. I will be pleased to be able to help them and they will be company for me.'

'You are aware they are destitute at the moment although I will be asking Mary to make provision for her daughters.'

Miss Walker sat up straight in her chair and stared at Kirsty. 'I am not concerned about money. I possess more than I need. But surely, Jessie must have her mother's share of my father's fortune.'

Kirsty frowned. 'I don't understand. Jessie worked as a servant in her aunt and uncle's house. She was dependent on their charity.'

'Charity, my foot.' Miss Walker leaned forward. 'When my father died he left me half his fortune and the other half he divided between Richard and his three children. Elizabeth had a share and when she died that share should have passed to Jessie.'

'Are you sure?'

'Of course, I'm sure. Leave it with me and I'll instruct my solicitor to look into this. Jessie should be a wealthy young woman.'

'I'm puzzled. Mary talked about inheriting half of her

father's estate when he died which gave me the impression she only had her dowry before that.'

An amused expression crossed Miss Walker's face. 'Mary was left half of her father's estate but she also received her share of her grandfather's fortune. She may not appear it but I think you will find Mary is not as poverty stricken as she claims to be. But you need not worry about her daughters I will be happy to provide for them until they come into their inheritance.'

Kirsty rose. 'Thank you, Miss Walker. I will make arrangements for the girls to come here.'

She closed the front door behind her when she left. Miss Walker had been too busy instructing Milly to prepare bedrooms for the girls to think about having her shown out.

62

Jessie stood at the door watching the motor car drive off. She was sure the policewoman meant well but Aunt Mary had always been scathing of her great aunt. She remembered her aunt talking about her to David, saying Elizabeth cheated their father out of half his inheritance. She didn't sound like the kind of woman who would look kindly on them.

Once the car passed out of sight Jessie returned to the house. Rose and Iris would be hungry and Uncle David's housekeeper took most of the food with her when she flounced out this morning.

She filled the kettle and placed it on the stove to heat. At least there were tea leaves in the caddy and, after a rummage in the cupboards, she found the remains of a loaf of bread and half a cheddar cheese.

Tears welled up in her eyes and she slumped into a chair at the kitchen table. She wasn't making a good job of looking after the girls and she had no money. What on earth would happen to them?

Raised voices and the clatter of feet on the stairs made her rise from her seat and, dashing the tears from her eyes, she turned to smile at Rose when she dashed through the door. Iris followed her a moment later.

'Is there anything to eat?' Iris was always hungry and seemed to have forgotten her anger with Jessie.

'I found bread and cheese.' Jessie sawed a slice from the loaf and deposited it on Iris's plate.

'Is that all?'

'I'm afraid so. It's all I could find.' She sliced more bread.

'When is Mama coming back?'

'I'm not sure but she said I had to look after you until she returned.' Aunt Mary had said no such thing and Jessie dreaded having to explain everything to them.

At the sound of the door knocker, she hurried out of the kitchen, thankful for the respite from further questioning.

'I have good news,' the policewoman said when Jessie opened the door.

Jessie motioned Kirsty inside. 'What good news?'

'I talked with your great aunt and found her to be most pleasant. She expressed concern for your welfare and offered you a home with her.'

'We don't want charity.' Jessie kept her voice low. She'd lived on charity all her life but her great aunt was a stranger which made it different.

'It's not charity. She says you will be company for her. Besides, she seems to think your mother left you some money when she died so you will be able to pay your way if that is what you wish.'

'She's wrong. My mother didn't have any money. Aunt Mary and Uncle Josiah told me my father left her penniless and they took her in so she wouldn't be put in the Poor House.'

'Well, once she gets her solicitor involved I'm sure things will become clearer. Now, if you collect your belongings and go and get Rose and Iris I'll take you to meet her.'

Jessie's thoughts were in turmoil as she walked to the kitchen. She didn't know Great Aunt Elizabeth and couldn't understand why she would offer them a home. According to Aunt Mary the woman was greedy and selfish as well as a cheat. Jessie couldn't imagine living with her would be pleasant. Well, she was used to working for her keep so she supposed that would ensure a roof over their heads until she could think of something better. She squared her shoulders and opened the kitchen door. Great Aunt Elizabeth was the only option they had for the time being.

She found Rose and Iris squabbling over the last piece of cheese and she grabbed a knife to slice the cheese into two pieces. 'After you've eaten that, get your coats. We're going to live with Great Aunt Elizabeth.'

The two girls stopped arguing. 'Who is Great Aunt Elizabeth?'

'Put your coats on and you'll soon find out.' Jessie rinsed the plates and left them draining.

The chauffeur standing beside the automobile held the rear door open when they emerged from the house.

Rose and Iris ran down the path. 'Are we going there by car?' Rose demanded.

'It will be a squeeze. But if Miss Kirsty doesn't mind sitting in the front with me I think you can all fit into the back seat.'

Within a few minutes, they drew up at the door of one of the largest houses Jessie had ever seen. The door opened before the engine stopped and a maid came running down the steps leading to the front door.

'Miss Walker said I must watch for you and bring you inside.'

'This is Rose and Iris,' the policewoman said as she helped them out of the car. 'And this is Milly, who is Miss Walker's maid.'

Jessie remained scrunched in the corner of the back seat. A tremor of fear rippled through her. If Miss Walker was as nice as the policewoman said, Rose and Iris would fit into this house better than she would. They were pretty and charming and everyone liked them. But Jessie always remained in the background convinced no one would like her because she didn't have their good looks and she was cursed with this awful squint in her eye.

'Come on, Jessie. Milly says we should go into the house where Miss Walker is waiting to meet you all.' The policewoman held her hand out.

Jessie grasped it and climbed out of the car. Rose and Iris were already at the top of the steps following Milly into the house.

'There's nothing to be afraid of,' the policewoman whispered, but she did not release her grip on Jessie's hand.

A tall woman with a kindly face came forward to meet Jessie as soon as she entered the house.

'And you must be Jessie,' she said. 'I would have known you anywhere. You look like your mother. I was sad when Elizabeth chose to go to Mary in her time of need. I wish she had come to me.' She reached out her arms and embraced her great niece.

A tear dropped on Jessie's head and the woman's arms felt warm and comforting. She relaxed. Never in her life had she experienced such love. Gradually her own arms went around the woman and the two of them rocked together as if they'd known one another all their lives.

63

Kirsty slipped away. Her task was done and she was no longer needed.

She smiled as the car travelled the few miles back to Dundee. The reunion of Elizabeth Walker with her great-nieces had been a success and even Jessie had thawed. Kirsty had no doubts they would be well-cared for although the trauma of the loss of their parents would no doubt affect Rose and Iris for years to come.

She was sure Elizabeth Walker would be up to the task of helping them to heal.

'I'll be going home after I report to Inspector Brewster,' Kirsty said when she got out of the car at the police station.

She marched across the courtyard and into the charge room.

Geordie looked up at her entry. He left the desk and his ledgers and crossed the room.

Leaning forward with his elbows on the counter top, he said, 'The inspector didn't expect you back today, miss.'

Kirsty narrowed her eyes. What did Brewster expect her to do? He knew she met with Jessie, and Mary Petrie's two daughters to look at options for their care. But now he had his prisoners under lock and key, perhaps he had no interest in the aftermath.

'I've come to make my report. Is Inspector Brewster in his office?'

As soon as the words were out of her mouth she regretted her sharp tone.

It wasn't Geordie's fault if Brewster was too insensitive to take an interest in the girls' welfare.

'Yes, miss.' Geordie turned back to the desk.

'Thanks, Geordie.' She hoped he hadn't taken umbrage.

Silence pervaded the corridor. Her boots clattered with a

hollow sound on the linoleum covered floor and she passed empty offices although a hint of cigarette smoke hung in the atmosphere. It was mid-afternoon and the constables would be out on their beats.

When she entered Brewster's office she found him staring at the ceiling deep in thought. She moved files from a chair and sat on it to wait for him to acknowledge her presence.

'I released Aggie earlier today.'

'Yes, sir.' If he expected her to comment any further he would be disappointed. She didn't intend to give him that pleasure.

He studied her for a moment before saying, 'I thought I told you to go home.' He sounded resigned. 'But when did you ever do what I told you?'

'I returned to make my report, sir.'

'Of course, you did.' He toyed with a pencil. 'Go ahead.'

'I managed to find a relative who agreed to provide a home for Jessie, as well as Mary Petrie's two daughters, Rose and Iris. She is their great aunt and she lives in Broughty Ferry so I took them to her and saw them settled.' She paused for breath. 'I informed Jessie of the charges against her uncle and aunt but Rose and Iris are not yet aware. I understand Jessie will explain to them when the time is right and she will be supported in this by Elizabeth Walker, her great aunt.'

'Good work,' Brewster said. 'I take it we should have no more worries in that area.'

'I did discover something else that may be of interest in respect of the criminal charges.'

Curiosity showed on Brewster's face.

'According to Elizabeth Walker, Jessie should have been left a considerable sum of money when her mother died but Jessie is unaware of that and believes she has been living on the charity of her aunt and uncle. It is possible her aunt and uncle took possession of her inheritance. Elizabeth Walker intends to ask her solicitor to investigate but I thought a criminal investigation might also be in order.'

'That will be difficult to prove but I think you are right. Will Elizabeth Walker cooperate with us?'

'I see no reason why she wouldn't. She is anxious to help the girls in any way she can. I can maintain contact with her if you like.'

'That can wait,' Brewster said. 'You are now officially off duty and I am ordering you to return home until you are fully recovered.'

He tapped the end of his pencil repeatedly on the desk to accentuate his words.

Kirsty opened her mouth to protest but Brewster cut in before she could say anything.

'I mean it, Kirsty. You look exhausted, you are pale and not yourself. I don't want to see you back here until you regain your strength.'

She rose from the chair. 'Yes, sir.'

She didn't have the energy to argue with him and he was right. Her experience yesterday had sapped her strength and all she wanted was to lie down and sleep.

'I'll walk you to the door,' Brewster said.

He didn't need to add, in case you need help. It was evident in his tone of voice and she hated being treated like a weak woman.

She summoned up the remains of her energy to say, 'I can manage. I'm not an invalid.'

Brewster laughed and grasped her elbow. 'I can see the Kirsty we all know is still lurking there. But you can protest all you like, I will still walk you to the car.'

His hand on her elbow felt strangely comforting although she couldn't help thinking he was making sure she left.

Ailsa came flying out of the house as soon as the car drew up at the door.

As Dougal helped Kirsty out, the child jumped from foot to foot unable to contain her excitement.

'Are you feeling better now?'

She grabbed Kirsty's hand and led her towards the house.

'I wanted to stay with you when you came yesterday but Mama said you were ill and I had to go Aunt Bea's. I didn't want to go but she made me. Mama says you're going to stay with us until Christmas. Are you?'

Ailsa's voice babbled on and on.

'Yes, I'm going to spend Christmas with you.'

Her arm went around Ailsa's shoulders and it felt good. Perhaps spending time with her parents wouldn't be so bad after all.

Also by Chris Longmuir

DUNDEE CRIME SERIES

Night Watcher
Dead Wood
Missing Believed Dead

KIRSTY CAMPBELL MYSTERIES

Devil's Porridge
The Death Game
Death of a Doxy

HISTORICAL SAGAS

A Salt Splashed Cradle

NONFICTION

Nuts & Bolts of Self-Publishing

CHRIS LONGMUIR

Chris Longmuir was born in Wiltshire and now lives in Angus. Her family moved to Scotland when she was two. After leaving school at fifteen, Chris worked in shops, offices, mills and factories, and was a bus conductor for a spell, before working as a social worker for Angus Council (latterly serving as Assistant Principal Officer for Adoption and Fostering).

Chris is a member of the Society of Authors, the Crime Writers Association and the Scottish Association of Writers. She writes short stories, articles and crime novels, and has won numerous awards. Her first published book, Dead Wood, won the Dundee International Book Prize and was published by Polygon. She designed her own website and confesses to being a techno-geek who builds computers in her spare time.

http://www.chrislongmuir.co.uk

Lightning Source UK Ltd.
Milton Keynes UK
UKHW011333080419
340670UK00001B/63/P